DADDY'S HOME!

Chutt-Riit always enjoyed visiting the quarters of his male offspring.

"What will it be this time?" he wondered, as he passed the outer guards.

Why the little sthondats, he thought affectionately. *They managed to put it together out of reach of the holo pickups.*

The adult put his hand to the door again, keying the locking sequence, then bounded backward four times his own length from a standing start. Even under the lighter gravity of Wunderland, it was a creditable feat. And necessary, for the massive panels rang and toppled as the rope-swung boulder slammed forward. The children had hung two cables from both towers, with the rock at the point of the V and a third rope to draw it back. As the doors bounced wide he saw the blade they had driven into the apex of the egg-shaped granite rock, long and barbed and polished to a wicked point.

Kittens, he thought. *Always going for the dramatic.*

MAN-KZIN WARS II

Larry Niven

with

Dean Ing,

Jerry Pournelle,

and

S.M. Stirling

A Baen Books Original

Baen Publishing Enterprises
P.O. Box 1403
Riverdale, NY 10471

ISBN: 0-671-72036-8

Cover art by Steve Hickman

First Printing, August 1989
Second Printing, July 1990
Third Printing, June 1991

Printed in the United States of America

Distributed by Simon & Schuster
1230 Avenue of the Americas
New York, NY 10020

CONTENTS

Introduction

The franchise universe lives!

When I first began sneaking into the playgrounds of other authors, I had my doubts. Still, Phil Farmer seemed to be having a lovely time reshaping the worlds he'd played in as a child. So I wrote a Dunsany story and an extrapolation of Lovecraft and an attempt at a *Black Cat* detective story and a study of Superman's sex life.

Fred Saberhagen invited me to write a *Berserker* story, and I found it indecently easy.

MEDEA: Harlan's World was a collaboration universe. Slow to become a book, it ultimately became a classic study of how creative minds may build and populate a solar system.

So Jim Baen and I invited selected authors to write stories set 14,000 years ago, when magic still worked. We filled two books with tales of the Warlock's era. (We also drove Niven half nuts. The idea was for Jim to do all the work and me to take all the credit. But Jim parted company with Ace Books, and I had to learn more than I ever wanted to know about being an editor!)

I entered a universe infested with lizard-like pirate-slavers, because of David Drake's urging, and because of a notion I found irresistable: the murder of Halley's Comet. When Susan Shwartz asked several of us to write new tales of the Thousand and One Nights, I rapidly realized that Scheherazade had overlooked a serious threat. I stayed out of *Thieves World*—too busy—but I was tempted.

Still, would readers and the publishing industry continue to support this kind of thing? It seemed like too much fun.

And now DC Comics has me reworking the background universe of Green Lantern! Green Lantern is almost as old as I am! But his mythos will be mine, for the next few years at least.

I'm having a wonderful time. I've got to say, being paid for this stuff feels like cheating.

What began with "The Warriors" has evolved further than my own ambitions would have carried it.

Jim Baen and I decided to open up the Man-Kzin Wars period of *known space*, because I don't have the background to tell war stories. Still, I had my doubts. I have friends who can write of war; but any writer good enough to be invited to play in my universe will have demonstrated that he can make his own. Would anyone accept my offer? I worried also that intruders might mess up the playground, by violating my background assumptions.

But the kzinti have been well treated, and I'm learning more about them than I ever expected. You too will be charmed and fascinated by kzinti family life as shown in "The Children's Hour," not to mention Pournelle's and Stirling's innovative use of stasis fields. Likewise there is Dean Ing's look at intelligent stone-age kzinti females: Ing finished his story for the first volume, then just kept writing. Now Pournelle and Stirling are talking about doing the same.

I too have found that *known space* stories keep getting longer. It's a fun universe, easier to enter than to leave.

One thing I hoped for when I opened up the Warlock's universe to other writers. I had run out of ideas. I hoped to be re-inspired. My wish was granted, and I have written several Warlock's-era stories since.

If the same doesn't hold for the era of the Man-Kzin Wars, it won't be the fault of the authors represented here. I'm having a wonderful time reading *known space* stories that I didn't have to write. If I do find myself re-inspired, these stories will have done it.

—Larry Niven

BRIAR PATCH

Dean Ing

If Locklear had been thinking straight, he never would have stayed in the god business. But when a man has been thrust into the Fourth Man-Kzin War, won peace with honor from the tigerlike Kzinti on a synthetic zoo planet, and released long-stored specimens so that his vast prison compound resembles the Kzin homeworld, it's hard for that man to keep his sense of mortality.

It's hard, that is, until someone decides to kill him. His first mistake was lust, impure and simple. A week after he paroled Scarface, the one surviving Kzin warrior, Locklear admitted his problem during supper. "All that caterwauling in the ravine," he said, refilling his bowl from the hearth stewpot, "is driving me nuts. Good thing you haven't let the rest of those Kzinti out of stasis; the racket would be unbelievable!"

Scarface wiped his muzzle with a brawny forearm and handed his own bowl to Kit, his new mate. The

3

darkness of the huge Kzersatz region was tempered only by coals, but Locklear saw those coals flicker in Scarface's cat eyes. "A condition of my surrender was that you release Kit to me," the big Kzin growled. "And besides: do humans mate so quietly?"

Because they were speaking Kzin, the word Scarface had used was actually "ch'rowl"—itself a sexual goad. Kit, who was refilling the bowl, let slip a tiny mew of surprise and pleasure. "Please, milord," she said, offering the bowl to Scarface. "Poor Rockear is already overstimulated. Is it not so?" Her huge eyes flicked to Locklear, whom she had grown to know quite well after Locklear waked her from age-long sleep.

"Dead right," Locklear agreed with a morose glance. "Not by the word; by the goddamn deed!"

"She is mine," Scarface grinned; a Kzin grin, the kind with big fangs and no amusement.

"Calm down. I may have been an animal psychologist, but I only have letches for human females," Locklear gloomed toward his Kzin companions. "And every night when I hear you two flattening the grass out there," he nodded past the half-built walls of the hut, "I get, uh, . . ." He did not know how to translate "horny" into Kzin.

"You get the urge to travel," Scarface finished, making it not quite a suggestion. The massive Kzin stared into darkness as if peering across the force walls surrounding Kzersatz. Those towering invisible walls separated the air, and lifeforms, of Kzersatz from other synthetic compounds of this incredible planet, Zoo. "I can see the treetops in the next compound as easily as you, Locklear. But I see no monkeys in them."

Before his defeat, Scarface had been "Tzak-Commander." The same strict Kzin honor that bound him to his surrender, forbade him to curse his captor as a monkey. But he could still sharpen the barb of his wit. Kit, with real affection for Locklear, did not approve. "Be nice," she hissed to her mate.

"Forget it," Locklear told her, stabbing with his Kzin *wtsai* blade for a hunk of meat in his stew. "Kit, he's stuck with his military code, and it won't let him insist that his captor get the hell out of here. But he's right. I still don't know if that next compound I call Newduvai is really Earthlike." He smiled at Scarface, remembering not to show his teeth, and added, "Or whether it has my kind of monkey."

"And we must not try to find out until your war wounds have completely healed," Kit replied.

The eyes of man and Kzin warrior met. "Whoa," Locklear said quickly, sparing Scarface the trouble. "*We* won't be scouting over there; I will, but you won't. I'm an ethologist," he went on, holding up a hand to bar Kit's interruption. "If Newduvai is as completely stocked as Kzersatz, somebody—maybe the Outsiders, maybe not, but damn' certain a long time ago—somebody intended all these compounds to be kept separate. Now, I won't say I haven't played god here a little . . ."

"And intend to play it over there a lot," said Kit, who had never yet surrendered to anyone.

"Hear me out. I'm not going to start mixing species from Kzersatz and Newduvai any more than I already have, and that's final." He pried experimentally at the scab running down his knife arm. "But I'm pretty much healed, thanks to your medkit, Scarface. And I meant it when I said you'd have free run of this place. It's intended for Kzinti, not humans. High time I took your lifeboat over those force walls to Newduvai."

"Boots will miss you," said Kit.

Locklear smiled, recalling the other Kzin female he'd released from stasis in a very pregnant condition. According to Kit, a Kzin mother would not emerge from her birthing creche until the eyes of her twins had opened—another week, at least. "Give her my love," he said, and swilled the last of his stew.

"A pity you will not do that yourself," Kit sighed.

"Milady." Scarface became, for the moment, every inch a Tzak-Commander. "Would you ask me to ch'rowl a human female?" He waited for Kit to control her mixed expression. "Then please be silent on the subject. Locklear is a warrior who knows what he fights for."

Locklear yawned. "There's an old song that says, 'Ain't gonna study war no more,' and a slogan that goes, 'Make love, not war.'"

Kit stood up with a fetching twitch of her tail. "I believe our leader has spoken, milord," she purred.

Locklear watched them swaying together in the night, and his parting call was plaintive. "Just try and keep it down, okay? A fellow needs his sleep."

The Kzin lifeboat was over ten meters long, well armed and furnished with emergency rations. In accord with their handshake armistice, Scarface had given flight instructions to his human pupil after disabling the hyperwave portion of its comm set. He had given no instructions on armament because Locklear, a peaceable man, saw no further use for anything larger than a sidearm. Neither of them could do much to make the lifeboat seating comfortable for Locklear, who was small even by human standards in an acceleration couch meant for a two-hundred-kilo Kzin.

Locklear paused in the airlock in midmorning and raised one arm in a universal peace sign. Scarface returned it. "I'll call you now and then, if those force walls don't stop the signal," Locklear called. "If you let your other Kzinti out of stasis, call and tell me how it works out."

"Keep your tail dry, Rockear," Kit called, perhaps forgetting he lacked that appendage—a compliment, of sorts.

"Will do," he called back as the airlock swung shut. Moments later, he brought the little craft to life and, cursing the cradle-rock motion that branded him a novice, urged the lifeboat into the yellow sky of Kzersatz.

Locklear made one pass, a "goodbye sweep," high above the region with its yellow and orange vegetation, taking care to stay well inside the frostline that defined those invisible force walls. He spotted the cave from the still-flattened grass where Kit had herded the awakened animals from the crypt and their sleep of forty thousand years, then steepened his climb and used aero boost to begin his trajectory. No telling whether the force walls stopped suddenly, but he did not want to find out by plowing into the damned things. It was enough to know they stopped below orbital height, and that he could toss the lifeboat from Kzersatz to Newduvai in a low-energy ballistic arc.

And he knew enough to conserve energy in the

craft's main accumulators because one day, when the damned stupid Man-Kzin War was over, he'd need the energy to jump from Zoo to some part of known space. Unless, he amended silently, somebody found Zoo first. The war might already be over, and certainly the warlike Kzinti must have the coordinates of Zoo . . .

Then he was at the top of his trajectory, seeing the planetary curvature of Zoo, noting the tiny satellite sunlets that bathed hundred-mile-diameter regions in light, realizing that a warship could condemn any one of those circular regions to death with one well-placed shot against its synthetic, automated little sun. He was already past the circular force walls now, and felt an enormous temptation to slow the ship by main accumulator energy. A good pilot could lower that lifeboat down between the walls of those force cylinders, in the hard vacuum between compounds. Outsiders might be lurking there, idly studying the specimens through invisible walls.

But Locklear was no expert with a Kzin lifeboat, not yet, and he had to use his wristcomp to translate the warning on the console screen. He set the wing extensions just in time to avoid heavy buffeting, thankful that he had not needed orbital speed to manage his brief trajectory. He bobbled a maneuver once, twice, then felt the drag of Newduvai's atmosphere on the lifeboat and gave the lifting surfaces full extension. He put the craft into a shallow bank to starboard, keeping the vast circular frostline far to portside, and punched in an autopilot instruction. Only then did he dare to turn his gaze down on Newduvai.

Like Kzersatz it boasted a big lake, but this one

glinted in a sun heartbreakingly like Earth's. A rugged jumble of cliffs soared into cloud at one side of the region, and green hills mounded above plains of mottled hues: tan, brown, green, Oh, God, all that green! He'd forgotten, in the saffron of Kzersatz, how much he missed the emerald of grass, the blue of sky, the darker dusty green of Earth forests. For it was, in every respect, perfectly Earthlike. He wiped his misting eyes, grinned at himself for such foolishness, and eased the lifeboat down to a lazy circular course that kept him two thousand meters above the terrain. If the builders of Zoo were consistent, one of those shallow creekbeds would begin not in a marshy meadow but in a horizontal shaft. And there he would find—he dared not think it through any further.

After his first complete circuit of Newduvai, he knew it had no herds of animals. No birds dotted the lakeshore; no bugs whacked his viewport. A dozen streams meandered and leapt down from the frostline where clouds dumped their moisture against cold encircling force walls. One stream ended in a second small lake with no obvious outlet, but none of the creeks or dry-washes began with a cave.

Mindful of his clumsiness in this alien craft, Locklear set it down in soft sand where a drywash delta met the kidney-shaped lake. After further consulting between his wristcomp and the ship's computer, he punched in his most important queries and listened to the ship cool while its sensors analyzed Newduvai.

Gravity: Earth normal. Atmosphere, solar flux, and temperature: all Earth normal. "And not a critter in sight," he told the cabin walls. In a burst of insight, he asked the computer to list anything that might be a health hazard to a Kzin. If man and Kzin could make steaks of each other, they probably should fear the same pathogens. The computer took its time, but its most fearsome finding was of tetanus in the dust.

He waited no longer, thrusting at the airlock in his hurry, filling his lungs with a rich soup of odors, and found his eyes brimming again as he stepped onto a little piece of Earth. Smells, he reflected, really got you back to basics. Scents of cedar, of dust, of grasses and yes, of wildflowers. Just like home—yet, in some skin-prickling way, not quite.

Locklear sat down on the sand then, with an earth-like sunlet baking his back from a turquoise sky, and he wept. Outsiders or not, any bunch that could engineer a piece of home on the rim of known space couldn't be all bad.

He was tasting the lake water's very faint brackish-ness when, in a process that took less than a minute, the sunlight dimmed and was gone. "But it's only noontime," he protested, and then laughed at himself and made a notation on his wristcomp, using its faint light to guide him back to the airlock.

As with Kzersatz, he saw no stars; and then he realized that the position of Newduvai's sun had been halfway to the horizon when—almost as it happened on Kzersatz—the daily ration of sunlight was quenched. Why should Newduvai's sun keep the same time as that of Kzersatz? It didn't; nor did it wink off as suddenly as that of Kzersatz.

He activated the still-functioning local mode of the lifeboat's comm set, intending to pass his findings on to Scarface. No response. Scarface's handset was an all-band unit; perhaps some wavelength could bounce off of debris from the Kzin cruiser scuttled in orbit— but Locklear knew that was a slender hope, and soon it seemed no hope at all. He spent the longest few hours of his life then, turning floodlights on the lake in the forlorn hope of seeing a fish leap, and with the vague fear that a tyrannosaur might pay him a social call. But no matter where he turned the lights he saw no gleam of eyes, and the sand was innocent of any tracks. Sleep would not come until he began to address the problem of the stasis crypt in logical ways.

Locklear came up from his seat with a bound, facing a sun that brightened as he watched. His wristcomp said not quite twelve hours had passed since the sunlet dimmed. His belly said it was late. His memory said yes, by God, there was one likely plan for locating that horizontal shaft: fly very near the frostline and scan every dark cranny that was two hundred meters or so inside the force walls. On Kzersatz, the stasis crypt had ended exactly beneath the frostline, perhaps a portal for those who'd built Zoo. And the front entrance had been two hundred meters inside the force walls.

He lifted the lifeboat slowly, ignoring hunger pangs, beginning to plot a rough map of Newduvai on the computer screen because he did not know how to make the computer do it for him. Soon, he passed a dry plateau with date palms growing in its declivities and followed the ship's shadow to more fertile soil. Near frostline, he set the aeroturbine reactor just above idle and, moving briskly a hundred meters above the ground, began a careful scan of the terrain because he was not expert enough with Kzin computers to automate the search.

After three hours he had covered more than half of

his sweep around Newduvai, past semi desert and
grassy fields to pine-dotted mountain slopes, and
the lifeboat's reactor coolant was overheating from
the slow pace. Locklear set the craft down nicely
near that smaller mountain lake, chopped all power
systems, and headed for scrubby trees in the near
distance. Scattered among the pines were cedar and
small oak. Nearer stood tall poplar and chestnut,
invaded by wild grape with immature fruit. But nearest of all, the reason for his landing here, were
gnarled little pear trees and, amid wild shoots of
rank growth, trees laden with small ripe plums. He
wolfed them down until juice dripped from his chin,
washed in the lake, and then found the pears unripe.
No matter: he'd seen dates, grapes, and chestnut,
which suggested a model of some Mediterranean
region. After identifying juniper, oleander, and hon-
eysuckle, he sent his wristcomp scurrying through its
megabytes and narrowed his opinion of the area: a
surrogate slice of Asia Minor.

He might have sat on sunwarmed stones until
dark, lulled by this sensation of being, somehow,
back home without a care. But then he glanced far
across the lower hills and saw, proceeding slowly
across a parched desert plateau many miles distant, a
whirlwind with its whiplike curve and bloom of dust
where it touched the soil.

"Uh-huh! That's how you reseed plants without
insect vectors," he said aloud to the builders of Zoo.
"But whirlwinds don't make honey, and they'll sting
anyway. Hell, even *I* can play god better than that,"
he said, and bore a pocketful of plums into the
lifeboat, filled once more with the itch to find the
cave that might not even exist on Newduvai.

But it was there, all right. Locklear saw it only because of the perfect arc of obsidian, gleaming through a tangle of brush that had grown around the cave mouth.

He made a botch of the landing because he was trembling with anticipation. A corner of his mind kept warning him not to assume everything here was the same as on Kzersatz, so Locklear stopped just outside that brush-choked entrance. His *wtsai* blade made short work of the brush, revealing a polished floor. He strode forward, *wtsai* in one hand, his big Kzin sidearm in the other, to the now-familiar luminous film that flickered, several meters inside the cave mouth, across an obsidian portal. He thrust his blade through the film and saw, as he had expected to see, stronger light flash behind the portal. Then he stepped through and stopped, listening.

He might have been back in the Kzersatz crypt: a quiet so deep his own breathing made echoes; the long obsidian central passage, with nine branches on each side, ending in a frost-covered force wall that filled the passageway. And the clear plastic containers ranked in the side passages were of three sizes on smooth metal bases, as expected. But Locklear took one look at the nearest specimen, spinning slowly in its stasis cage, and knew that here the resemblance to Kzersatz ended forever.

The monster lay in something like a fetal crouch, tumbling slowly in response to the grav polarizer as it had been doing for many thousands of years. It was black, with great forward-curving horns and heavy shoulders, and when released—*if* anyone dared, he amended—it would stand six feet at the shoulder.

Locklear figured its weight at a ton. Some European zoologists had once tried to breed cattle back to this brute, but with scant success, and Locklear had not seen so much as a sketch of it since his undergrad work. It was a bull aurochs, a beast which had survived on Earth into historic times; and counting the cows, Locklear realized there were over forty of them.

No point in kidding himself about his priorities. Locklear walked past the stasized camels and gerbils, hurried faster beyond small horses and cheetahs and bats, began to trot as he ran to the next passage past lions and hares and grouse, and was sprinting as he passed whole schools of fish (without water? Why the hell not? They were in stasis, he reminded himself—) in their respective containers. He was out of breath by the time he dashed between specimens of reindeer and saw the monkeys.

NO! A mistake any Kzin might have made, but: "How could I play such a shameful joke on myself?" They were in fetal curls, and some of them boasted a lot of body hair. And each of them, Locklear realized, was human.

In a kind of reverence he studied them all, careful to avoid touching the metal bases which, on Kzersatz, opened the cages and released the specimens. Narrow-headed and swarthy they were, no taller than he, with heavy brow ridges and high cheekbones. Noses like prizefighters; forearms like blacksmiths; and some had pendulous mammaries and a few had—had— "Tits," he breathed. "There's a difference! Thank you, God."

Men and women like these had first been studied in a river valley near old Dusseldorf, hardy folk who had preceded modern humans on Earth and, in all probability, had intermarried with them until forty or fifty thousand years before. Locklear, rubbing at the gooseflesh on his arms, began to study each of the stasized nudes with great care. He would need every possible advantage because they would be disoriented, perhaps even furious, when they waked. And the last thing Locklear needed was to start off on the wrong foot with a frenzied Neanderthaler.

Only an idiot would release a mob of Neanderthal hunters into a tiny world without taking steps to protect endangered game animals. The killing of a dozen deer might doom the rest of that species to slow extinction here. On the other hand, Locklear might have released all the animals and waited for a season or more. But certain of the young women in stasis were not exactly repellant, and he did not intend to wait a year before making their acquaintance. Besides, his notes on a Neanderthal community could make him famous on a dozen worlds, and Locklear was anxious to get on with it.

His second option was to wake the people and guide them, by force if necessary, outside to fruits and grains. But each of them would see those stasized animals, probably as meat on the hoof, and might not respond to his demands. It was beyond belief that any of them would speak a language he knew. Then it struck him that he already knew how to disassemble a stasis cage, and that he had as much time as he needed. With a longing glance backward, Locklear retraced his steps to the lifeboat and started looking for something with wheels.

But Kzin lifeboats do not carry cargo dollies, and the sun of Newduvai had dimmed before he found a way to remove the wheeled carriage below the reactor's heat exchanger unit. Evidently the unit needed replacement often enough that Kzin engineers installed a carriage with it. That being so, Locklear decided not to use the lifeboat's reactor any more than he had to.

He worked until hunger and aching muscles drove him to the cabin where he cut slices of bricklike Kzin rations and ate plums for dessert. But before he fell asleep, Locklear made some decisions that might save his hide. The lifeboat must be hidden away from inquisitive savage fingers; he would even camouflage the stasis crypt so that those savages would not know what lay inside; and it was absolutely crucial that he present himself as a shaman of great power. Without a few tawdry magics, he might not be able to distance himself as an observer; might even be challenged to combat by some strong male. And Locklear remembered those hornlike fingernails and bulging muscles all too well. He saw no sense in shooting a man, even a Neanderthal, merely to prove a point that could be made in peaceable ways.

He spent over a week preparing his hardware. His trials on Kzersatz had taught him how, when all you've got is a hammer, the whole world is a nail; and that you must hammer out a few other tools as soon as possible. He soon found the lifeboat's military toolbox complete with wire, pistol-grip arc welder, and motorized drill.

He took time off to gather fruit and to let his frustrations drain away. It was hard not to throw rocks at the sky when he commanded a state-of-the-art Kzin craft, yet could not cannibalize much of it for the things he needed. "Maybe I should release a dog from stasis so I could kick it," he told himself aloud, while attaching an oak branch as a wagon tongue for the wheeled carriage. But lacking any other game, he figured, the dog would probably attack before he did.

Then he used oak staves to lever a cage base up, with flat stones as blocks, and eased his makeshift wagon beneath. The doe inside was heavy with young. Most likely, she would retreat far from him before bearing her fawns, and he knew what to do with the tuneable grav polarizer below that cage. Soon the clear plastic container sat gleaming in the sun, and Locklear poked hard at the base before retreating to the cave mouth.

As on Kzersatz, the container levered up, the red doe sank to the cage base, and the base slid forward. A moment later the creature moved, stood with lovely slender limbs shaking, and then saw him waving an oak stave. She reached grassy turf in one graceful bound and sped off with leaps he watched in admiration. Then, feeling somehow more lonely as the doe vanished, he sighed and disconnected the plastic container, then set about taking the entire cage to pieces. Already experienced with these gadgets, he would need at least two of the grav polarizer units before he could move stasized specimens outside with ease.

Disconnected from the stasis unit, a polarizer toroid with its power source and wiring could be tuned to lift varied loads; for example, a container housing a school of fish. The main thing was to avoid tipping it, which Locklear managed by wiring the polarizer securely to the underside of his wheeled carriage. Another hour saw him tugging his burden to the airlock, where he wrestled that entire, still-functioning

cageful of fish inside. The fish, he saw, had sucking
mouths meant for bottom-feeding on vegetable trash.
They looked rather like carp or tilapia. Raising the
lifeboat with great care, he eased toward the big lake
some miles distant. It was no great trick to dump the
squirming mass of life from the airlock port into the
lake from a height of two meters, and then he cele-
brated by landing near the first laden fig tree he saw.
Munching and lazing in the sun, he decided that his
fortunes were looking up. But then, Locklear had
been wrong before . . .

He knew that his next steps must be planned
carefully. Before hiding the Kzin craft away he must
duplicate the airboat he had built on Kzersatz. After
an exhaustive search—meanwhile mapping Newduvai's
major features—he felled and stripped slender pines,
hauling them in the lifeboat to his favorite spot near
the small mountain lake. By now he had found a
temporary spot in a barren cleft near frostline to hide
the lifeboat itself, and began by stripping off its
medium-caliber beam weapons from extension struts.
The strut skins were attached by long screws, which
Locklear saved. The weapon wiring came in handy,
too, as he began fitting the raftlike platform of his
airboat together. When he realized that the lifeboat's
slings and emergency seats could be stripped for a
fabric sail, he began to feel a familiar excitement.

This airboat was larger than his first, with its single
sail and swiveling double-pole keel for balance. With
wires for rigging, he could hunker down just behind
the mast and operate the gravity control vernier
through a slot in the flat deck. He could carry over
two hundred kilos of ballast, the mass of a stasis cage
with a human specimen inside, far from the crypt

before setting that specimen free. "I'll have to carry the cage back, of course. Who knows what trouble a savage might create, fiddling with a stasis cage?" He snorted at himself; he'd almost said "monkeying," and it was dangerous to assume he was smarter than these ancient people. But wasn't he, really? If Neanderthalers had died out on Earth, they must have been inferior in some way. Well, he was sure as hell going to find out.

If his new airboat was larger than the first, it was also more unwieldy. He used it to ferry logs to his cabin site at the small lake, cursing his need to tack in the light breezes, wishing he had a better propulsion system, for over a week before the solution hit him.

At the time he was debating the release of more animals. The mammoths, he promised himself, would come last. No wonder the builders of Newduvai had left them nearest the crypt entrance! Their cage tops would each make a dandy greenhouse and their grav polarizers would lift tons. *Or push tons*.

"Some things don't change," he told himself, laughing aloud. "I was dumb on Kzersatz and I've been dumb here." So he released the hares, gerbils, grouse, and some other species of bird with beaks meant for crunching seeds. He promptly installed their grav units around his airboat seat for propulsion, removing the mast and keel poles for reuse as cabin roof beams. That was the day Locklear nearly killed himself caroming off the lake's surface at sixty miles an hour, whooping like a fool. Now the homemade craft was no longer a boat; it was a scooter, and would scoot with an extra fifty kilos of cargo.

It might have been elation with the sporty performance of his scooter that made him so optimistic, failing to remember that you have to kill pessimists, but optimists do it themselves. The log cabin, five meters square with fireplace and frond-thatched shed roof, needed only a pallet of sling fabric and fragrant boughs beneath. A *big* pallet, he decided. It had been Kit who taught him that he should have food and shelter ready before waking strangers in strange lands. He had figs and apricot slices drying, Kzin rations for the strong of tooth, and Kzin-sized drinking vessels from the lifeboat. He moved a few more items, including a clever Kzin memory pad with electronic stylus and screen, from lifeboat to cabin, then attached a ten-meter cable harness from the scooter to the lifeboat's overhead weapon pylon.

It was only necessary then to set the scooter's bottom grav unit to slight buoyancy, and to pilot the Kzin lifeboat very slowly, towing the scooter.

The cleft where he landed had become a soggy meadow from icemelt near the frostline high on Newduvai's perimeter, protected on one side by the towering force wall and on the other by jagged basalt. The lifeboat could not be seen from below, and if his first aerial visitors were Kzinti, they'd have to fly dangerously near that force wall before they saw it. He sealed the lifeboat and then hauled the scooter down hand over hand, puffing with exertion, letting the scooter bounce harmlessly off the lifeboat's hull as he clambered aboard. Then he cast off and twiddled with those grav unit verniers until the wind whistled in his ears en route to the stasis crypt. He was already expert at modifying stasis units, and he would have lots of them to play with. If he had to protect himself from a wild woman, he could hardly wish for anything better.

He trundled the crystal cage into sunlight still wondering if he'd chosen the right—specimen? Subject? "Woman, dammit; woman!" He was trying to wear too many hats, he knew, with the one labeled "lecher" perched on top. He landed the scooter near his cabin, placed bowls of fruit and water nearby, and pressed the cage baseplate, retreating beyond his offerings.

She sank to the cage floor but only shifted position, still asleep, the breeze moving strands of chestnut hair at her cheeks. She was small and muscular, her breasts firm and immature, pubic hair sparse, limbs slender and marked with scratches; and yes, he realized as he moved nearer, she had a forty-thousand-year-old zit on her little chin. Easily the best-looking choice in the crypt, not yet fully developed into the Neanderthal body shape, she seemed capable of sleep in any position and was snoring lightly to prove it.

A *genuine teen-ager*, he mused, grinning. Aloud he said, "Okay, Lolita, up and at 'em." She stirred; a hand reached up as if tugging at an invisible blanket. "You'll miss the school shuttle," he said louder. It had never failed back on Earth with his sister.

It didn't fail here, either. She waked slowly, blinking as she sat up in lithe, nude, heartbreaking innocence. But her yawn snapped in two as she focused on him, and her pantomime of snatching a stone and hurling it at Locklear was convincing enough to make him duck. She leaped away scrabbling for real stones, and between her screams and her clods, all in Locklear's direction, she seemed to be trying to cover herself.

He retreated, but not far enough, and grabbed a

chunk of dirt only after taking one clod on his thigh.
He threatened a toss of his own, whereupon she
ducked behind the cage, watching him warily.

Well, it wouldn't matter what he said, so long as
he said it calmly. His tone and gestures would have
to serve. "You're a real little shit before breakfast,
Lolita," he said, smiling, tossing his clod gently
toward the bowls.

She saw the food then, frowning. His open hands
and strained smile invited her to the food, and she
moved toward it still holding clods ready. Wolfing
plums, she paused to gape as he pulled a plum from
a pocket and began to eat. "Never seen pockets, hm?
Stick around, little girl, I'll show you lots of interesting things." The humor didn't work, even on himself; and at his first step toward her she ran like a
deer.

Every time he pointed to himself and said his
name, she screamed something brief. She moved
around the area, checking out the cabin, draping a
vine over her breasts, and after an hour Locklear
gave up. He'd made a latchcord for the cabin door,
so she couldn't do much harm. She watched from
fifty meters distance with great wondering brown
eyes as he waved, lifted the scooter, and sped away
with her cage and a new idea.

An hour later he returned with a second cage,
cursing as he saw Lolita trying to smash his cabin
window with an oak stave. The clear plastic, of cage
material, was tough stuff and he laughed as the scooter
settled nearby, pretending he didn't itch to whack
her rump. She began a litany of stone-age curses,
then, as she saw the new cage and its occupant.
Locklear actually had to mount the scooter and chase

her off before she would quit pelting him with anything she could throw.

He made the same preparations as before, this time with shreds of smelly Kzin rations as well, and stood leaning against the cage for long moments, facing Lolita who lurked fifty meters away, to make his point. The young woman revolving slowly inside the cage was at his mercy. Then he pressed the baseplate, turned his back as the plastic levered upward, and strode off a few paces with a sigh. This one was a Neanderthal and no mistake: curves a little too broad to be exciting, massive forearms and calves, pug nose, considerable body hair. *Nice tits, though. Stop it, fool!*

The young woman stirred, sat up, looked around, then let her big jaw drop comically as she stared at Locklear, whose smile was a very rickety construction. She cocked her head at him, impassive, an instant before he spoke.

"You're no beauty, lady, so maybe you won't throw rocks at *me*. Too late for breakfast," he continued in his sweetest tones and a pointing finger. "How about lunch?"

She saw the bowls. Slowly, with caution and surprising grace, she stepped from the scooter's deck still eyeing him without smile or frown. Then she squatted to inspect the food, knees apart, facing him, and Locklear grew faint at the sight. He looked away quickly, flushing, aware that she continued to stare at him while sampling human and Kzin rations with big strong teeth and wrinklings of her nose that made her oddly attractive. *More attractive. Why the hell doesn't she cover up or something?*

He pulled another plum from a pocket, and this

magic drew a smile from her as they ate. He realized she was through eating when she wiped sticky fingers in her straight black hair, and stepped back by reflex as she stepped toward him. She stopped, with a puzzled inclination of her head, and smiled at him. That was when he stood his ground and let her approach. He had hoped for something like this, so the watching Lolita could see that he meant no harm.

When the woman stood within arm's length of him she stopped. He put a hand on his breast. "Me Locklear you Jane," he said.

"(Something,)" she said. Maybe *Kh-roofeh*.

He was going to try saying it himself when she startled him into a wave of actual physical weakness. With eyes half-closed, she cupped her full breasts in both hands and smiled. He looked at her erect nipples, feeling the rush of blood to his face, and showed her his hands in a broad helpless shrug. Whereupon, she took his hands and placed them on her breasts, and now her big black eyes were not those of a savage Neanderthal but a sultry smiling Levantine woman who knew how to make a point. Two points.

Three points, as he felt a rising response and knew her hands were seeking that rise, hands that had never known velcrolok closures yet seemed to have an intelligence of their own. His whole body was tingling now as he caressed her, and when her hands found that fabric closure, she shared a fresh smile with him, and tried to pull him down on the ground with her.

So he took her hands in his and walked her to the cabin. She "hmm"ed when he pulled the latchcord loop to open the door, and "ahh"ed when she saw the big pallet, and then offered those swarthy full breasts again and put her face against the hollow of his throat, and toyed inside his velcrolok closure until he astonished her by pulling his entire flight suit off, and offered her body in ways simple and sophisticated, and Locklear accepted all the offers he could, and made a few of his own, all of which she accepted expertly.

He had his first sensation of something eerie, something just below his awareness, as he lay inert on his back bathed in honest sweat, his partner lying face-down more or less across him like one stick abandoned across another stick after both had been rubbed to kindle a blaze. He saw a movement at his window and knew it was Lolita, peering silently in. He sighed.

His partner sighed, too, and turned toward the window with a quick, vexed burst of some command. The face disappeared.

He chuckled, "Did you hear the little devil, or smell her?" Actually, his partner had more of the *eau de sweatsock* perfume than Lolita did; now more pronounced than ever. He didn't care. If the past half-hour had been any omen, he might never care again.

She stretched then, and sat up, dragging a heel that was rough as a rasp across his calf. Her heavy ragged nails had scratched him, and he was oily from God knew what mixture of greases in her long hair. He didn't give a damn about that either, reflecting that a man should allow a few squeaks in the hinges of the pearly gates.

She said something then, softly, with that tilt of her head that suggested inquiry. "Locklear," he replied, tapping his chest again.

Her look was somehow pitying then, as she repeated her phrase, placing one hand on her head, the other on his.

"Oh yeah, you're my girl and I'm your guy," he said, nodding, placing his hands on hers.

She sat quite still for a moment, her eyes sad on his. Then, delighting him, she placed one hand on his breast and managed a passable, "Loch-leah."

He grinned and nodded, then cocked his head and placed a hand between her (wonderful!) breasts. No homecoming queen, but dynamite in deep shadows . . .

He paid more attention as she said, approximately, "Ch'roofh," and when he repeated it she laughed, closing her eyes with downcast chin. *A big chin, a really whopping big one to be honest about it*, and then he caught her gaze, not angry but perhaps reproachful, and again he felt the passage of something like a cold breeze through his awareness.

She rubbed his gooseflesh down for him, responding to his "ahh"s, and presently she astonished him again by beginning to query him on the names of things. Locklear knew that he could thoroughly confuse her if he insisted on perfectly grammatical tenses, cases, and syntax. He tried to keep it simple, and soon learned that "head down, eyes shut" was the same as a negative headshake. "Chin elevated, smiling" was the same as a nod—and now he realized he'd seen her giving him yesses that way from the first moment she awoke. A smile or a frown was the same for her as for him—but that heads-up smile was a definite gesture.

She drew him outside again presently, studying the terrain with lively curiosity, miming actions and listening as he provided words, responding with words of her own.

The name he gave her was, in part, because it was faintly like the one she'd offered; and in part because she seemed willing to learn his ways while revealing ancient ways of her own. He named her "Ruth." Locklear felt crestfallen when, by midafternoon, he realized Ruth was learning his language much faster than he was learning hers. And then, as he glanced over her shoulder to see little Lolita creeping nearer, he began to understand why.

Ruth turned quickly, with a shouted command and warning gestures, and Lolita dropped the sharpened stick she'd been carrying. Locklear knew beyond doubt that Lolita had made no sound in her approach. There was only one explanation that would fit all his data: Ruth unafraid of him from the first; offering herself as if she knew his desires; keeping track of Lolita without looking; and her uncanny speed in learning his language.

And that moment when she'd placed her hand on his head, with an inquiry that was somehow pitying. Now he copied her gesture with one hand on his own head, the other on hers, and lowered his head, eyes shut. "No," he said. "Locklear, no telepath. Ruth, yes?"

"Ruth, yes." She pointed to Lolita then. "No— telpat."

She needed another ten minutes of pantomime, attending to his words and obviously to his thoughts as he spoke them, to get her point across. Ruth was a "gentle," but like Locklear himself, Lolita was a "new."

When darkness came to Newduvai, Lolita got chummier in a hurry, complaining until Ruth let her into the cabin. Despite that, Ruth didn't seem to like the girl much and accepted Locklear's name for her, shortening it to "Loli." Ruth spoke to her in their common tongue, not so much gutteral as throaty, and Locklear had a strong impression that they were old acquaintances. Either of them could tend a fire expertly, and both were wary of the light from his Kzin memory screen until they found that it would not singe a curious finger.

Locklear was bothered on two counts by Loli's insistence on taking pieces of Kzin plastic film to make a bikini suit: first because Ruth plainly thought it silly, and second because the kid was more appealing with it than she was when stark naked. At least the job kept Loli silently occupied, listening and watching as Locklear got on with the business of talking with Ruth.

Their major breakthrough for the evening came when Locklear got the ideas of past and future, "before" and "soon," across to Ruth. Her telepathy was evidently the key to her quick grasp of his language; yet it seemed to work better with emotional states than with abstract ideas, and she grew upset when Loli became angry with her own first clumsy efforts at making her panties fit. Clearly, Ruth was a lady who liked her harmony.

For Ruth was, despite her rude looks, a lady—when she wasn't in the sack. Even so, when at last Ruth had seen to Loli's comfort with spare fabric and Locklear snapped off the light, he felt inviting hands on him again. "No thanks," he said, chuckling, patting her shoulder, even though he wanted her again. And Ruth *knew* he did, judging from her sly insistence.

"No. Loli here," he said finally, and felt Ruth shrug as if to say it didn't matter. Maybe it didn't matter to Neanderthals, but—"Soon," he promised, and shared a hug with Ruth before they fell asleep.

During the ensuing week, he learned much. For one thing, he learned that Loli was a chronic pain in the backside. She ate like a Kzin warrior. She liked to see if things would break. She liked to spy. She interfered with Locklear's pace during his afternoon "naps" with Ruth by whacking on the door with sticks and stones, until he swore he would ". . . hit Loli soon."

But Ruth would not hear of that. "Hit Loli, same hit Ruth head. Locklear like hit Ruth head?"

But one afternoon, when she saw Locklear studying her with friendly intensity, Ruth spoke to Loli at some length. The girl picked up her short spear and, crooning her happiness, loped off into the forest. Ruth turned to Locklear smiling. "Loli find fruitwater, soon Ruth make fruitfood." A few minutes of miming showed that she had promised to make some kind of dessert, if Loli could find a beehive for honey.

Locklear had seen beehives in stasis, but explained that there were very few animals loose on Newduvai, and no hurtbugs.

"No hurtbugs? Loli no find, long time. Good," Ruth replied firmly, and led him by the hand into their cabin, and "good" was the operative word.

On his next trip to the crypt, Locklear needed all day for his solitary work. He might put it off forever, but it was clear by now that he must populate Newduvai with game before he released their most fearsome predators. The little horses needed only to see daylight before galloping off. Camels were quicker still, and the deer bounded off like golf balls down a freeway. The predators would simply have to wait until the herds were larger, and the day was over before he could rig grav polarizers to trundle mammoths to the mouth of the crypt. His last job of the day was his most troublesome, releasing small cages of bees near groves of fruit trees and wildflowers.

Locklear and Ruth managed to convey a lot with only a few hundred words, though some of those words had to do multiple duty while Ruth expanded her vocabulary. When she said "new," for example, it often carried a stigma. Neanderthals, he decided, were very conservative folk, and they sensed a lie before you told it. If Ruth was any measure, they also had little aptitude for math. She understood one and two and many. She understood "none," but not as a number. If there wasn't any, she conveyed to him, why try to count it? She had him there.

Eventually, between food-gathering forays, he used pebbles and sketches to tell Ruth of the many, many other animals and people he could bring to the scene. She was no sketch artist; in fact, she insisted, women were not supposed to draw things—especially hunt-things. Ah, he said, magics were only for men? Yes, she said, then mystified him with pantomimes of sleep and pain. That was for men, too, and food-gathering was for women.

He pursued the mystery, sketching with the Kzin memo screen. At last, when she pretended to cut her throat with his *wtsai* knife, he understood, and added the word "kill" to her vocabulary. Men hunted and killed.

Dry-mouthed, he asked, "Man like kill Locklear?"

Now it was her turn to be mystified. "No kill. Why kill magic man?"

Because, he replied, "Locklear like Ruth, one-two other men like Ruth. Kill Locklear for Ruth?"

He had never seen her laugh aloud, but he saw it now, the big teeth gleaming, breasts shaking with merriment. "Locklear like Ruth, good. Many man like Ruth, good."

He was silent for a long time, fighting the temptation to tell her that many men liking Ruth was *not* good. Then: "Ruth like many man?"

She had learned to nod by now, and did it happily. The next five minutes were troubled ones for Locklear. Ruth did not seem to understand monogamy in any form. Apparently, everybody took pot luck in the sex department and was free to accept or reject. Some people were simply more popular than others. "Many man like Ruth," she said. "Many, many, many . . ."

"Okay, for Christ's sake, I get the idea," he exploded, and again he saw that look of sadness—or perhaps pain. "Locklear see, Ruth popular with man." It seemed to be their first quarrel. Tentatively, he said, "Locklear little popular with woman."

"Much popular with Ruth," she said, and began to rub his shoulders. That was the day she asked him about her appearance, and he responded tho best way he could. She thought it silly to trim her strong, useful nails; sillier to wash her hair. Still, she did it, and he claimed she was pretty, and she knew he lied.

When it occurred to him to ask how he could look nice for her, Ruth said, "Locklear pretty now." But he never thought to wonder if *she* might be lying.

Whatever Ruth said about women and hunting, it did not seem to apply to Loli. While aloft in the scooter one day to study distribution of the animals,

Locklear saw the girl chasing a hare across a meadow. She was no slouch with a short spear and nailed the hare on her second toss, dispatching it with a stone after a brief struggle. He lowered the scooter very, very slowly, watching her tear at the animal, disgusted when he realized she was eating it raw.

She saw his shadow when the scooter was hovering very near, and sat there blushing, looking at him with the innards of the hare across her lap.

She understood few of his words—or seemed to, at the cabin—but his tone was clear enough. "You couldn't share it, you little bastard. No, you sneak out here and stuff yourself." She began to suck her thumb, pouting. Then perhaps Loli realized the boss must be placated; she tried a smile on her blood-streaked face and held her grisly trophy out.

"No. Ruth. Give to Ruth," he scowled, pointing toward the cabin. She elevated her chin and smiled, and he flew off grumbling. He couldn't much blame the kid; Kzin rations and fruit were getting pretty tiresome, and the gruel Ruth made from grain wasn't all that exciting without bits of meat. It was going to be rougher on the animals when he woke the men.

And why wake them at all? You've got it good here, he reminded himself in Sequence Umpteen of his private dialogue. *You have your own little world and a harem of one, and you know when her period comes so you know when not to play. And one of these days, Loli will be a knockout, I suspect. A much niftier dish than poor Ruth, who doesn't know what a skag she'd be in modern society, thank God.*

Moments like this made him squirm. Setting Ruth's looks aside, he had no complaint, not even about the country itself. *Not much seasonal change, no danger-*

ous animals unless you want to release them, cer-
tainly none of the most dangerous animal of all.
Except for Kzinti, of course. One on one, they were
meaner predators than men—even Neanderthal
savages.

"That's why I have to release 'em," he said to the
wind. "If a fully-manned Kzin ship comes, I'll need
an army." He no longer kidded himself about schol-
arship and the sociology of *homo neanderthalensis*,
which was strictly a secondary item. It was sobering
to look yourself over and see self-interest riding you
like a hunchback. So he flew directly to the crypt
and spent the balance of the day releasing the whop-
pers: aurochs and bison, which didn't make him sweat
much, and a half-dozen mammoths, which did.

A mammoth, he found, was a flighty beast not
given to confrontations. He could set one shambling
off with a shout, its trunk high like a periscope
tasting the breeze. Every one of them turned into
the wind and disappeared toward the frostline, and
now the crypt held only its most dangerous creatures.

He returned to the cabin perilously late, the sun
of Newduvai dying while he was still a hundred
meters from the wisp of smoke rising from the cabin.
He landed blind near the cabin, very slowly but with
a jolt, and saw the faint gleam of the Kzin light leap
from the cabin window. Ruth might not have a head
for figures, but she'd seen him snap that light on fifty
times. *And she must've sensed my panic. I wonder
how far off she can do that. . . .*

Ruth already had succulent broiled haunches of
Loli's hare, keeping them warm over coals, and it
wrenched his heart as he saw she was drooling as she
waited for him. He wiped the corner of her mouth,

kissed her anyhow, and sat at the rough pole table while she brought his supper. Loli had obviously eaten, and watched him as if fearful that he would order her outside.

Hauling mammoths, even with a grav polarizer, is exhausting work. After finishing off a leg of hare, and falling asleep at the table, Locklear was only half-aware when Ruth picked him up and carried him to their pallet as easily as she would have carried a child.

The next day, he had Ruth convey to Loli that she was not to hunt without permission. Then, with less difficulty than he'd expected, he sketched and quizzed her about the food of a Neanderthal tribe. Yes, they hunted everything: bugs to mammoths, it was all protein, but chiefly they gathered roots, grains, and fruits.

That made sense. Why risk getting killed hunting when tubers didn't fight back? He posed his big question then. If he brought a tribe to Newduvai (this brought a smile of anticipation to her broad face), and forbade them to hunt without his permission, would they obey?

Gentles might, she said. New people, such as Loli, were less obedient. She tried to explain why, conveying something about telepathy and hunting, until he waved the question aside. If he showed her sleeping gentles, would she tell him which ones were good? Oh yes, she said, adding a phrase she knew he liked: "No problem."

But it took him an hour to get Ruth on the scooter. That stuff was all very well for great magic men, she implied, but women's magics were more prosaic. After a few minutes idling just above the turf, he sped

up, and she liked that fine. Then he slowed and lifted
the scooter a bit. By noon, he was cruising fast as
they surveyed groups of aurochs, solitary gazelles,
and skittish horses from high above. It was she,
sampling the wind with her nose, who directed him
higher and then pointed out a mammoth, a huge
specimen using its tusks to find roots.

He watched the huge animal briefly, estimating
how many square miles a mammoth needed to feed,
and then made a decision that saddened him. Earth
had kept right on turning when the last mammoths
disappeared. Newduvai could not afford many of
them, ripping up foliage by the roots. Perhaps the
Outsiders didn't care about that, but Locklear did. If
you had to start sawing off links in your food chain,
best if you started at the top. And he didn't want to
pursue that thought by himself. At the very top was
man. And Kzin. It was the kind of thing he'd like to
discuss with Scarface, but he'd made two trips to the
lifeboat without a peep from its all-band comm set.

Finally, he flew to the crypt and set his little craft
down nearby, reassuring Ruth as they walked inside.
She paused for flight when she saw the rest of the
mammoths, slowly tumbling inside their cages. "Much,
much, much magic," she said, and patted him with
great confidence.

But it was the sight of forty Neanderthals in stasis
that really affected Ruth. Her face twisted with re-
morse, she turned from the nearest cage and faced
Locklear with tears streaming down her cheeks.
"Locklear kill?"

"No, no! Sleep," he insisted, miming it.

She was not convinced. "No sleeptalk," she protested, placing a hand on her head and pointing

toward the rugged male nearby. And doubtless she was right; in stasis you didn't even dream.

"Before, Locklear take Ruth from little house," he said, tapping the cage, and then she remembered, and wanted to take the man out then and there. Instead, he got her help in moving the cage onto his improvised dolly and outside to the scooter.

They were halfway to the cabin and a thousand feet up on the heavily-laden scooter when Ruth somehow struck the cage base with her foot. Locklear saw the transparent plastic begin to rise, shouted, and nearly turned the scooter on its side as he leaped to slam the plastic down.

"Good God! You nearly let a wild man loose on a goddamn raft, a thousand feet in the air," he raged, and saw her cringe, holding her head in both hands. "Okay, Ruth. Okay, no problem," he continued more slowly, and pointed at the cage base. "Ruth no hit little house more. Locklear hit, soon."

They remained silent until they landed, and Locklear had time to review Newduvai's first in-flight airline emergency. Ruth had not feared a beating. No, it was his own panic that had punished her. That figured: a Kzin telepath sometimes suffered when someone nearby was suffering.

He brought food and water from the cabin, placed it near the scooter, then paused before pressing the cage base. "Ruth: gentle man talk in head same Ruth talk in head?"

"Yes, all gentles talk in head." She saw what he was getting at. "Ruth talk to man, say Locklear much, much good magic man."

He pointed again at the man, a muscular young specimen who, without so much body hair, might have excited little comment at a collegiate wrestling match. "Ruth friend of man?"

She blushed as she replied: "Yes. Friend long time."

"That's what I was afraid of," he muttered with a heavy sigh, pressed the baseplate, and then stepped back several paces, nearly bumping into the curious Loli.

The man's eyes flicked open. Locklear could see the heavy muscles tense, yet the man moved only his eyes, looking from him to Ruth, then to him again. When he did move, it was as though he'd been playing possum for forty thousand years, and his movements were as oddly graceful as Ruth's. He held up both hands, smiling, and it was obvious that some silent message had passed between them.

Locklear advanced with the same posture. A flat touch of hands, and then the man turned to Ruth with a burst of throaty speech. He was no taller than Locklear, but immensely more heavily-boned and muscled. He stood as erect as any man, unconcerned in his nakedness, and after a double handclasp with Ruth he made a smiling motion toward her breasts.

Again, Locklear saw the deeper color of flushing over her face and, after a head-down gesture of negation, she said something while staring at the young man's face. Puzzled, he glanced at Locklear with a comical half-smile, and Locklear tried to avoid looking at the man's budding erection. He told the man his name, and got a reply, but as usual Locklear gave him a name that seemed appropriate. He called him "Minuteman."

After a quick meal of fruit and water, Ruth did the translating. From the first, Minuteman accepted the fact that Locklear was one of the "new" people. After

Locklear's demonstrations with the Kzin memo screen
and a levitation of the scooter, Minuteman gave him
more physical space, perhaps a sign of deference. Or
perhaps wariness; time would tell.

Though Loli showed no fear of Minuteman, she
spoke little to him and kept her distance—with an
egg-sized stone in her little fist at all times. Minuteman treated Loli as a guest might treat an unwel-
come pet. *Oh yes*, thought Locklear, *he knows her,
all righty.* . . .

The hunt, Locklear claimed, was a celebration to
welcome Minuteman, but he had an ulterior motive.
He made his point to Ruth, who chattered and gestured and, no doubt, silently communed with Minuteman for long moments. It would be necessary for
Minuteman to accompany Locklear on the scooter,
but without Ruth if they were to lug any sizeable
game back to the cabin.

When Ruth stopped, Minuteman said something
more. "Yes, no problem," Ruth said then.

Minuteman, his facial scars writhing as he grinned,
managed, "Yes, no problem," and laughed when
Locklear did. *Amazing how fast these people adapt*,
Locklear thought. *He wakes up on a strange planet,
and an hour later he's right at home. A wonderful
trusting kind of innocence; even childlike.* Then
Locklear decided to see just how far that trust went,
and gestured for Minuteman to sit down on the
scooter after he wrestled the empty stasis cage to the
ground.

Soon they were scudding along just above the
trees at a pace guaranteed to scare the hell out of any
sensible Neanderthal, Minuteman desperately trying
to make a show of confidence in the leadership of

this suicidal shaman, and Locklear was satisfied on
two counts, with one count yet to come. First, the
scooter's pace near trees was enough to make Minuteman hold on for dear life. Second, the young
Neanderthal would view Locklear's easy mastery of
the scooter as perhaps the very greatest of magics—
and maybe Minuteman would pass that datum on,
when the time came.

The third item was a shame, really, but it had to
be done. A shaman without the power of ultimate
punishment might be seen as expendable, and
Locklear had to show that power. He showed it after
passing over specimens of aurochs and horse, both
noted with delight by Minuteman.

The goat had been grazing not far from three does
until he saw the scooter swoop near. He was an old
codger, probably driven off by the younger buck
nearby, and Locklear recalled that the gestation period for goats was only five months—and besides, he
told himself, the Outsiders could be pretty dumb in
some matters. You didn't need twenty bucks for
twenty does.

All of the animals bounded toward a rocky slope,
and Minuteman watched them as Locklear maneuvered, forcing the old buck to turn back time and
again. When at last the buck turned to face them,
Locklear brought the scooter down, moving straight
toward the hapless old fellow. Minuteman did not
turn toward Locklear until he heard the report of the
Kzin sidearm which Locklear held in both hands,
and by that time the scooter was only a man's height
above the rocks.

At the report, the buck slammed backward, stumbling, shot in the breast. Minuteman ducked away

from the sound of the shot, seeing Locklear with the sidearm, and then began to shout. Locklear let the scooter settle but Minuteman did not wait, leaping down, rushing at the old buck which still kicked in its death agony.

By the time Locklear had the scooter resting on the slope, Minuteman was tearing at the buck's throat with his teeth, trying to dodge flinty hooves, the powerful arms locked around his prey. In thirty seconds the buck's eyes were glazing and its movements grew more feeble by the moment. Locklear put away the sidearm, feeling his stomach churn. Minuteman was drinking the animal's blood; sucking it, in fact, in a kind of frenzy.

When at last he sat up, Minuteman began to massage his temples with bloody fingers—perhaps a ritual, Locklear decided. The young Neanderthal's gaze at Locklear was not pleasant, though he was suitably impressed by the invisible spear that had noisily smashed a man-sized goat off its feet leaving nothing more than a tiny hole in the animal's breast. Locklear went through a pantomime of shooting, and Minuteman gestured his "yes." Together, they placed the heavy carcass on the scooter and returned to the cabin. Minuteman seemed oddly subdued for a hunter who had just chewed a victim's throat open.

Locklear guffawed at what he saw at the cabin: in the cage so recently vacated by Minuteman was Loli, revolving in the slow dance of stasis. Ruth explained, "Loli like little house, like sleep. Ruth like for Loli sleep. Many like for Loli sleep long time," she added darkly.

It was Ruth who butchered the animal with the *wtsai*, while talking with Minuteman. Locklear watched smugly, noting the absence of flies. Damned if he was going to release those from their cages, nor the mosquitoes, locusts, and other pests which lay with the predators in the crypt. Why would any god worth his salt pester a planet with flies, anyhow? The butterflies might be worth the trouble.

He was still ruminating on these matters when Ruth handed him the *wtsai* and entered the cabin silently. She seemed preoccupied, and Minuteman had wandered off toward the oaks so, just to be sociable, he said, "Minuteman see Locklear kill with magic. Minuteman like?"

She built a smoky fire, stretching skewers of stringy meat above the smoke, before answering. "No good, talk bad to magic man."

"It's okay, Ruth. Talk true to Locklear."

She propped the cabin door open to adjust the draft, then sat down beside him. "Minuteman feel bad. Locklear no kill meat fast, meat hurt long time. Meat feel much, much bad, so Minuteman feel much bad before kill meat. Locklear new person, no feel bad. Loli no feel bad. Minuteman no want hunt with Locklear."

As she attended to the barbecue and Locklear continued to ferret out more of this mystery, he grew more chastened. Neanderthal boys, learning to kill for food, began with animals that did not have a highly developed nervous system. Because when the animal felt pain, all the gentles nearby felt some of it, too, especially women and girls. Neanderthal hunt teams were all-male affairs, and they learned every trick of stealth and quick kills because a clumsy kill meant a slow one. Minuteman had known that, lacking a club, he himself would feel the least pain if the goat bled to death quickly.

And large animals? You dug pit traps and visited them from a distance, or drove your prey off a distant cliff if you could. Neanderthal telepathy did not work much beyond twenty meters. The hunter who approached a wounded animal to pierce its throat with a spear was very brave, or very hungry. Or he was one of the new people, perfectly capable of irritating or even fighting a gentle without feeling the slightest psychic pain. The gentle Neanderthal, of course, was not protected against the new person's reflected pain. No wonder Ruth took care of Loli without liking her much!

He asked if Loli was the first "new" Ruth had seen. No, she said, but the only one they had allowed in the tribe. A hunt team had found her wandering alone, terrified and hungry, when she was only as high as a man's leg. Why hadn't the hunters run away? They had, Ruth said, but even then Loli had been quick on her feet. Rather than feel her gnawing fear and hunger on the perimeter of their camp, they had taken her in. And had regretted it ever since, ". . . long time. Long, long, long time!"

Locklear knew that he had gained a crucial insight; a Neanderthal behaved gently because it was in his own interests. It was, at least, until modern Cro-Magnon man appeared without the blessing, and the curse, of telepathy.

Ruth's first telepathic greeting to the waking Minuteman had warned that he was in the presence of a great shaman, a "new" but nonetheless a good man. Minuteman had been so glad to see Ruth that he had proposed a brief roll in the grass, which involved great pleasure to participants—and it was expected that the audience could share their joy by telepathy.

But Ruth knew better than that, reminding her friend that Locklear was not telepathic. Besides, she had the strongest kind of intuition that Locklear did not want to see her enjoying any other man. Peculiar, even bizarre; but new people were hard to figure. . . .

It was clear now, why Ruth's word "new" seemed to have an unpleasant side. New people were savage people. *So much for labels*, Locklear told himself. *Modern man is the real savage!*

Ruth took Loli out of stasis for supper, perhaps to share in the girl's pleasure at such a feast. Through Ruth, Locklear explained to Minuteman that he regretted giving pain to his guest. He would be happy to let gentles do the hunting, but all animals belonged to Locklear. No animals must be hunted without prior permission. Minuteman was agreeable, especially with a mouthful of succulent goat rib in his big lantern jaws. Tonight, Minuteman could share the cabin. Tomorrow he must choose a site for a camp, for Locklear would soon bring many, many more gentles.

Locklear fell asleep slowly, no thanks to the ache in his jaws. The others had wolfed down that barbecued goat as if it had been well-aged porterhouse, but he had been able to choke only a little of it down after endless chewing because, savory taste or not, that old goat had been tough as a Kzin's knuckles.

He wondered how Kit and Scarface were getting along, on the other side of those force walls. He really ought to fire up the lifeboat and visit them soon. Just as soon as he got things going here. With his mind-bending discovery of the truly gentle nature of Neanderthals, he was feeling very optimistic about the future. And modestly hungry. And very, very sleepy.

*   *   *

Minuteman spent two days quartering the vast circular expanse of Newduvai while Locklear piloted the scooter. In the process, he picked up a smatter of modern words though it was Ruth, in the evenings, who straightened out misunderstandings. Minuteman's clear choice for a major encampment was beside Newduvai's big lake, near the point where a stream joined the "big water." The site was a day's walk from the cabin, and Minuteman stressed that his choice might not be the choice of tribal elders. Besides, gentles tended to wander from season to season.

Though tempted by his power to command, Locklear decided against using it unless absolutely necessary. He would release them all and let them sort out their world, with the exception of excess hunting or tribal warfare. That didn't seem likely, but: "Ruth," he asked after the second day of recon, "see all people in little houses in cave?"

"Yes," she said firmly. "Many many in tribe of Minuteman and Ruth. Many many in other tribe."

But "many many" could mean a dozen or less. "Ruth see all in other tribe before?"

"Many times," she assured him. "Others give killstones, Ruth tribe give food."

"You trade with them," he said. After she had studied his face a moment, she agreed. He persisted: "Bad trades? Problem?"

"No problem," she said. "Trade one, two man or woman sometimes, before big fire."

He asked about that, of course, and got an answer to a question he hadn't thought to ask. Ruth's last memory before waking on Newduvai—and Minuteman's, too—was of the great fire that had driven

several tribes to the base of a cliff. There, with trees
bursting into flame nearby, the men had gathered
around their women and children, beginning their
song to welcome death. It was at that moment when
the Outsiders must have put them in stasis and
whisked them off to the rim of Known Space.

Almost an ethical decision, Locklear admitted.
Almost. "No little gentles in cave," he reminded
Ruth. "Locklear much sorry."

"No good, think of little gentles," she said glumly.
And with that, they passed to matters of tribal leadership. The old men generally led, though an old
woman might have followers. It seemed a loose kind
of democracy and, when some faction disagreed, they
could simply move out—perhaps no farther than a
short walk away.

Locklear soon learned why the gentles tended to
stay close: "Big, bad animals eat gentles," Ruth said.
"New people take food, kill gentles," she added.
Lions, wolves, bears—and modern man—were their
reasons for safety in numbers.

Ruth and Minuteman had both seen much of
Newduvai from the air by now. To check his own
conclusions, Locklear said, "Plenty food for many
people. Plenty for many, many, many people?"

Plenty, said Ruth, for all people in little houses; no
problem. Locklear ended the session on that note
and Minuteman, perhaps with some silent urging
from Ruth, chose to sleep outside.

Again, Locklear had a trouble getting to sleep,
even after a half-hour of delightful tussle with the
willing, homely, gentle Ruth. He could hardly wait
for morning and his great social experiment.

*   *   *

His work would have gone much faster with Minuteman's muscular help, but Locklear wanted to share
the crypt's secrets with as few as possible. The lake
site was only fifteen minutes from the crypt by scooter,
and there were no predators to attack a stasis cage,
so Locklear transported the gentles by twos and left
them in their cages, cursing his rotten time-manage-
ment. It soon was obvious that the job would take
two days and he'd set his heart on results now, now,
now!

He was setting the scooter down near his cabin
when Minuteman shot from the doorway, began to
lope off, and then turned, approaching Locklear with
the biggest, ugliest smile he could manage. He chattered away with all the innocence of a ferret in a
birdhouse, his maleness in repose but rather large
for that innocence. And wet.

Ruth waved from the cabin doorway.

"Right," Locklear snarled, too exhausted to let his
anger kindle to white-hot fury. "Minuteman, I named
you well. Your pants would be down, if you had any.
Ahh, the hell with it."

Loli was asleep in her cage, and Minuteman found
employment elsewhere as Locklear ate chopped goat,
grapes, and gruel. He did not look at Ruth, even
when she sat near him as he chewed.

Finally he walked to the pallet, looking from it to
Ruth, shook his head and then lay down.

Ruth cocked her head in that way she had. "Like
Ruth stay at fire?"

"I don't give a good shit. Yes, Ruth stay at fire.
Good." Some perversity made him want her, but it
was not as strong as his need for sleep. And rejecting
her might be a kind of punishment, he thought
sleepily. . . .

Late the next afternoon, Locklear completed his airlift and returned to the cabin. He could see Minuteman sitting disconsolate, chin in hands, at the edge of the clearing. Apparently, no one had seen fit to take Loli from stasis. He couldn't blame them much. Actually, he thought as he entered the cabin, he had no logical reason to blame them for anything. They enjoyed each other according to their own tradition, and he was out of step with it. *Damn' right, and I don't know if I could ever get in step.*

He called Minuteman in. "Many, many gentles at big water," he said. "No big bad meat hurt gentles. Like see gentles now?" Minuteman wanted to very much. So did Ruth. He urged them onto the scooter and handed Ruth her woven basket full of dried apricots, giving both hindquarters of the goat to Minuteman without comment. Soon they were flitting above conifers and poplars, and then Ruth saw the dozens of cages glistening beside the lake.

"Gentles, gentles," she exclaimed, and began to weep. Locklear found himself angry at her pleasure, the anger of a wronged spouse, and set the scooter down abruptly some distance from the stasis cages.

Minuteman was off and running instantly. Ruth disembarked, turned, held a hand out. "Locklear like wake gentles? Ruth tell gentles, Locklear good, much good magics."

"Tell 'em anything you like," he barked, "after you screw 'em all!"

In the distance, Minuteman was capering around the cages, shouting in glee. After a moment, Ruth said, "Ruth like go back with Locklear."

"The hell you will! No, Ruth like push-push with many gentles. Locklear no like." And he twisted a vernier hard, the scooter lifting quickly.

Plaintively, growing faint on the breeze: "Ruth hurt in head. Like Locklear much . . ." And whatever else she said was lost.

He returned to the hidden Kzin lifeboat, hating the idea of the silent cabin, and monitored the comm set for hours. It availed him nothing, but its boring repetitions eventually put him to sleep.

For the next week, Locklear worked like a man demented. He used a stasis cage, as he had on Kzersatz, to store his remaining few hunks of smoked goat. He flew surveillance over the new encampment, so high that no one would spot him, which meant that he could see little of interest, beyond the fact that they were building huts of bundled grass and some dark substance, perhaps mud. The stasis cages lay in disarray; he must retrieve them soon.

It was pure luck that he spotted a half-dozen deer one morning, a half-day's walk from the encampment, running as though from a predator. Presently, hovering beyond big chestnut trees, he saw them: men, patiently herding their prey toward an arroyo. He grinned to himself and waited until a rise of ground would cover his maneuver. Then he swooped low behind the deer, swerving from side to side to group them, yelping and growling until he was hoarse. By that time, the deer had put a mile between themselves and their real pursuers.

No better time than now to get a few things straight. Locklear swept the scooter toward the encampment at a stately pace, circling twice, hearing thin shouts as the Neanderthals noted his approach. He watched them carefully, one hand checking his Kzin sidearm. They might be gentle but a few already carried spears and they were, after all, experts at the quick kill. He let the scooter hover at knee height, a constant reminder of his great magics, and noted the great stir he made as the scooter glided silently to a stop at the edge of the camp.

He saw Ruth and Minuteman emerge from one of the dozen beehive-shaped, grass-and-wattle huts. No, it wasn't Ruth; he admitted with chagrin that they all looked very much alike. The women paused first, and then he did spot Ruth, waving at him, a few steps nearer. The men moved nearer, falling silent now, laying their new spears and stone axes down as if by prearrangement. They stopped a few paces ahead of the women.

An older male, almost covered in curly gray hair, continued to advance using a spear—no, it was only a long walking staff—to aid him. He too stopped, with a glance over his shoulder, and then Locklear saw a bald old fellow with a withered leg hobbling past the younger men. Both of the oldsters advanced together then, full of years and dignity without a stitch of clothes. The gray man might have been sixty, with a little pot belly and knobby joints suggesting arthritis. The cripple was perhaps ten years younger but stringy and meatless, and his right thigh had been hideously smashed a long time before. His right leg was inches too short, and his left hip seemed disfigured from years of walking to compensate.

Locklear knew he needed Ruth now, but feared to risk violating some taboo so soon. "Locklear," he said, showing empty hands, then tapping his breast.

The two old men cocked their heads in a parody of Ruth's familiar gesture, then the curly one began to speak. Of course it was all gibberish, but the walking staff lay on the ground now and their hands were empty.

Wondering how much they would understand telepathically, Locklear spoke with enough volume for Ruth to hear. "Gentles hunt meat in hills," he said. "Locklear no like." He was not smiling.

The old men used brief phrases to each other, and then the crippled one turned toward the huts. Ruth began to walk forward, smiling wistfully at Locklear as she stopped next to the cripple.

She waited to hear a few words from each man, and then faced Locklear. "All one tribe now, two leaders," she said. "Skywater and Shortleg happy to see great shaman who save all from big fire. Ruth happy see Locklear, too," she added softly.

He told her about the men hunting deer, and that it must stop; they must make do without meat for awhile. She translated. The old men conferred, and their gesture for "no" was the same as Ruth's. They replied through Ruth that young men had always hunted, and always would.

He told them that the animals were his, and they must not take what belonged to another. The old men said they could see that he felt in his head the animals were his, but no one owned the great mother land, and no one could own her children. They felt much bad for him. He was a very, very great shaman, but not so good at telling gentles how to live.

With great care, having chosen the names Cloud and Gimp for the old fellows, he explained that if many animals were killed, soon there would be no more. One day when many little animals were born, he would let them hunt the older ones.

The gist of their reply was this: Locklear obviously

thought he was right, but they were older and therefore wiser. And because they had never run out of
game no matter how much they killed, they *never
could* run out of game. If it hadn't already happened,
it wouldn't ever happen.

Abruptly, Locklear motioned to Cloud and had
Ruth translate: he could prove the scarcity of game if
Cloud would ride the scooter as Ruth and Minute-
man had ridden it.

Much silent discussion and some out loud. Then
old Cloud climbed aboard and in a moment, the
scooter was above the trees.

From a mile up, they could identify most of the
game animals, especially herd beasts in open plains.
There weren't many to see. "No babies at all,"
Locklear said, trying to make gestures for "small."
"Cloud, gentles *must* wait until babies are born."
The old fellow seemed to understand Locklear's
thoughts well enough, and spoke a bit of gibberish,
but his head gesture was a Neanderthal "no."

Locklear, furious now, used the verniers with aban-
don. The scooter fled across parched arroyo and broken hill, closer to the ground and now so fast that
Locklear himself began to feel nervous. Old Cloud
sensed his unease, grasping handholds with gnarled
knuckles and hunkering down, and Locklear knew a
savage elation. *Serve the old bastard right if I splat-
tered him all over Newduvai.* And then he saw the
old man staring at his eyes, and knew that the thought
had been received.

"No, I won't do it," he said. But a part of him had
wanted to; *still* wanted to out of sheer frustration.
Cloud's face was a rigid mask of fear, big teeth showing, and Locklear slowed the scooter as he approached
the encampment again.

Cloud did not wait for the vehicle to settle, but debarked as fast as painful old joints would permit and stood facing his followers without a sound.

After a moment, with dozens of Neanderthals staring in stunned silence, they all turned their backs, a wave of moans rising from every throat. Ruth hesitated, but she too faced away from Locklear.

"Ruth! No hurt Cloud. Locklear no like hurt gentles."

The moans continued as Cloud strode away. "Locklear need to talk to Ruth!" And then as the entire tribe began to walk away, he raised his voice: "No hurt gentles, Ruth!"

She stopped, but would not look at him as she replied. "Cloud say new people hurt gentles and not know. Locklear hurt Cloud before, want kill Cloud. Locklear go soon soon," she finished in a sob. Suddenly, then, she was running to catch the others.

Some of the men were groping for spears now. Locklear did not wait to see what they might do with them. A half-hour later he was using the dolly in the crypt, ranking cage upon cage just inside the obscuring film. With several lion cages stacked like bricks at the entrance, no sensible Neanderthal would go a step further. Later, he could use disassembled stasis units as booby traps as he had done on Kzersatz. But it was nearly dark when he finished, and Locklear was hurrying. Now, for the first time ever on Newduvai, he felt gooseflesh when he thought of camping in the open.

For days, he considered a return to Kzersatz in the lifeboat, meanwhile improving the cabin with Loli's help. He got that help very simply, by refusing to let her sleep in her stasis cage unless she did help. Loli was very bright, and learned his language quickly because she could not rely on telepathy. Operating on the sour-grape theory, he told himself that Ruth had been mud-fence ugly; he hadn't felt any real affection for a Neanderthal bimbo. Not *really* . . .

He managed to ignore Loli's budding charms by reminding himself that she was no more than twelve or so, and gradually she began to trust him. He wondered how much that trust would suffer if she found he was taking her from stasis only on the days he needed help.

As the days faded into weeks, the cabin became a two-room affair with a connecting passage for firewood and storage. Loli, after endless scraping and soaking of the stiff goathide in acorn water, fashioned herself a one-piece garment. She taught Locklear how repeated boiling turned acorns into edible nuts, and wove mats of plaited grass for the cabin.

He let her roam in search of small game once a week until the day she returned empty-handed. He was cutting hinge material of stainless steel from a stasis cage with Kzin shears at the time, and smiled. "Don't feel bad, Loli. There's plenty of meat in storage." The more he used complete sentences, the more she seemed to be picking up the lingo.

She shrugged, picking at a scab on one of her little feet. "Loli not hurt. Gentles hunt Loli." She read his stare correctly. "Gentles not try to hurt Loli; this many follow and hide," she said, holding up four fingers and making a comical pantomime of a stealthy hunter.

He held up four fingers. "Four," he reminded her. "Did they follow you here?"

"Maybe want to follow Loli here," she said, grinning. "Loli think much. Loli go far far—"

"Very far," he corrected.

"Very far to dry place, gentles no follow feet there. Loli hide, run very far where gentles not see. Come back to Locklear."

Yes, they'd have trouble tracking her through those desert patches, he realized, and she could've doubled back unseen in the arroyos. Or she might have been followed after all. "Loli is smart," he said, patting her shoulder, "but gentles are smart, too. Gentles maybe want to hurt Locklear."

"Gentles cover big holes, spears in holes, come back, maybe find kill animal. Maybe kill Locklear."

Yeah, they'd do it that way. Or maybe set a fire to burn him out of the cabin. "Loli, would you feel bad if the gentles killed me?"

In her vast innocence, Loli thought about it before answering. "Little while, yes. Loli don't like to live alone. Gentles all time like to play," she said, with a bump-and-grind routine so outrageous that he burst out laughing. "Locklear don't trade food for play," she added, making it obvious that Neanderthal men *did*.

"Not until Loli is older," he said with brutal honesty.

"Loli is a woman," she said, pouting as though he had slandered her.

To shift away from this dangerous topic he said, "Yes, and you can help me make this place safe from gentles." That was the day he began teaching the girl how to disassemble cages for their most potent parts, the grav polarizers and stasis units.

They burned off the surrounding ground cover bit by bit during the nights to avoid telltale smoke, and

Loli assured him that Neanderthals never ventured from camp on nights as dark as Newduvai's. Sooner or later, he knew, they were bound to discover his little homestead and he intended to make it a place of terrifying magics.

As luck would have it, he had over two months to prepare before a far more potent new magic thundered across the sky of Newduvai.

Locklear swallowed hard the day he heard that long roll of synthetic thunder, recognizing it for what it was. He had told Loli about the Kzinti, and now he warned her that they might be near, and saw her coltish legs flash into the forest as he sent the scooter scudding close to the ground toward the heights where his lifeboat was hidden. He would need only one close look to identify a Kzin ship.

Dismounting near the lifeboat, peering past an outcrop and shivering because he was so near the cold force walls, he saw a foreshortened dot hovering near Newduvai's big lake. Winks of light streaked downward from it; he counted five shots before the ship ceased firing, and knew that its target had to be the big encampment of gentles.

"If only I had those beam cannons I took apart," he growled, unconsciously taking the side of the Neanderthals as tendrils of smoke fingered the sky. But he had removed the weapon pylon mounts long before. He released a long-held breath as the ship dwindled to a dot in the sky, hunching his shoulders, wondering how he could have been so naive as to foreswear war altogether. Killing was a bitter draught, yet not half so bitter as dying.

The ship disappeared. Ten minutes later he saw it

again, making the kind of circular sweep used for cartography, and this time it passed only a mile distant, and he gasped—for it was not a Kzin ship. The little cruiser escort bore Interworld Commission markings.

"The goddamn tabbies must have taken one of ours," he muttered to himself, and cursed as he saw the ship break off its sweep. No question about it: they were hovering very near his cabin.

Locklear could not fight from the lifeboat, but at least he had plenty of spare magazines for his Kzin sidearm in the lifeboat's lockers. He crammed his pockets with spares, expecting to see smoke roiling from his homestead as he began to skulk his scooter low toward home. His little vehicle would not bulk large on radar. And the tabbies might not realize how soon it grew dark on Newduvai. Maybe he could even the odds a little by landing near enough to snipe by the light of his burning cabin. He sneaked the last two hundred meters afoot, already steeling himself for the sight of a burning cabin.

But the cabin was not burning. And the Kzinti were not pillaging because, he saw with utter disbelief, the armed crew surrounding his cabin was human. He had already stood erect when it occurred to him that humans had been known to defect in previous wars—and he was carrying a Kzin weapon. He placed the sidearm and spare magazines beneath a stone overhang. Then Locklear strode out of the forest rubber-legged, too weak with relief to be angry at the firing on the village.

The first man to see him was a rawboned, ruddy private with the height of a belter. He brought his assault rifle to bear on Locklear, then snapped it to "port arms." Three others spun as the big belter shouted, "Gomulka; We've got one!"

A big fireplug of a man, wearing sergeant's stripes, whirled and moved away from a cabin window, motioning a smaller man beneath the other window to stay put. Striding toward the belter, he used the heavy bellow of command. "Parker; escort him in! Schmidt, watch the perimeter."

The belter trotted toward Locklear while an athletic specimen with a yellow crew-cut moved out to watch the forest where Locklear had emerged. Locklear took the belter's free hand and shook it repeatedly. They walked to the cabin together, and the rest of the group relaxed visibly to see Locklear all but capering in his delight. Two other armed figures appeared from across the clearing, one with curves too lush to be male, and Locklear invited them all in with, "There are no Kzinti on this piece of the planet; welcome to Newduvai."

Leaning, sitting, they all found their ease in Locklear's room, and their gazes were as curious as Locklear's own. He noted the varied shoulder patches: We Made It, Jinx, Wunderland. The woman, wearing the bars of a lieutenant, was evidently a Flatlander like himself. Commander Curt Stockton wore a Canyon patch, standing wiry and erect beside the woman, with pale gray eyes that missed nothing.

"I was captured by a Kzin ship," Locklear explained, "and marooned. But I suppose that's all in the records; I call the planet 'Zoo' because I think the Outsiders designed it with that in mind."

"We had these co-ordinates, and something vague about prison compounds, from translations of Kzin records," Stockton replied. "You must know a lot about this Zoo place by now."

"A fair amount. Listen, I saw you firing on a village near the big lake an hour ago. You mustn't do it again, commander. Those people are real Earth Neanderthals, probably the only ones in the entire galaxy."

The blocky sergeant, David Gomulka, slid his gaze to lock on Stockton's and shrugged big sloping shoulders. The woman, a close-cropped brunette whose cinched belt advertised her charms, gave Locklear a brilliant smile and sat down on his pallet. "I'm Grace Agostinho; Lieutenant, Manaus Intelligence Corps, Earth. Forgive our manners, Mr. Locklear, we've been in heavy fighting along the Rim and this isn't exactly what we expected to find."

"Me neither," Locklear smiled, then turned serious. "I hope you didn't destroy that village."

"Sorry about that," Stockton said. "We may have caused a few casualties when we opened fire on those huts. I ordered the firing stopped as soon as I saw they weren't Kzinti. But don't look so glum, Locklear; it's not as if they were human."

"Damn right they are," Locklear insisted. "As you'll soon find out, if we can get their trust again. I've even taught a few of 'em some of our language. And that's not all. But hey, I'm dying of curiosity without any news from outside. Is the war over?"

Commander Stockton coughed lightly for attention and the others seemed as attentive as Locklear. "It looks good around the core worlds, but in the Rim sectors it's still anybody's war." He jerked a thumb toward the two-hundred-ton craft, twice the length of a Kzin lifeboat, that rested on its repulsor jacks at the edge of the clearing with its own small pinnace clinging to its back. "The *Anthony Wayne* is the kind of cruiser escort they don't mind turning over to small combat teams like mine. The big brass gave us this mission after we captured some Kzinti files from a tabby dreadnaught. Not as good as R & R back home, but we're glad of the break." Stockton's grin was infectious.

"I haven't had time to set up a distillery," Locklear said, "or I'd offer you drinks on the house."

"A man could get parched here," said a swarthy little private.

"Good idea, Gazho. You're detailed to get some medicinal brandy from the med stores," said Stockton.

As the private hurried out, Locklear said, "You could probably let the rest of the crew out to stretch their legs, you know. Not much to guard against on Newduvai."

"What you see is all there is," said a compact private with high cheekbones and a Crashlander medic patch. Locklear had not heard him speak before. Softly accented, laconic; almost a scholar's diction. But that's what you might expect of a military medic.

Stockton's quick gaze riveted the man as if to say, "that's enough." To Locklear he nodded. "Meet Soichiro Lee; an intern before the war. Has a tendency to act as if a combat team is a democratic outfit but," his glance toward Lee was amused now, "he's a good sawbones. Anyhow, the *Wayne* can take care of herself. We've set her auto defenses for voice recognition when the hatch is closed, so don't go wandering closer than ten meters without one of us. And if one of those hairy apes throws a rock at her, she might just burn him for his troubles."

Locklear nodded. "A crew of seven; that's pretty thin."

Stockton, carefully: "You want to expand on that?"

Locklear: "I mean, you've got your crew pretty thinly spread. The tabbies have the same problem, though. The bunch that marooned me here had only four members."

Sergeant Gomulka exhaled heavily, catching Stockton's glance. "Commander, with your permission: Locklear here might have some ideas about those tabby records."

"Umm. Yeah, I suppose," with some reluctance. "Locklear, apparently the Kzinti felt there was some valuable secret, a weapon maybe, here on Zoo. They intended to return for it. Any idea what it was?"

Locklear laughed aloud. "Probably it was me. It ought to be the whole bleeding planet," he said. "If you stand near the force wall and look hard, you can see what looks like a piece of the Kzin homeworld close to this one. You can't imagine the secrets the other compounds might have. For starters, the life forms I found in stasis had been here forty thousand years, near as I can tell, before I released 'em."

"*You* released them?"

"Maybe I shouldn't have, but—" He glanced shyly toward Lieutenant Agostinho. "I got pretty lonesome."

"Anyone would," she said, and her smile was more than understanding.

Gomulka rumbled in evident disgust, "Why would a lot of walking fossils be important to the tabby war effort?"

"They probably wouldn't," Locklear admitted. "And anyhow, I didn't find the specimens until after the Kzinti left." He could not say exactly why, but this did not seem the time to regale them with his adventures on Kzersatz. Something just beyond the tip of his awareness was flashing like a caution signal.

Now Gomulka looked at his commander. "So that's not what we're looking for," he said. "Maybe it's not on this Newduvai dump. Maybe next door?"

"Maybe. We'll take it one dump at a time," said Stockton, and turned as the swarthy private popped into the cabin. "Ah. I trust the Armagnac didn't insult your palate on the way, Nathan," he said.

Nathan Gazho looked at the bottle's broken seal, then began to distribute nested plastic cups, his breath already laced with his quick nip of the brandy. "You don't miss much," he grumbled.

But I'm missing something, Locklear thought as he touched his half-filled cup to that of the sloe-eyed, langourous lieutenant. *Slack discipline? But combat troops probably ignore the spit and polish. Except for this hotsy who keeps looking at me as if we shared a secret, they've all got the hand calluses and haircuts of shock troops. No, it's something else . . .*

He told himself it was reluctance to make himself a hero; and next he told himself they wouldn't believe him anyway. And then he admitted that he wasn't sure exactly why, but he would tell them nothing about his victory on Kzersatz unless they asked. *Maybe because I suspect they'd round up poor Scarface, maybe hunt him down and shoot him like a mad dog no matter what I said. Yeah, that's reason enough. But something else, too.*

Night fell, with its almost audible thump, while they emptied the Armagnac. Locklear explained his scholarly fear that the gentles were likely to kill off animals that no other ethologist had ever studied on the hoof; mentioned Ruth and Minuteman as well; and decided to say nothing about Loli to these hardbitten troops. Anse Parker, the gangling belter, kept bringing the topic back to the tantalizingly vague secret mentioned in Kzin files. Parker, Locklear decided, thought himself subtle but managed only to be transparently cunning.

Austin Schmidt, the wide-shouldered blond, had little capacity for Armagnac and kept toasting the day when ". . . all this crap is history and I'm a man of means," singing that refrain from an old barracks ballad in a surprisingly sweet tenor. Locklear could not warm up to Nathan Gazho, whose gaze took inventory of every item in the cabin. The man's expensive wristcomp and pinky ring mismatched him like earrings on a weasel.

David Gomulka was all noncom, though, with a veteran's gift for controlling men and a sure hand in measuring booze. If the two officers felt any unease when he called them "Curt" and "Grace," they managed to avoid showing it. Gomulka spun out the tale of his first hand-to-hand engagement against a Kzin penetration team with details that proved he knew how the tabbies fought. Locklear wanted to say, "That's right; that's how it is," but only nodded.

It was late in the evening when the commander cut short their speculations on Zoo, stood up, snapped the belt flash from its ring and flicked it experimentally. "We could all use some sleep," he decided, with the smile of a young father at his men, some of whom where older than he. "Mr. Locklear, we have more than enough room. Please be our guest in the *Anthony Wayne* tonight."

Locklear, thinking that Loli might steal back to the cabin if she were somewhere nearby, said, "I appreciate it, commander, but I'm right at home here. Really."

A nod, and a reflective gnawing of Stockton's lower lip. "I'm responsible for you now, Locklear. God knows what those Neanderthals might do, now that we've set fire to their nests."

"But—" The men were stretching out their kinks, paying silent but close attention to the interchange.

"I must insist. I don't want to put it in terms of command, but I *am* the local sheriff here now, so to speak." The engaging grin again. "Come on, Locklear, think of it as repaying your hospitality. Nothing's certain in this place, and—" his last phrase bringing soft chuckles from Gomulka, "they'd throw me in the brig if I let anything happen to you now."

The taciturn Parker led the way, and Locklear smiled in the darkness thinking how Loli might wonder at the intensely bright, intensely magical beams that bobbed toward the ship. After Parker called out his name and a long number, the ship's hatch steps dropped at their feet and Locklear knew the reassurance of climbing into an Interworld ship with its familiar smells, whines, and beeps.

Parker and Schmidt were loudly in favor of a nightcap, but Stockton's, "Not a good idea, David," to the sergeant was met with a nod and barked commands by Gomulka. Grace Agostinho made a similar offer to Locklear.

"Thanks anyway. You know what I'd really like?"

"Probably," she said, with a pursed-lipped smile.

He was blushing as he said, "Ham sandwiches. Beer. A slice of thrillcake," and nodded quickly when she hauled a frozen shrimp teriyaki from their food lockers. When it popped from the radioven, he sat near the ship's bridge to eat it, idly noting a few dark foodstains on the bridge linolamat and listening to Grace tell of small news from home. The Amazon dam, a new "must-see" holo musical, a controversial cure for the common cold; the kind of tremendous trifles that cemented friendships.

She left him briefly while he chased scraps on his plate, and by the time she returned most of the crew had secured their pneumatic cubicle doors. "It's always satisfying to feed a man with an appetite," said Grace, smiling at his clean plate as she slid it into the galley scrubber. "I'll see you're fed well on the *Wayne*." With hands on her hips, she said, "Well: Private Schmidt has sentry duty. He'll show you to your quarters."

He took her hand, thanked her, and nodded to the slightly wavering Schmidt who led the way back toward the ship's engine room. He did not look back but, from the sound of it, Grace entered a cubicle where two men were arguing in subdued tones.

Schmidt showed him to the rearmost cubicle but not the rearmost dozen bunks. Those, he saw, were ranked inside a cage of duralloy with no privacy whatever. Dark crusted stains spotted the floor inside and outside the cage. A fax sheet lay in the passageway. When Locklear glanced toward it, the private saw it, tried to hide a startle response, and then essayed a drunken grin.

"Gotta have a tight ship," said Schmidt, banging his head on the duralloy as he retrieved the fax and balled it up with one hand. He tossed the wadded fax into a flush-mounted waste receptacle, slid the cubicle door open for Locklear, and managed a passable salute. "Have a good one, pal. You know how to adjust your rubberlady?"

Locklear saw that the mattresses of the two bunks were standard models with adjustable inflation and webbing. "No problem," he replied, and slid the door closed. He washed up at the tiny inset sink, used the urinal slot below it, and surveyed his clothes after removing them. They'd all seen better days. Maybe he could wangle some new ones. He was sleepier than he'd thought, and adjusted his rubberlady for a soft setting, and was asleep within moments.

He did not know how long it was before he found himself sitting bolt-upright in darkness. He knew what was wrong, now: *everything*. It might be possible for a little escort ship to plunder records from a derelict mile-long Kzin battleship. It was barely possible that the same craft would be sent to check on some big Kzin secret—*but not without at least a cruiser, if the Kzinti might be heading for Zoo*.

He rubbed a trickle of sweat as it counted his ribs. He didn't have to be a military buff to know that ordinary privates do not have access to medical lockers, and the commander had told Gazho to get that brandy from med stores. Right; and all those motley shoulder patches didn't add up to a picked combat crew, either. And one more thing: even in his half-blotted condition, Schmidt had snatched that fax sheet up as though it was evidence against him. Maybe it was . . .

He waved the overhead lamp on, grabbed his ratty flight suit, and slid his cubicle door open. If anyone asked, he was looking for a cleaner unit for his togs.

A low thrum of the ship's sleeping hydraulics; a slightly louder buzz of someone sleeping, most likely Schmidt while on sentry duty. *Not much discipline at all. I wonder just how much commanding Stock-*

ton really does. Locklear stepped into the passage-way, moved several paces, and eased his free hand into the waste receptacle slot. Then he thrust the fax wad into his dirty flight suit and padded silently back, cursing the sigh of his door. A moment later he was colder than before.

The fax was labeled, "PRISONER RIGHTS AND PRIVILEGES," and had been signed by some Provost Marshall—or a doctor, to judge from its illegibility. He'd bet anything that fax had fallen, or had been torn, from those duralloy bars. Rust-colored crusty stains on the floor; a similar stain near the ship's bridge; but no obvious damage to the ship from Kzin weapons.

It took all his courage to go into the passageway again, flight suit in hand, and replace the wadded fax sheet where he'd found it. And the door seemed much louder this time, almost a sob instead of a sigh.

Locklear felt like sobbing, too. He lay on his rubberlady in the dark, thinking about it. A hundred scenarios might explain some of the facts, but only one matched them all: the *Anthony Wayne* had been a prisoner ship, but now the prisoners were calling themselves "commander" and "sergeant," and the real crew of the *Anthony Wayne* had made those stains inside the ship with their blood.

He wanted to shout it, but demanded it silently: *So why would a handful of deserters fly to Zoo?* Before he fell at last into a troubled sleep, he had asked it again and again, and the answer was always the same: somehow, one of them had learned of the Kzin records and hoped to find Zoo's secret before either side did.

These people would be deadly to anyone who

knew their secret. And almost certainly, they'd never buy the truth, that Locklear himself was the secret because the Kzinti had been so sure he was an Interworld agent.

Locklear awoke with a sensation of dread, then a brief upsurge of joy at sleeping in modern accomodations, and then he remembered his conclusions in the middle of the night, and his optimism fell off and broke.

To mend it, he decided to smile with the innocence of a Candide and plan his tactics. If he could get to the Kzin lifeboat, he might steer it like a slow battering ram and disable the *Anthony Wayne*. Or they might blow him to flinders in midair—and what if his fears were wrong, and despite all evidence this combat team was genuine? In any case, disabling the ship meant marooning the whole lot of them together. It wasn't a plan calculated to lengthen his life expectancy; maybe he would think of another.

The crew was already bustling around with breakfasts when he emerged, and yes, he could use the ship's cleaning unit for his clothes. When he asked for spare clothing, Soichiro Lee was first to deny it to him. "Our spares are still—contaminated from a previous engagement," he explained, with a meaningful look toward Gomulka.

I bet they are, with blood, Locklear told himself as he scooped his synthesized eggs and bacon. Their uniforms all seemed to fit well. Probably their own, he decided. The stylized winged gun on Gomulka's patch said he could fly gunships. Lee might be a medic, and the sensuous Grace might be a real intelligence officer—and all could be renegades.

Stockton watched him eat, friendly as ever, arms folded and relaxed. "Gomulka and Gazho did a recon in our pinnace at dawn," he said, sucking a tooth. "Seems your apemen are already rebuilding at another site; a terrace at this end of the lake. A lot closer to us."

"I wish you could think of them as people," Locklear said. "They're not terribly bright, but they don't swing on vines."

Chuckling: "Bright enough to be nuisances, perhaps try and burn us out if they find the ship here," Stockton said. "Maybe bright enough to know what it is the tabbies found here. You said they can talk a little. Well, you can help us interrogate 'em."

"They aren't too happy with me," Locklear admitted as Gomulka sat down with steaming coffee. "But I'll try on one condition."

Gomulka's voice carried a rumble of barely hidden threat. "Conditions? You're talking to your commander, Locklear."

"It's a very simple one," Locklear said softly. "No more killing or threatening these people. They call themselves 'gentles,' and they are. The New Smithson, or half the Interworld University branches, would give a year's budget to study them alive."

Grace Agostinho had been working at a map terminal, but evidently with an ear open to their negotiations. As Stockton and Gomulka gazed at each other in silent surmise, she took the few steps to sit beside Locklear, her hip warm against his. "You're an ethologist. Tell me, what could the Kzinti do with these gentles?"

Locklear nodded, sipped coffee, and finally said, "I'm not sure. Study them hoping for insights into the underlying psychology of modern humans, maybe."

Stockton said, "But you said the tabbies don't know about them."

"True; at least I don't see how they could. But you asked. I can't believe the gentles would know what you're after, but if you have to ask them, of course I'll help."

Stockton said it was necessary, and appointed Lee acting corporal at the cabin as he filled most of the pinnace's jumpseats with himself, Locklear, Agostinho, Gomulka, and the lank Parker. The little craft sat on downsloping delta wings that ordinarily nested against the *Wayne*'s hull, and had intakes for gas-reactor jets. "Newest piece of hardware we have," Stockton said, patting the pilot's console. It was Gomulka, however, who took the controls.

Locklear suggested that they approach very slowly, with hands visibly up and empty, as they settled the pinnace near the beginnings of a new gentles campsite. The gentles, including their women, all rushed for primitive lances but did not flee, and Anse Parker was the only one carrying an obvious weapon as the pinnace's canopy swung back. Locklear stepped forward, talking and smiling, with Parker at their backs. He saw Ruth waiting for old Gimp, and said he was much happy to see her, which was an understatement. Minuteman, too, had survived the firing on their village.

Cloud had not. Ruth told him so immediately. "Locklear make many deaths to gentles," she accused. Behind her, some of the gentles stared with faces that were anything but gentle. "Gentles not like talk to Locklear, he says. Go now. Please," she added, one of the last words he'd taught her, and she said it with urgency. Her glance toward Grace

Agostinho was interested, not hostile but perhaps pitying.

Locklear moved away from the others, farther from the glaring Gimp. "More new people come," he called from a distance, pleading. "Think gentles big, bad animals. Stop when they see gentles; much much sorry. Locklear say not hurt gentles more."

With her head cocked sideways, Ruth seemed to be testing his mind for lies. She spoke with Gimp, whose face registered a deep sadness and, perhaps, some confusion as well. Locklear could hear a buzz of low conversation between Stockton nearby and Gomulka, who still sat at the pinnace controls.

"Locklear think good, but bad things happen," Ruth said at last. "Kill Cloud, many more. Gentles not like fight. Locklear know this," she said, almost crying now. "Please go!"

Gomulka came out of the pinnace with his sidearm drawn, and Locklear turned toward him, aghast. "No shooting! You promised," he reminded Stockton.

But: "We'll have to bring the ape-woman with the old man," Stockton said grimly, not liking it but determined. Gomulka stood quietly, the big sloping shoulders hunched.

Stockton said, "This is an explosive situation, Locklear. We must take those two for interrogation. Have the woman tell them we won't hurt them unless their people try to hunt us."

Then, as Locklear froze in horrified anger, Gomulka bellowed, *"Tell 'em!"*

Locklear did it and Ruth began to call in their language to the assembled throng. Then, at Gomulka's command, Parker ran forward to grasp the pathetic old Gimp by the arm, standing more than a head taller than the Neanderthal. That was the moment when Minuteman, who must have understood only a little of their parley, leaped weaponless at the big belter.

Parker swept a contemptuous arm at the little fellow's reach, but let out a howl as Minuteman, with those blacksmith arms of his, wrenched that arm as one would wave a stick.

The report was shattering, with echoes slapping off the lake, and Locklear whirled to see Gomulka's two-handed aim with the projectile sidearm. "No! Goddammit, these are human beings," he screamed, rushing toward the fallen Minuteman, falling on his knees, placing one hand over the little fellow's breast as if to stop the blood that was pumping from it. The gentles panicked at the thunder from Gomulka's weapon, and began to run.

Minuteman's throat pulse still throbbed, but he was in deep shock from the heavy projectile and his pulse died as Locklear watched helpless. Parker was already clubbing old Gimp with his rifle-butt and Gomulka, his sidearm out of sight, grabbed Ruth as she tried to interfere. The big man might as well have walked into a train wreck while the train was still moving.

Grace Agostinho seemed to know she was no fighter, retreating into the pinnace. Stockton, whipping the ornamental braid from his epaulets, began to fashion nooses as he moved to help Parker, whose left arm was half-useless. Locklear came to his feet, saw Gomulka's big fist smash at Ruth's temple, and dived into the fray with one arm locked around Gomulka's bull neck, trying to haul him off-balance. Both of Ruth's hands grappled with Gomulka's now, and

Locklear saw that she was slowly overpowering him
while her big teeth sought his throat, only the whites
of her eyes showing. It was the last thing Locklear
would see for awhile, as someone raced up behind
him.

He awoke to a gentle touch and the chill of anti-
septic spray behind his right ear, and focused on the
real concern mirrored on Stockton's face. He lay in
the room he had built for Loli, Soichiro Lee kneeling
beside him, while Ruth and Gimp huddled as far as
they could get into a corner. Stockton held a standard issue parabellum, arms folded, not pointing the
weapon but keeping it in evidence. "Only a mild
concussion," Lee murmured to the commander.

"You with us again, Locklear?" Stockton got a nod
in response, motioned for Lee to leave, and sighed.
"I'm truly sorry about all this, but you were interfering with a military operation. Gomulka is—he has a
lot of experience, and a good commander would be
stupid to ignore his suggestions."

Locklear was barely wise enough to avoid saying
that Gomulka did more commanding than Stockton
did. Pushing himself up, blinking from the headache
that split his skull like an axe, he said, "I need some
air."

"You'll have to get it right here," Stockton said,
"because I can't—won't let you out. Consider yourself under arrest. Behave yourself and that could
change." With that, he shouldered the woven mat
aside and his slow footsteps echoed down the connecting corridor to the other room.

Without a door directly to the outside, he would
have to run down that corridor where armed yahoos

waited. Digging out would make noise and might take hours. Locklear slid down against the cabin wall, head in hands. When he opened them again he saw that poor old Gimp seemed comatose, but Ruth was looking at him intently. "I wanted to be friend of all gentles," he sighed.

"Yes. Gentles know," she replied softly. "New people with gentles not good. Stok-Tun not want hurt, but others not care about gentles. Ruth hear in head," she added, with a palm against the top of her head.

"Ruth must not tell," Locklear insisted. "New people maybe kill if they know gentles hear that way."

She gave him a very modern nod, and even in that hopelessly homely face, her shy smile held a certain beauty. "Locklear help Ruth fight. Ruth like Locklear much, much; even if Locklear is— now."

"Ruth, 'new' means 'ugly,' doesn't it? New, new," he repeated, screwing his face into a hideous caricature, making claws of his hands, snarling in exaggerated mimicry.

He heard voices raised in muffled excitement in the other room, and Ruth's head was cocked again momentarily. "Ugly?" She made faces, too. "Part yes. New means not same as before but also ugly, maybe bad."

"All the gentles considered me the ugly man. Yes?"

"Yes," she replied sadly. "Ruth not care. Like ugly man if good man, too."

"And you knew I thought you were, uh . . ."

"Ugly? Yes. Ruth try and fix before."

"I know," he said, miserable. "Locklear like Ruth for that and many, many more things."

Quickly, as boots stamped in the corridor, she

said, "Big problem. New people not think Locklear tell truth. New woman—"

Schmidt's rifle barrel moved the mat aside and he let it do his gesturing to Locklear. "On your feet, buddy, you've got some explaining to do."

Locklear got up carefully so his head would not roll off his shoulders. Stumbling toward the doorway he said to Ruth: "What about new woman?"

"Much, much new in head. Ruth feel sorry," she called as Locklear moved toward the other room.

They were all crowded in, and seven pairs of eyes were intent on Locklear. Grace's gaze held a liquid warmth but he saw nothing warmer than icicles in any other face. Gomulka and Stockton sat on the benches facing him across his crude table like judges at a trial. Locklear did not have to be told to stand before them.

Gomulka reached down at his own feet and grunted with effort, and the toolbox crashed down on the table. His voice was not its usual command timbre, but menacingly soft. "Gazho noticed this was all tabby stuff," he said.

"Part of an honorable trade," Locklear said, dry-mouthed. "I could have killed a Kzin and didn't."

"They trade you a fucking LIFEBOAT, too?"

Those goddamn pinnace sorties of his! The light of righteous fury snapped in the big man's face, but Locklear stared back. "Matter of fact, yes. The Kzin is a cat of his word, sergeant."

"Enough of your bullshit, I want the truth!"

Now Locklear shifted his gaze to Stockton. "I'm telling it. Enough of your bullshit, too. How did your bunch of bozos get out of the brig, Stockton?"

Parker blurted, "How the hell did—" before Gomulka spun on his bench with a silent glare. Parker blushed and swallowed.

"We're asking the questions, Locklear. The tabbies must've left you a girlfriend, too," Stockton said quietly. "Lee and Schmidt both saw some little hotsy queen of the jungle out near the perimeter while we were gone. Make no mistake, they'll hunt her down and there's nothing I can say to stop them."

"Why not, if you're a commander?"

Stockton flushed angrily, with a glance at Gomulka that was not kind. "That's my problem, not yours. Look, you want some straight talk, and here it is: Agostinho has seen the goddamned translations from a tabby dreadnaught, and there *is* something on this godforsaken place they think is important, and we were in this Rim sector when—when we got into some problems, and she told me. I'm an officer, I really am, believe what you like. But we have to find whatever the hell there is on Zoo."

"So you can plea-bargain after your mutiny?"

"That's ENOUGH," Gomulka bellowed. "You're a little too cute for your own good, Locklear. But if you're ever gonna get off this ball of dirt, it'll be after you help us find what the tabbies are after."

"It's me," Locklear said simply. "I've already told you."

Silent consternation, followed by disbelief. "And what the fuck are you," Gomulka spat.

"Not much, I admit. But as I told you, they captured me and got the idea I knew more about the Rim sectors than I do."

"How much Kzinshit do you think I'll swallow?" Gomulka was standing, now, advancing around the table toward his captive. Curt Stockton shut his eyes and sighed his helplessness.

Locklear was wondering if he could grab anything from the toolbox when a voice of sweet reason stopped Gomulka. "Brutality hasn't solved anything here yet," said Grace Agostinho. "I'd like to talk to Locklear alone." Gomulka stopped, glared at her, then back at Locklear. "I can't do any worse than you have, David," she added to the fuming sergeant.

Beckoning, she walked to the doorway and Gazho made sure his rifle muzzle grated on Locklear's ribs as the ethologist followed her outside. She said, "Do I have your honorable parole? Bear in mind that even if you try to run, they'll soon have you and the girl who's running loose, too. They've already destroyed some kind of flying raft; yours, I take it," she smiled.

Damn, hell, shit, and blast! "Mine. I won't run, Grace. Besides, you've got a parabellum."

"Remember that," she said, and began to stroll toward the trees while the cabin erupted with argument. Locklear vented more silent damns and hells; she wasn't leading him anywhere near his hidden Kzin sidearm.

Grace Agostinho, surprisingly, first asked about Loli. She seemed amused to learn he had waked the girl first, and that he'd regretted it at his leisure. Gradually, her questions segued to answers. "Discipline on a warship can be vicious," she mused as if to herself. "Curt Stockton was—is a career officer, but it's his view that there must be limits to discipline. His own commander was a hard man, and—"

"Jesus Christ; you're saying he mutinied like Fletcher Christian?"

"That's not entirely wrong," she said, now very feminine as they moved into a glade, out of sight of the cabin. "David Gomulka is a rougher sort, a man of some limited ideas but more of action. I'm afraid Curt filled David with ideas that, ah, . . ."

"Stockton started a boulder downhill and can't stop it," Locklear said. "Not the first time a man of ideas has started something he can't control. How'd you get into this mess?"

"An affair of the heart; I'd rather not talk about it. When I'm drawn to a man, . . . well, I tend to show it," she said, and preened her hair for him as she leaned against a fallen tree. "You must tell them what they want to know, my dear. These are desperate men, in desperate trouble."

Locklear saw the promise in those huge dark eyes and gazed into them. "I swear to you, the Kzinti thought I was some kind of Interworld agent, but they dropped me on Zoo for safekeeping."

"And were you?" Softly, softly, catchee monkey . . .

"Good God, no! I'm an—"

"Ethologist. I heard it. But the Kzin suspicion does seem reasonable, doesn't it?"

"I guess, if you're paranoid." *God, but this is one seductive lieutenant.*

"Which means that David and Curt could sell you to the Kzinti for safe passage, if I let them," she said, moving toward him, her hands pulling apart the closures on his flight suit. "But I don't think that's the secret, and I don't think *you* think so. You're a fascinating man, and I don't know when I've been so attracted to anyone. Is this so awful of me?"

He knew damned well how powerfully persuasive a woman like Grace could be with that voluptuous willowy sexuality of hers. And he remembered Ruth's warning, and believed it. But he would rather drown in honey than in vinegar, and when she turned her face upward, he found her mouth with his, and willingly let her lust kindle his own.

Presently, lying on forest humus and watching Grace comb her hair clean with her fingers, Locklear's breathing slowed. He inventoried her charms as she shrugged into her flight suit again; returned her impudent smile; began to readjust his togs. "If this be torture," he declaimed like an actor, "make the most of it."

"Up to the standards of your local ladies?"

"Oh yes," he said fervently, knowing it was only a small lie. "But I'm not sure I understand why you offered."

She squatted becomingly on her knees, brushing at his clothing. "You're very attractive," she said. "And mysterious. And if you'll help us, Locklear, I promise to plumb your mysteries as much as you like—and vice-versa."

"An offer I can't refuse, Grace. But I don't know how I can do more than I have already."

Her frown held little anger; more of perplexity. "But I've told you, my dear: we must have that Kzin secret."

"And you didn't believe what I said."

Her secret smile again, teasing: "Really, darling, you must give me some credit. I *am* in the intelligence corps."

He did see a flash of irritation cross her face this time as he laughed. "Grace, this is crazy," he said, still grinning. "It may be absurd that the Kzinti thought I was an agent, but it's true. I think the planet itself is a mind-boggling discovery, and I said so first thing off. Other than that, what can I say?"

"I'm sorry you're going to be this way about it," she said with the pout of a nubile teen-ager, then hitched up the sidearm on her belt as if to remind him of it.

She's sure something, he thought as they strode back to his clearing. *If I had any secret to hide, could she get it out of me with this kind of attention? Maybe—but she's all technique and no real passion. Exactly the girl you want to bring home to your friendly regimental combat team . . .*

Grace motioned him into the cabin without a word and, as Schmidt sent him into the room with Ruth and the old man, he saw both Gomulka and Stockton leave the cabin with Grace. *I don't think she has affairs of the heart*, he reflected with a wry smile. *Affairs of the glands beyond counting, but maybe no heart to lose. Or no character?*

He sat down near Ruth, who was sitting with Gimp's head in her lap, and sighed. "Ruth much smart about new woman. Locklear see now," he said and, gently, kissed the homely face.

The crew had a late lunch but brought none for their captives, and Locklear was taken to his judges in the afternoon. He saw hammocks slung in his room, evidence that the crew intended to stay awhile. Stockton, as usual, began as pleasantly as he could. "Locklear, since you're not on Agostinho's list of known intelligence assets in the Rim sectors, then maybe we've been peering at the wrong side of the coin."

"That's what I told the tabbies," Locklear said.

"Now we're getting somewhere. Actually, you're a Kzin agent; right?"

Locklear stared, then tried not to laugh. "Oh, Jesus, Stockton! Why would they drop me here, in that case?"

Evidently, Stockton's pleasant side was loosely attached under trying circumstances. He flushed angrily. "You tell us."

"You can find out damned fast by turning me over to Interworld authorities," Locklear reminded him.

"And if you turn out to be a plugged nickel," Gomulka snarled, "you're home free and we're in deep shit. No, I don't think we will, little man. We'll do anything we have to do to get the facts out of you. If it takes shooting hostages, we will."

Locklear switched his gaze to the bedeviled Stockton and saw no help there. At this point, a few lies might help the gentles. "A real officer, are you? Shoot these poor savages? Go ahead, actually you might be doing me a favor. You can see they hate my guts! The only reason they didn't kill me today is that they think I'm one of you, and they're scared to. Every one you knock off, or chase off, is just one less who's out to tan my hide."

Gomulka, slyly: "So how'd you say you got that tabby ship?"

Locklear: "On Kzersatz. Call it grand theft, I don't give a damn." Knowing they would explore Kzersatz sooner or later, he said, "The tabbies probably thought I hightailed it for the Interworld fleet but I could barely fly the thing. I was lucky to get down here in one piece."

Stockton's chin jerked up. "Do you mean there's a Kzin force right across those force walls?"

"There was; I took care of them myself."

Gomulka stood up now. "Sure you did. I never heard such jizm in twenty years of barracks brags. Grace, you never did like a lot of hollering and blood. Go to the ship." Without a word, and with the same liquid gaze she would turn on Locklear—and perhaps on anyone else—she nodded and walked out.

As Gomulka reached for his captive, Locklear grabbed for the heavy toolbox. That little hand welder would ruin a man's entire afternoon. Gomulka nodded, and suddenly Locklear felt his arms gripped from behind by Schmidt's big hands. He brought both feet up, kicked hard against the table, and as the table flew into the faces of Stockton and Gomulka, Schmidt found himself propelled backward against the cabin wall.

Shouting, cursing, they overpowered Locklear at last, hauling the top of his flight suit down so that its arms could be tied into a sort of straitjacket. Breathing hard, Gomulka issued his final backhand slap toward Locklear's mouth. Locklear ducked, then spat into the big man's face.

Wiping spittle away with his sleeve, Gomulka muttered, "Curt, we gotta soften this guy up."

Stockton pointed to the scars on Locklear's upper body. "You know, I don't think he softens very well, David. Ask yourself whether you think it's useful, or whether you just want to do it."

It was another of those ideas Gomulka seemed to value greatly because he had so few of his own. "Well goddammit, what would you do?"

"Coercion may work, but not this kind." Studying the silent Locklear in the grip of three men, he came near smiling. "Maybe give him a comm set and drop him among the Neanderthals. When he's good and ready to talk, we rescue him."

A murmur among the men, and a snicker from Gazho. To prove he did have occasional ideas, Gomulka replied, "Maybe. Or better, maybe drop him next door on Kzinkatz or whatever the fuck he calls it." His eyes slid slowly to Locklear.

To Locklear, who was licking a trickle of blood from his upper lip, the suggestion did not register for a count of two beats. When it did, he needed a third beat to make the right response. Eyes wide, he screamed.

"Yeah," said Nathan Gazho.

"Yeah, right," came the chorus.

Locklear struggled, but not too hard. "My God! They'll— They EAT people, Stockton!"

"Well, it looks like a voice vote, Curt," Gomulka drawled, very pleased with his idea, then turned to Locklear. "But that's democracy for you. You'll have a nice comm set and you can call us when you're ready. Just don't forget the story about the boy who cried 'wolf.' But when you call, Locklear—" the big sergeant's voice was low and almost pleasant, "—be ready to deal."

Locklear felt a wild impulse, as Gomulka shoved him into the pinnace, to beg, "Please, Bre'r Fox, don't throw me in the briar patch!" He thrashed a bit and let his eyes roll convincingly until Parker, with a choke hold, pacified him half-unconscious.

If he had any doubts that the pinnace was orbitrated, Locklear lost them as he watched Gomulka at work. Parker sat with the captive though Lee, beside Gomulka, faced a console. The three pirates negotiated a three-way bet on how much time would pass before Locklear begged to be picked up. His comm set, roughly shoved into his ear with its button switch, had fresh batteries but Lee reminded him again that they would be returning only once to bail him out. The pinnace, a lovely little craft, arced up to orbital height and, with only its transparent canopy between him and hard vac, Locklear found real fear added to his pretense. After pitchover, tiny bursts of light at the wingtips steadied the pinnace as it began its re-entry over the saffron jungles of Kzersatz.

Because of its different schedule, the tiny programmed sunlet of Kzersatz was only an hour into its morning. "Keep one eye on your sweep screen," Gomulka said as the roar of deceleration died away.

"I am," Lee replied grimly. "Locklear, if we get jumped by a tabby ship I'll put a burst right into your guts, first thing."

As Locklear made a show of moaning and straining at his bonds, Gomulka banked the pinnace for its mapping sweep. Presently, Lee's infrared scanners flashed an overlay on his screen and Gomulka nodded, but finished the sweep. Then, by manual control, he slowed the little craft and brought it at a leisurely pace to the I R blips, a mile or so above the alien veldt. Lee brought the screen's video to high magnification.

Anse Parker saw what Locklear saw. "Only a few tabbies, huh? And you took care of 'em, huh? You son of a bitch!" He glared at the scene, where a dozen Kzinti moved unaware amid half-submerged huts and cooking fires, and swatted Locklear across the back of his head with an open hand. "Looks like they've gone native," Parker went on. "Hey, Gomulka: they'll be candy for us."

"I noticed," Gomulka replied. "You know what? If we bag 'em now, we're helping this little shit. We can come back any time we like, maybe have ourselves a tabby-hunt."

"Yeah; show 'em what it's like," Lee snickered, "after they've had their manhunt."

Locklear groaned for effect. *A village ready-made in only a few months! Scarface didn't waste any time getting his own primitives out of stasis. I hope to God he doesn't show up looking glad to see me.* To avoid that possibility he pleaded, "Aren't you going to give me a running chance?"

"Sure we are," Gomulka laughed. "Tabbies will pick up your scent anyway. Be on you like flies on a turd." The pinnace flew on, unseen from far below, Lee bringing up the video now and then. Once he said, "Can't figure out what they're hunting in that field. If I didn't know Kzinti were strict carnivores I'd say they were farming."

Locklear knew that primitive Kzinti ate vegetables as well, and so did their meat animals; but he kept his silence. It hadn't even occurred to these piratical deserters that the Kzinti below might be as prehistoric as Neanderthalers. Good; let them think they understood the Kzinti! *But nobody knows 'em like I do*, he thought. It was an arrogance he would recall with bitterness very, very soon.

Gomulka set the pinnace down with practiced ease behind a stone escarpment and Parker, his gaze nervously sweeping the jungle, used his gunbarrel to urge Locklear out of the craft.

Soichiro Lee's gentle smile did not match his final words: "If you manage to hide out here, just remember we'll pick up your little girlfriend before long. Probably a better piece of snatch than the Manaus machine," he went on, despite a sudden glare from Gomulka. "How long do you want us to use her, asshole? Think about it," he winked, and the canopy's "thunk" muffled the guffaws of Anse Parker.

Locklear raced away as the pinnace lifted, making it look good. They had tossed Bre'r Rabbit into his personal briar patch, never suspecting he might have friends here.

He was thankful that the village lay downhill as he began his one athletic specialty, long-distance jogging, because he could once again feel the synthetic gravity of Kzersatz tugging at his body. He judged that he was a two-hour trot from the village and paced himself carefully, walking and resting now and then. And planning.

As soon as Scarface learned the facts, they could set a trap for the returning pinnace. And then, with captives of his own, Locklear could negotiate with Stockton. It was clear by now that Curt Stockton considered himself a leader of virtue—because he was a man of ideas. David Gomulka was a man of action without many important ideas, the perfect model of a playground bully long after graduation.

And Stockton? He would've been the kind of clever kid who decided early that violence was an inferior way to do things, because he wasn't very good at it himself. Instead, he'd enlist a Gomulka to stand nearby while the clever kid tried to beat you up with words; debate you to death. And if that finally failed, he could always sigh, and walk away leaving the bully to do his dirty work, and imagine that his own hands were clean.

But Kzersatz was a whole 'nother playground, with different rules. Locklear smiled at the thought and jogged on.

An hour later he heard the beast crashing in panic through orange ferns before he saw it, and realized that it was pursued only when he spied a young male flashing with sinuous efficiency behind.

No one ever made friends with a Kzin by interrupting its hunt, so Locklear stood motionless among palmferns and watched. The prey reminded him of a pygmy tyrannosaur, almost the height of a man but with teeth meant for grazing on foliage. The Kzin bounded nearer, disdaining the *wtsai* knife at his belt, and screamed only as he leaped for the kill.

The prey's armored hide and thrashing tail made the struggle interesting, but the issue was never in doubt. A Kzin warrior was trained to hunt, to kill, and to eat that kill, from kittenhood. The roars of the lizard dwindled to a hissing gurgle; the tail and the powerful legs stilled. Only after the Kzin vented his victory scream and ripped into his prey did Locklear step into the clearing made by flattened ferns.

Hands up and empty, Locklear called in Kzin, "The Kzin is a mighty hunter!" To speak in Kzin, one needed a good falsetto and plenty of spit. Locklear's command was fair, but the young Kzin reacted as though the man had spouted fire and brimstone. He paused only long enough to snatch up his kill, a good hundred kilos, before bounding off at top speed.

Crestfallen, Locklear trotted toward the village

again. He wondered now if Scarface and Kit, the mate Locklear had freed for him, had failed to speak of mankind to the ancient Kzin tribe. In any case, they would surely respond to his use of their language until he could get Scarface's help. Perhaps the young male had simply raced away to bring the good news.

And perhaps, he decided a half-hour later, he himself was the biggest fool in Known Space or beyond it. They had ringed him before he knew it, padding silently through foliage the same mottled yellows and oranges as their fur. Then, almost simultaneously, he saw several great tigerish shapes disengage from their camouflage ahead of him, and heard the scream as one leapt upon him from behind.

Bowled over by the rush, feeling hot breath and fangs at his throat, Locklear moved only his eyes. His attacker might have been the same one he surprised while hunting, and he felt needle-tipped claws through his flight suit.

Then Locklear did the only things he could: kept his temper, swallowed his terror, and repeated his first greeting: "The Kzin is a mighty hunter."

He saw, striding forward, an old Kzin with ornate bandolier straps. The oldster called to the others, "It is true, the beast speaks the Hero's Tongue! It is as I prophesied." Then, to the young attacker, "Stand away at the ready," and Locklear felt like breathing again.

"I am Locklear, who first waked members of your clan from age-long sleep," he said in that ancient dialect he'd learned from Kit. "I come in friendship. May I rise?"

A contemptuous gesture and, as Locklear stood

up, a worse remark. "Then you are the beast that lay with a palace *prret*, a courtesan. We have heard. You will win no friends here."

A cold tendril marched down Locklear's spine. "May I speak with my friends? The Kzinti have things to fear, but I am not among them."

More laughter. "The Rockear beast thinks it is fearsome," said the young male, his ear-umbrellas twitching in merriment.

"I come to ask help, and to offer it," Locklear said evenly.

"The priesthood knows enough of your help. Come," said the older one. And that is how Locklear was marched into a village of prehistoric Kzinti, ringed by hostile predators twice his size.

His reception party was all-male, its members staring at him in frank curiosity while prodding him to the village. They finally left him in an open area surrounded by huts with his hands tied, a leather collar around his neck, the collar linked by a short braided rope to a hefty stake. When he squatted on the turf, he noticed the soil was torn by hooves here and there. Dark stains and an abbatoir odor said the place was used for butchering animals. The curious gazes of passing females said he was only a strange animal to them. The disappearance of the males into the largest of the semi-submerged huts suggested that he had furnished the village with something worth a town meeting.

At last the meeting broke up, Kzin males striding from the hut toward him, a half-dozen of the oldest emerging last, each with a four-fingered paw tucked into his bandolier belt. Prominent scars across the breasts of these few were all exactly similar; some kind of self-torture ritual, Locklear guessed. Last of all with the ritual scars was the old one he'd spoken with, and this one had *both* paws tucked into his belt. *Got it; the higher your status, the less you need to keep your hands ready, or to hurry.*

The old devil was enjoying all this ceremony, and so were the other big shots. Standing in clearly-separated rings behind them were the other males with a few females, then the other females, evidently the entire tribe. Locklear spotted a few Kzinti whose expressions and ear-umbrellas said they were either sick or unhappy, but all played their obedient parts.

Standing before him, the oldster reached out and raked Locklear's face with what seemed to be only a ceremonial insult. It brought welts to his cheek anyway. The oldster spoke for all to hear. "You began the tribe's awakening, and for that we promise a quick kill."

"I waked several Kzinti, who promised me honor," Locklear managed to say.

"Traitors? They have no friends here. So *you*— have no friends here," said the old Kzin with pompous dignity. "This the priesthood has decided."

"You are the leader?"

"First among equals," said the high priest with a smirk that said he believed in no equals.

"While this tribe slept," Locklear said loudly, hoping to gain some support, "a mighty Kzin warrior came here. I call him Scarface. I return in peace to see him, and to warn you that others who look like me may soon return. They wish you harm, but I do not. Would you take me to Scarface?"

He could not decipher the murmurs, but he knew amusement when he saw it. The high priest stepped forward, untied the rope, handed it to the nearest of the husky males who stood behind the priests. "He would see the mighty hunter who had new ideas," he said. "Take him to see that hero, so that he will fully appreciate the situation. Then bring him back to the ceremony post."

With that, the high priest turned his back and, followed by the other priests, walked away. The dozens of other Kzinti hurried off, carefully avoiding any backward glances. Locklear said, to the huge specimen tugging on his neck rope, "I cannot walk quickly with hands behind my back."

"Then you must learn," rumbled the big Kzin, and lashed out with a foot that propelled Locklear forward. *I think he pulled that punch,* Locklear thought. *Kept his claws retracted, at least.* The Kzin led him silently from the village and along a path until hidden by foliage. Then, "You are the Rockear," he said, slowing. "I am (something as unpronounceable as most Kzin names)," he added, neither friendly nor unfriendly. He began untying Locklear's hands with, "I must kill you if you run, and I will. But I am no priest," he said, as if that explained his willingness to ease a captive's walking.

"You are a stalwart," Locklear said. "May I call you that?"

"As long as you can," the big Kzin said, leading the way again. "I voted to my priest to let you live, and teach us. So did most heroes of my group."

Uh-huh; they have priests instead of senators. But this smells like the old American system before direct elections. "Your priest is not bound to vote as you say?" A derisive snort was his answer, and he persisted. "Do you vote your priests in?"

"Yes. For life," said Stalwart, explaining everything.

"So they pretend to listen, but they do as they like," Locklear said.

A grunt, perhaps of admission or of scorn. "It was always thus," said Stalwart, and found that Locklear could trot, now. Another half-hour found them moving across a broad veldt, and Locklear saw the scars of a grass fire before he realized he was in familiar surroundings. Stalwart led the way to a rise and then stopped, pointing toward the jungle. "There," he said, "is your scarfaced friend."

Locklear looked in vain, then back at Stalwart. "He must be blending in with the ferns. You people do that very—"

"The highest tree. What remains of him is there."

And then Locklear saw the flying creatures he had called "batowls," tiny mites at a distance of two hundred meters, picking at tatters of something that hung in a net from the highest tree in the region. "Oh, my God! Won't he die there?"

"He is dead already. He underwent the long ceremony," said Stalwart, "many days past, with wounds that killed slowly."

Locklear's glare was incriminating: "I suppose you voted against that, too?"

"That, and the sacrifice of the palace *prret* in days past," said the Kzin.

Blinking away tears, for Scarface had truly been a cat of his word, Locklear said, "Those *prret*. One of them was Scarface's mate when I left. Is she—up there, too?"

For what it was worth, the big Kzin could not

meet his gaze. "Drowning is the dishonorable punishment for females," he said, pointing back toward
Kzersatz's long shallow lake. "The priesthood never
avoids tradition, and she lies beneath the water.
Another *prret* with kittens was permitted to rejoin
the tribe. She chose to be shunned instead. Now and
then, we see her. It is treason to speak against the
priesthood, and I will not."

Locklear squeezed his eyes shut; blinked; turned
away from the hideous sight hanging from that distant tree as scavengers picked at its bones. "And I
hoped to help your tribe! A pox on all your houses,"
he said to no one in particular. He did not speak to
the Kzin again, but they did not hurry as Stalwart
led the way back to the village.

The only speaking Locklear did was to the comm
set in his ear, shoving its pushbutton switch. The
Kzin looked back at him in curiosity once or twice,
but now he was speaking Interworld, and perhaps
Stalwart thought he was singing a death song.

In a way, it was true—though not a song of his
own death, if he could help it. "Locklear calling the
Anthony Wayne," he said, and paused.

He heard the voice of Grace Agostinho reply,
"Recording."

"They've caught me already, and they intend to
kill me. I don't much like you bastards, but at least
you're human. I don't care how many of the male
tabbies you bag; when they start torturing me I
won't be any further use to you."

Again, Grace's voice replied in his ear: "Recording."

Now with a terrible suspicion, Locklear said, "Is
anybody there? If you're monitoring me live, say
'monitoring.'"

His comm set, in Grace's voice, only said, "Recording."

Locklear flicked off the switch and began to walk even more slowly, until Stalwart tugged hard on the leash. Any Kzin who cared to look, as they re-entered the village, would have seen a little man bereft of hope. He did not complain when Stalwart retied his hands, nor even when another Kzin marched him away and fairly flung him into a tiny hut near the edge of the village. Eventually they flung a bloody hunk of some recent kill into his hut, but it was raw and, with his hands tied behind him, he could not have held it to his mouth.

Nor could he toggle his comm set, assuming it would carry past the roof thatch. He had not said he would be in the village, and they would very likely kill him along with everybody else in the village when they came. *If* they came.

He felt as though he would drown in cold waves of despair. A vicious priesthood had killed his friends and, even if he escaped for a time, he would be hunted down by the galaxy's most pitiless hunters. And if his own kind rescued him, they might cheerfully beat him to death trying to learn a secret he had already divulged. And even the gentle Neanderthalers hated him, now.

Why not just give up? I don't know why, he admitted to himself, and began to search for something to help him fray the thongs at his wrists. He finally chose a rough-barked post, sitting down in front of it and staring toward the Kzin male whose lower legs he could see beneath the door matting.

He rubbed until his wrists were as raw as that meat lying in the dust before him. Then he rubbed until his muscles refused to continue, his arms cramping horribly. By that time it was dark, and he kept falling into an exhausted, fitful sleep, starting to scratch at his bonds every time a cramp woke him. The fifth time he awoke, it was to the sounds of scratching again. And a soft, distant call outside, which his guard answered just as softly. It took Locklear a moment to realize that those scratching noises were not being made by *him*.

The scratching became louder, filling him with a dread of the unknown in the utter blackness of the Kzersatz night. Then he heard a scrabble of clods tumbling to the earthen floor. Low, urgent, in the fitz-rowr of a female Kzin: "Rockear, quickly! Help widen this hole!"

He wanted to shout, remembering Boots, the new mother of two who had scorned her tribe; but he whispered hoarsely: "Boots?"

An even more familiar voice than that of Boots. "She is entertaining your guard. Hurry!"

"Kit! I can't, my hands are tied," he groaned. "Kit, they said you were drowned."

"Idiots," said the familiar voice, panting as she worked. A very faint glow preceded the indomitable Kit, who had a modern Kzin beltpac and used its glowlamp for brief moments. Without slowing her frantic pace, she said softly, "They built a walkway into the lake and—dropped me from it. But my mate, your friend Scarface, knew what they intended. He told me to breathe—many times just before I fell. With all the stones—weighting me down, I simply walked on the bottom, between the pilings—and untied the stones beneath the planks near shore.

Idiots," she said again, grunting as her fearsome claws ripped away another chunk of Kzersatz soil. Then, "Poor Rockear," she said, seeing him writhe toward her.

In another minute, with the glowlamp doused, Locklear heard the growling curses of Kit's passage into the hut. She'd said females were good tunnelers, but not until now had he realized just how good. The nearest cover must be a good ten meters away . . . "Jesus, don't bite my hand, Kit," he begged, feeling her fangs and the heat of her breath against his savaged wrists. A moment later he felt a flash of white-hot pain through his shoulders as his hands came free. He'd been cramped up so long it hurt to move freely. "Well, by God it'll just have to hurt," he said aloud to himself, and flexed his arms, groaning.

"I suppose you must hold to my tail," she said. He felt the long, wondrously luxuriant tail whisk across his chest and, because it was totally dark, did as she told him. Nothing short of true and abiding friendship, he knew, would provoke her into such manhandling of her glorious, her sensual, her fundamental tail.

They scrambled past mounds of soft dirt until Locklear felt cool night air on his face. "You may quit insulting my tail now," Kit growled. "We must wait inside this tunnel awhile. You take this: I do not use it well."

He felt the cold competence of the object in his hand and exulted as he recognized it as a modern Kzin sidearm. Crawling near with his face at her shoulder, he said, "How'd you know exactly where I was?"

"Your little long-talker, of course. We could hear

you moaning and panting in there, and the magic tools of my mate located you."

But I didn't have it turned on. Ohhh-no; I didn't KNOW it was turned on! The goddamned thing is transmitting all the time . . . He decided to score one for Stockton's people, and dug the comm set from his ear. Still in the tunnel, it wouldn't transmit well until he moved outside. Crush it? Bury it? Instead, he snapped the magazine from the sidearm and, after removing its ammunition, found that the tiny comm set would fit inside. Completely enclosed by metal, the comm set would transmit no more until he chose.

He got all but three of the rounds back in the magazine, cursing every sound he made, and then moved next to Kit again. "They showed me what they did to Scarface. I can't tell you how sorry I am, Kit. He was my friend, and they will pay for it."

"Oh, yes, they will pay," she hissed softly. "Make no mistake, he is still your friend."

A thrill of energy raced from the base of his skull down his arms and legs. "You're telling me he's alive?"

As if to save her the trouble of a reply, a male Kzin called softly from no more than three paces away: "Milady; do we have him?"

"Yes," Kit replied.

"Scarface! Thank God you're—"

"Not now," said the one-time warship commander. "Follow quietly."

Having slept near Kit for many weeks, Locklear recognized her steam-kettle hiss as a sufferer's sigh. "I know your nose is hopeless at following a spoor, Rockear. But try not to pull me completely apart this time." Again he felt that long bushy tail pass across his breast, but this time he tried to grip it more gently as they sped off into the night.

Sitting deep in a cave with rough furniture and booby-trapped tunnels, Locklear wolfed stew under the light of a Kzin glowlamp. He had slightly scandalized Kit with a hug, then did the same to Boots as the young mother entered the cave without her kittens. The guard would never be trusted to guard anything again, said the towering Scarface, but that rescue tunnel was proof that a Kzin had helped. Now they'd be looking for Boots, thinking she had done more than lure a guard thirty meters away.

Locklear told his tale of success, failure, and capture by human pirates as he finished eating, then asked for an update of the Kzersatz problem. Kit, it turned out, had warned Scarface against taking the priests from stasis but one of the devout and not entirely bright males they woke had done the deed anyway.

Scarface, with his small hidden cache of modern equipment, had expected to lead; had he not been Tzak-Commander, once upon a time? The priests had seemed to agree—long enough to make sure they could coerce enough followers. It seemed, said Scarface, that ancient Kzin priests hadn't the slightest compunctions about lying, unlike modern Kzinti. He had tried repeatedly to call Locklear with his all-band comm set, without success. Depending on long custom, demanding that tradition take precedence over new ways, the priests had engineered the capture of Scarface and Kit in a hook-net, the kind of cruel device that tore at the victim's flesh at the slightest movement.

Villagers had spent days in building that walkway out over a shallowly sloping lake, a labor of loathing for Kzinti who hated to soak in water. Once it was extended to the point where the water was four meters deep, the rough-hewn dock made an obvious reminder of ceremonial murder to any female who might try, as Kit and Boots had done ages before, to liberate herself from the ritual prostitution of yore.

And then, as additional mental torture, they told their bound captives what to expect, and made Scarface watch as Kit was thrown into the lake. Boots, watching in horror from afar, had then watched the torture and disposal of Scarface. She was amazed when Kit appeared at her birthing bower, having seen her disappear with great stones into deep water. The next day, Kit had killed a big ruminant, climbing that tree at night to recover her mate and placing half of her kill in the net.

"My medkit did the rest," Scarface said, pointing to ugly scar tissue at several places on his big torso. "These scum have never seen anyone recover from deep body punctures. Antibiotics can be magic, if you stretch a point."

Locklear mused silently on their predicament for long minutes. Then: "Boots, you can't afford to hang around near the village anymore. You'll have to hide your kittens and—"

"They have my kittens," said Boots, with a glitter of pure hate in her eyes. "They will be cared for as long as I do not disturb the villagers."

"Who told you that?"

"The high priest," she said, mewling pitifully as

she saw the glance of doubt pass between Locklear and Scarface. The priests were accomplished liars.

"We'd best get them back soon," Locklear suggested. "Are you sure this cave is secure?"

Scarface took him halfway out one tunnel and, using the glowlamp, showed him a trap of horrifying simplicity. It was a grav polarizer unit from one of the biggest cages, buried just beneath the tunnel floor with a switch hidden to one side. If you reached to the side carefully and turned the switch off, that hidden grav unit wouldn't hurl you against the roof of the tunnel as you walked over it. If you didn't, it did. Simple. Terrible. "I like it," Locklear smiled. "Any more tricks I'd better know before I plaster myself over your ceiling?"

There were, and Scarface showed them to him. "But the least energy expended, the least noise and alarm to do the job, the best. Instead of polarizers, we might bury some stasis units outside, perhaps at the entrance to their meeting hut. Then we catch those *kshat* priests, and use the lying scum for target practice."

"Good idea, and we may be able to improve on it. How many units here in the cave?"

That was the problem; two stasis units taken from cages were not enough. They needed more from the crypt, said Locklear.

"They destroyed that little airboat you left me, but I built a better one," Scarface said with a flicker of humor from his ears.

"So did I. Put a bunch of polarizers on it to push yourself around and ignored the sail, didn't you?" He saw Scarface's assent and winked.

"Two units might work if we trap the priests one

by one," Scarface hazarded. "But they've been meddling in the crypt. We might have to fight our way in. And you . . ." he hesitated.

"And I have fought better Kzinti before, and here I stand," Locklear said simply.

"That you do." They gripped hands, and then went back to set up their raid on the crypt. The night was almost done.

When surrendering, Scarface had told Locklear nothing of his equipment cache. With two sidearms he could have made life interesting for a man; interesting and short. But his word had been his bond, and now Locklear was damned glad to have the stuff.

They left the females to guard the cave. Flitting low across the veldt toward the stasis crypt with Scarface at his scooter controls, they planned their tactics. "I wonder why you didn't start shooting those priests the minute you were back on your feet," Locklear said over the whistle of breeze in their faces.

"The kittens," Scarface explained. "I might kill one or two priests before the cowards hid and sent innocent fools to be shot, but they are perfectly capable of hanging a kitten in the village until I gave myself up. And I did not dare raid the crypt for stasis units without a warrior to back me up."

"And I'll have to do," Locklear grinned.

"You will," Scarface grinned back; a typical Kzin grin, all business, no pleasure.

They settled the scooter near the ice-rimmed force wall and moved according to plan, making haste slowly to avoid the slightest sound, the huge Kzin's head swathed in a bandage of leaves that suggested a wound while—with luck—hiding his identity for a few crucial seconds.

Watching the Kzin warrior's muscular body slide among weeds and rocks, Locklear realized that Scarface was still not fully recovered from his ordeal. *He made his move before he was ready because of me, and I'm not even a Kzin. Wish I thought I could match that kind of commitment,* Locklear mused as he took his place in front of Scarface at the crypt entrance. His sidearm was in his hand. Scarface had sworn the priests had no idea what the weapon was and, with this kind of ploy, Locklear prayed he was right. Scarface gripped Locklear by the neck then, but gently, and they marched in together expecting to meet a guard just inside the entrance.

No guard. No sound at all—and then a distant hollow slam, as of a great box closing. They split up then, moving down each side corridor, returning to the main shaft silently, exploring side corridors again. After four of these forays, they knew that no one would be at their backs.

Locklear was peering into the fifth when, glancing back, he saw Scarface's gesture of caution. Scuffing steps down the side passage, a mumble in Kzin, then silence. Then Scarface resumed his hold on his friend's neck and, after one mutual glance of worry, shoved Locklear into the side passage.

"Ho, see the beast I captured," Scarface called, his voice booming in the wide passage, prompting exclamations from two surprised Kzin males.

Stasis cages lay in disarray, some open, some with transparent tops ripped off. One Kzin, with the breast scars and bandoliers of a priest, hopped off the cage he used as a seat, and placed a hand on the butt of

his sharp *wtsai*. The other bore scabs on his breast
and wore no bandolier. He had been tinkering with
the innards of a small stasis cage, but whirled, jaw
agape.

"It must have escaped after we left, yesterday,"
said the priest, looking at the "captive," then with
fresh curiosity at Scarface. "And who are—"

At that instant, Locklear saw what levitated, spinning, inside one of the medium-sized cages; spinning
almost too fast to identify. But Locklear knew what it
had to be, and while the priest was staring hard at
Scarface, the little man lost control.

His cry was in Interworld, not Kzin: "You filthy
bastard!" Before the priest could react, a roundhouse
right with the massive barrel of a Kzin pistol took
away both upper and lower incisors from the left side
of his mouth. Caught this suddenly, even a two-
hundred kilo Kzin could be sent reeling from the
blow, and as the priest reeled to his right, Locklear
kicked hard at his backside.

Scarface clubbed at the second Kzin, the corridor
ringing with snarls and zaps of warrior rage. Locklear
did not even notice, leaping on the back of the fallen
priest, hacking with his gunbarrel until the *wtsai*
flew from a smashed hand, kicking down with all his
might against the back of the priest's head. The
priest, at least twice Locklear's bulk, had lived a life
much too soft, for far too long. He rolled over, eyes
wide not in fear but in anger at this outrage from a
puny beast. It is barely possible that fear might have
worked.

The priest caught Locklear's boot in a mouthful of
broken teeth, not seeing the sidearm as it swung at
his temple. The thump was like an iron bar against a

melon, the priest falling limp as suddenly as if some switch had been thrown.

Sobbing, Locklear dropped the pistol, grabbed handfuls of ear on each side, and pounded the priest's head against cruel obsidian until he felt a heavy grip on his shoulder.

"He is dead, Locklear. Save your strength," Scarface advised. As Locklear recovered his weapon and stumbled to his feet, he was shaking uncontrollably. "You must hate our kind more than I thought," Scarface added, studying Locklear oddly.

"He wasn't your kind. I would kill a man for the same crime," Locklear said in fury, glaring at the second Kzin who squatted, bloody-faced, in a corner holding a forearm with an extra elbow in it. Then Locklear rushed to open the cage the priest had been watching.

The top levered back, and its occupant sank to the cage floor without moving. Scarface screamed his rage, turning toward the injured captive. "You experiment on tiny kittens? Shall we do the same to you now?"

Locklear, his tears flowing freely, lifted the tiny Kzin kitten—a male—in hands that were tender, holding it to his breast. "It's breathing," he said. "A miracle, after getting the centrifuge treatment in a cage meant for something far bigger."

"Before I kill you, do something honorable," Scarface said to the wounded one. "Tell me where the other kitten is."

The captive pointed toward the end of the passage. "I am only an acolyte," he muttered. "I did not enjoy following orders."

Locklear sped along the cages and, at last, found

Boot's female kitten revolving slowly in a cage of the proper size. He realized from the prominence of the tiny ribs that the kitten would cry for milk when it waked. *If* it waked. "Is she still alive?"

"Yes," the acolyte called back. "I am glad this happened. I can die with a less-troubled conscience."

After a hurried agreement and some rough questioning, they gave the acolyte a choice. He climbed into a cage hidden behind others at the end of another corridor and was soon revolving in stasis. The kittens went into one small cage. Working feverishly against the time when another enemy might walk into the crypt, they disassembled several more stasis cages and toted the working parts to the scooter, then added the kitten cage and, barely, levitated the scooter with its heavy load.

An hour later, Scarface bore the precious cage into the cave and Locklear, following with an armload of parts, heard the anguish of Boots. "They'll hear you from a hundred meters," he cautioned as Boots gathered the mewing, emaciated kittens in her arms.

They feared at first that her milk would no longer flow but presently, from where Boots had crept into the darkness, Kit returned. "They are suckling. Do not expect her to be much help from now on," Kit said.

Scarface checked the magazine of his sidearm. "One priest has paid. There is no reason why I cannot extract full payment from the others now," he said.

"Yes, there is," Locklear replied, his fingers flying with hand tools from the cache. "Before you can get 'em all, they'll send devout fools to be killed while they escape. You said so yourself. Scarface, I don't want innocent Kzin blood on my hands! But after my old promise to Boots, I saw what that maniac was doing and—let's just say *my* honor was at stake." He knew that any modern Kzin commander would understand that. Setting down the wiring tool, he shuddered and waited until he could speak without a tremor in his voice. "If you'll help me get the wiring rigged for these stasis units, we can hide them in the right spot and take the entire bloody priesthood in one pile."

"All at once? I should like to know how," said Kit, counting the few units that lay around them.

"Well, I'll tell you how," said Locklear, his eyes bright with fervor. They heard him out, and then their faces glowed with the same zeal.

When their traps lay ready for emplacement, they slept while Kit kept watch. Long after dark, as Boots lay nearby cradling her kittens, Kit waked the others and served a cold broth. "You take a terrible chance, flying in the dark," she reminded them.

"We will move slowly," Scarface promised, "and the village fires shed enough light for me to land. Too bad about the senses of inferior species," he said, his ear umbrellas rising with his joke.

"How would you like a nice cold bath, tabby?" Locklear's question was mild, but it held an edge.

"Only monkeys *need* to bathe," said the Kzin, still amused. Together they carried their hardware outside and, by the light of a glowlamp, loaded the scooter while Kit watched for any telltale glow of eyes in the distance.

After a hurried nuzzle from Kit, Scarface brought the scooter up swiftly, switching the glowlamp to its pinpoint setting and using it as seldom as possible.

Their forward motion was so slow that, on the two occasions when they blundered into the tops of towering fernpalms, they jettisoned nothing more than soft curses. An hour later, Scarface maneuvered them over a light yellow strip that became a heavily trodden path and began to follow that path by brief glowlamp flashes. The village, they knew, would eventually come into view.

It was Locklear who said, "Off to your right."

"The village fires? I saw them minutes ago."

"Oh shut up, supercat," Locklear grumped. "So where's our drop zone?"

"Near," was the reply, and Locklear felt their little craft swing to the side. At the pace of a weed seed, the scooter wafted down until Scarface, with one leg hanging through the viewslot of his craft, spat a short, nasty phrase. One quick flash of the lamp guided him to a level landing spot and then, with admirable panache, Scarface let the scooter settle without a creak.

If they were surprised now, only Scarface could pilot his scooter with any hope of getting them both away. Locklear grabbed one of the devices they had prepared and, feeling his way with only his feet, walked until he felt a rise of turf. Then he retraced his steps, vented a heavy sigh, and began the emplacement.

Ten minutes later he felt his way back to the scooter, tapping twice on one of its planks to avoid getting his head bitten off by an all-too-ready Scarface. "So far, so good," Locklear judged.

"This had better work," Scarface muttered.

"Tell me about it," said the retreating Locklear, grunting with a pair of stasis toroids. After the stasis units were all in place, Locklear rested at the scooter before creeping off again, this time with the glowlamp and a very sloppy wiring harness.

When he returned for the last time, he virtually fell onto the scooter. "It's all there," he said, exhausted, rubbing wrists still raw from his brief captivity. Scarface found his bearings again, but it was another hour before he floated up an arroyo and then used the lamp for a landing light.

He bore the sleeping Locklear into the cave as a man might carry a child. Soon they both were snoring, and Locklear did not hear the sound that terrified the distant villagers in late morning.

Locklear's first hint that his plans were in shreds came with rough shaking by Scarface. "Wake up! The monkeys have declared war," were the first words he understood.

As they lay at the main cave entrance, they could see sweeps of the pinnace as it moved over the Kzin village. Small energy beams lanced down several times, at targets too widely spaced to be the huts. "They're targeting whatever moves," Locklear ranted, pounding a fist on hard turf. "And I'll bet the priests are hiding!"

Scarface brought up his all-band set and let it scan. In moments, the voice of David Gomulka grated from the speaker. ". . . kill 'em all. Tell 'em, Locklear! And when they do let you go, you'd better be ready to talk; over."

"I can talk to 'em any time I like, you know," Locklear said to his friend. "The set they gave me may have a coded carrier wave."

"We must stop this terror raid," Scarface replied, "before they kill us all!"

Locklear stripped his sidearm magazine of its rounds and fingered the tiny ear set from its metal cage, screwing it into his ear. "Got me tied up," he said, trying to ignore the disgusted look from Scarface at this unseemly lie. "Are you receiving . . ."

"We'll home in on your signal," Gomulka cut in.

Locklear quickly shoved the tiny set back into the butt of his sidearm. "No, you won't," he muttered to himself. Turning to Scarface: "We've got to transmit from another place, or they'll triangulate on me."

Racing to the scooter, they fled to the arroyo and skimmed the veldt to another spot. Then, still moving, Locklear used the tiny set again. "Gomulka, they're moving me."

The sergeant, furiously: "Where the fuck—?"

Locklear: "If you're shooting, let the naked savages alone. The real tabbies are the ones with bandoliers, got it? Bag 'em if you can but the naked ones aren't combatants."

He put his little set away again but Scarface's unit, on "receive only," picked up the reply. "Your goddamn signal is shooting all over hell, Locklear. And whaddaya mean, not combatants? I've never had a chance to hunt tabbies like this. No little civilian shit is gonna tell us we can't teach 'em what it's like to be hunted! You got that, Locklear?"

They continued to monitor Gomulka, skating back near the cave until the scooter lay beneath spreading ferns. Fleeing into the safety of the cave, they agreed on a terrible necessity. "They intend to take ears and tails as trophies, or so they say," Locklear admitted. "You must find the most peaceable of your tribe,

Boots, and bring them to the cave. They'll be cut down like so many vermin if you don't "

"No priests, and no acolytes," Scarface snarled. "Say nothing about us but you may warn them that no priest will leave this cave alive! That much, my honor requires."

"I understand," said Boots, whirling down one of the tunnels.

"And you and I," Scarface said to Locklear, "must lure that damned monkeyship away from this area. We cannot let them see Kzinti streaming in here."

In early afternoon, the scooter slid along rocky highlands before settling beneath a stone overhang. "The best cover for snipers on Kzersatz, Locklear. I kept my cache here, and I know every cranny and clearing. We just may trap that monkeyship, if I am clever enough at primitive skills."

"You want to trap them here? Nothing simpler," said Locklear, bringing out his tiny comm set.

But it was not to be so simple.

Locklear, lying in the open on his back with one hand under saffron vines, watched the pinnace thrumm overhead. The clearing, ringed by tall fernpalms, was big enough for the *Anthony Wayne*, almost capacious for a pinnace. Locklear raised one hand in greeting as he counted four heads inside the canopy: Gomulka, Lee, Gazho, and Schmidt. Then he let his head fall back in pretended exhaustion, and waited.

In vain. The pinnace settled ten meters away, its engines still above idle, and the canopy levered up; but the deserter crew had beam rifles trained on the surrounding foliage and did not accept the bait. "They may be back soon," Locklear shouted in Interworld.

He could hear the faint savage ripping at vegetation nearby, and wondered if they heard it, too. "Hurry!"

"Tell us now, asshole," Gomulka boomed, his voice coming both from the earpiece and the pinnace. "The secret, *now*, or we leave you for the tabbies!"

Locklear licked his lips, buying seconds. "It's—It's some kind of drive. The Outsiders built it here," he groaned, wondering feverishly what the devil his tongue was leading him into. He noted that Gazho and Lee had turned toward him now, their eyes blazing with greed. Schmidt, however, was studying the tallest fernpalm, and suddenly fired a thin line of fire slashing into its top, which was already shuddering.

"Not good enough, Locklear," Gomulka called. "We've got great drives already. Tell us where it is."

"In a cavern. Other side of—valley," Locklear said, taking his time. "Nobody has an—instantaneous drive but Outsiders," he finished.

A whoop of delight, then, from Gomulka, one second before that fernpalm began to topple. Schmidt was already watching it, and screamed a warning in time for the pilot to see the slender forest giant begin its agonizingly slow fall. Gomulka hit the panic button.

Too late. The pinnace, darting forward with its canopy still up, rose to meet the spreading top of the tree Scarface had cut using claws and fangs alone. As the pinnace was borne to the ground, its canopy twisting off its hinges, the swish of foliage and squeal of metal filled the air. Locklear leaped aside, rolling away.

Among the yells of consternation, Gomulka's was loudest. "Schmidt, you dumb fuck!"

"It was him," Schmidt yelled, coming upright again to train his rifle on Locklear—who fired first. If that slug had hit squarely, Schmidt would have been dead meat but its passage along Schmidt's forearm left only a deep bloody crease.

Gomulka, every inch a warrior, let fly with his own sidearm though his nose was bleeding from the impact. But Locklear, now protected by another tree, returned the fire and saw a hole appear in the canopy next to the wide-staring eyes of Nathan Gazho.

When Scarface cut loose from thirty meters away, Gomulka made the right decision. Yelling commands, laying down a cover of fire first toward Locklear, then toward Scarface, he drove his team out of the immobile pinnace by sheer voice command while he peered past the armored lip of the cockpit.

Scarface's call, in Kzin, probably could not be understood by the others, but Locklear could not have agreed more. "Fight, run, fight again," came the snarling cry.

Five minutes later after racing downhill, Locklear dropped behind one end of a fallen log and grinned at Scarface, who lay at its other end. "Nice aim with that tree."

"I despise chewing vegetable matter," was the reply. "Do you think they can get that pinnace in operation again?"

"With safety interlocks? It won't move at more than a crawl until somebody repairs the—" but Locklear fell silent at a sudden gesture.

From uphill, a stealthy movement as Gomulka scuttled behind a hillock. Then to their right, another brief rush by Schmidt who held his rifle one-handed now. This advance, basic to any team using

projectile weapons, would soon overrun their quarry.
The big blond was in the act of dropping behind a
fern when Scarface's round caught him squarely in
the breast, the rifle flying away, and Locklear saw
answering fire send tendrils of smoke from his log.
He was only a flicker behind Scarface, firing blindly
to force their heads down, as they bolted downhill
again in good cover.

Twice more, during the next hour, they opened
up at long range to slow Gomulka's team. At that
range they had no success. Later, drawing nearer to
the village, they lay behind stones at the lip of an
arroyo. "With only three," Scarface said with satis-
faction. "They are advancing more slowly."

"And we're wasting ammo," Locklear replied. "I
have, uh, two eights and four rounds left. You?"

"Eight and seven. Not enough against beam rifles." The big Kzin twisted, then, ear umbrellas cocked
toward the village. He studied the sun's position,
then came to some internal decision and handed
over ten of his precious remaining rounds. "The
brush in the arroyo's throat looks flimsy, Locklear,
but I could crawl under its tops, so I know you can.
Hold them up here, then retreat under the brushtops
in the arroyo and wait at its mouth. With any luck I
will reach you there."

The Kzin warrior was already leaping toward the
village. Locklear cried softly, "Where are you going?"

The reply was almost lost in the arroyo: "For
reinforcements."

The sun had crept far across the sky of Kzersatz
before Locklear saw movement again, and when he
did it was nearly too late. A stone descended the

arroyo, whacking another stone with the crack of
bowling balls; Locklear realized that someone had
already crossed the arroyo. Then he saw Soichiro
Lee ease his rifle into sight. Lee simply had not
spotted him.

Locklear took two-handed aim very slowly and
fired three rounds, full-auto. The first impact puffed
dirt into Lee's face so that Locklear did not see the
others clearly. It was enough that Lee's head blossomed,
snapping up and back so hard it jerked his torso, and
the rifle clattered into the arroyo.

The call of alarm from Gazho was so near it spooked
Locklear into firing blindly. Then he was bounding
into the arroyo's throat, sliding into chest-high brush
with spreading tops.

Late shadows were his friends as he waited, hoping one of the men would go for the beam rifle in
plain sight. Now and then he sat up and lobbed a
stone into brush not far from Lee's body. Twice,
rifles scorched that brush. Locklear knew better than
to fire back without a sure target while pinned in
that ravine.

When they began sending heavy fire into the throat
of the arroyo, Locklear hoped they would exhaust
their plenums, but saw a shimmer of heat and knew
his cover could burn. He wriggled away downslope,
past a trickle of water, careful to avoid shaking the
brush. It was then that he heard the heavy reports of
a Kzin sidearm toward the village.

He nearly shot the rope-muscled Kzin that sprang
into the ravine before recognizing Scarface, but within
a minute they had worked their way together. "Those
kshat priests," Scarface panted, "have harangued a

dozen others into chasing me. I killed one priest; the others are staying safely behind."

"So where are our reinforcements?"

"The dark will transform them."

"But we'll be caught between enemies," Locklear pointed out.

"Who will engage each other in darkness, a dozen fools against three monkeys."

"Two," Locklear corrected. But he saw the logic now, and when the sunlight winked out a few minutes later he was watching the stealthy movement of Kzin acolytes along both lips of the arroyo.

Mouth close to Locklear's ear, Scarface said, "They will send someone up this watercourse. Move aside; my *wtsai* will deal with them quietly."

But when a military flare lit the upper reaches of the arroyo a few minutes later, they heard battle screams and suddenly, comically, two Kzin warriors came bounding directly between Locklear and Scarface. Erect, heads above the brushtops, they leapt toward the action and were gone in a moment.

Following with one hand on a furry arm, Locklear stumbled blindly to the arroyo lip and sat down to watch. Spears and torches hurtled from one side of the upper ravine while thin energy bursts lanced out from the other. Blazing brush lent a flickering light as well, and at least three great Kzin bodies surged across the arroyo toward their enemies.

"At times," Scarface said quietly as if to himself, "I think my species more valiant than stupid. But they do not even know their enemy, nor care."

"Same for those deserters," Locklear muttered, fascinated at the firefight his friend had provoked. "So how do we get back to the cave?"

"This way," Scarface said, tapping his nose, and set off with Locklear stumbling at his heels.

The cave seemed much smaller when crowded with a score of worried Kzinti, but not for long. The moment they realized that Kit was missing, Scarface demanded to know why.

"Two acolytes entered," explained one male, and Locklear recognized him as the mild-tempered Stalwart. "They argued three idiots into helping take her back to the village before dark."

Locklear, in quiet fury: "No one stopped them?"

Stalwart pointed to bloody welts on his arms and neck, then at a female lying curled on a grassy pallet. "I had no help but her. She tried to offer herself instead."

And then Scarface saw that it was Boots who was hurt but nursing her kittens in silence, and no cave could have held his rage. Screaming, snarling, claws raking tails, he sent the entire pack of refugees pelting into the night, to return home as best they could. It was Locklear's idea to let Stalwart remain; he had, after all, shed his blood in their cause.

Scarface did not subside until he saw Locklear, with the Kzin medkit, ministering to Boots. "A fine ally, but no expert in Kzin medicine," he scolded, choosing different unguents.

Boots, shamed at having permitted acolytes in the cave, pointed out that the traps had been disarmed for the flow of refugees. "The priesthood will surely be back here soon," she added.

"Not before afternoon," Stalwart said. "They never mount ceremonies during darkness. If I am any judge, they will drown the beauteous *prret* at high noon."

Locklear: "Don't they ever learn?"

Boots: "No. They are the priesthood," she said as if explaining everything, and Stalwart agreed.

"All the same," Scarface said, "they might do a better job this time. You," he said to Stalwart; "could you get to the village and back here in darkness?"

"If I cannot, call me acolyte. You would learn what they intend for your mate?"

"Of course he must," Locklear said, walking with him toward the main entrance. "But call before you enter again. We are setting deadly traps for anyone who tries to return, and you may as well spread the word."

Stalwart moved off into darkness, sniffing the breeze, and Locklear went from place to place, switching on traps while Scarface tended Boots. This tender care from a Kzin warrior might be explained as gratitude; even with her kittens, Boots had tried to substitute herself for Kit. Still, Locklear thought, there was more to it than that. He wondered about it until he fell asleep.

Twice during the night, they were roused by tremendous thumps and, once, a brief Kzin snarl. Scarface returned each time licking blood from his arms. The second time he said to a bleary-eyed Locklear, "We can plug the entrances with corpses if these acolytes keep squashing themselves against our ceilings." The grav polarizer traps, it seemed, made excellent sentries.

Locklear did not know when Stalwart returned but, when he awoke, the young Kzin was already speaking with Scarface. True to their rigid code, the priests fully intended to drown Kit again in a noon

ceremony using heavier stones and, afterward, to lay
siege to the cave.

"Let them; it will be empty," Scarface grunted.
"Locklear, you have seen me pilot my little craft. I
wonder . . ."

"Hardest part is getting around those deserters, if
any," Locklear said. "I can cover a lot of ground
when I'm fresh."

"Good. Can you navigate to where Boots had her
birthing bower before noon?"

"If I can't, call me acolyte," Locklear said, smiling.
He set off at a lope just after dawn, achingly alert.
Anyone he met, now, would be a target.

After an hour, he was lost. He found his bearings
from a promontory, loping longer, walking less, and
was dizzy with fatigue when he climbed a low cliff to
the overhang where Scarface had left his scooter.
Breathing hard, he was lowering his rump to the
scooter when the rifle butt whistled just over his
head.

Nathan Gazho, who had located the scooter after
scouring the area near the pinnace, felt fierce glee
when he saw Locklear's approach. But he had not
expected Locklear to drop so suddenly. He swung
again as Locklear, almost as large as his opponent,
darted in under the blow. Locklear grunted with the
impact against his shoulder, caught the weapon by
its barrel, and used it like a pry-bar with both hands
though his left arm was growing numb. The rifle
spun out of reach. As they struggled away from the
ten-meter precipice, Gazho cursed—the first word
by either man—and snatched his utility knife from
its belt clasp, reeling back, his left forearm out. His
crouch, the shifting of the knife, its extraordinary

honed edge: marks of a man who had fought with knives before.

Locklear reached for the Kzin sidearm but he had placed it in a lefthand pocket and now that hand was numb. Gazho darted forward in a swordsman's balestra, flicking the knife in a short arc as he passed. By that time Locklear had snatched his own *wtsai* from its sheath with his right hand. Gazho saw the long blade but did not flinch, and Locklear knew he was running out of time. Standing four paces away, he pump-faked twice as if to throw the knife. Gazho's protecting forearm flashed to the vertical at the same instant when Locklear leaped forward, hurling the *wtsai* as he squatted to grasp a stone of fist size.

Because Locklear was no knife-thrower, the weapon did not hit point-first; but the heavy handle caught Gazho squarely on the temple and, as he stumbled back, Locklear's stone splintered his jaw. Nathan Gazho's legs buckled and inertia carried him backward over the precipice, screaming.

Locklear heard the heavy thump as he was fumbling for his sidearm. From above, he could see the broken body twitching, and his single round from the sidearm was more kindness than revenge. Trembling, massaging his left arm, he collected his *wtsai* and the beam rifle before crawling onto the scooter. Not until he levitated the little craft and guided it ineptly down the mountainside did he notice the familiar fittings of the standard-issue rifle. It had been fully discharged during the firefight, thanks to Scarface's tactic.

Many weeks before—it seemed a geologic age by now—Locklear had found Boots's private bower by accident. The little cave was hidden behind a low waterfall near the mouth of a shallow ravine, and once he had located that ravine from the air it was only a matter of following it, keeping low enough to avoid being seen from the Kzin village. The sun was almost directly overhead as Locklear approached the rendezvous. If he'd cut it too close . .

Scarface waved him down near the falls and sprang onto the scooter before it could settle. "Let me fly it," he snarled, shoving Locklear aside in a way that suggested a Kzin on the edge of self-control. The scooter lunged forward and, as he hung on, Locklear told of Gazho's death.

"It will not matter," Scarface replied as he piloted the scooter higher, squinting toward the village, "if my mates dies this day." Then his predator's eyesight picked out the horrifying details, and he began to gnash his teeth in uncontrollable fury.

When they were within a kilometer of the village, Locklear could see what had pushed his friend beyond sanity. While most of the villagers stood back as if to distance themselves from this pomp and circumstance, the remaining acolytes bore a bound, struggling burden toward the lakeshore. Behind them marched the bandoliered priests, arms waving beribboned lances. They were chanting, a cacophony like metal chaff thrown into a power transformer, and Locklear shuddered.

Even at top speed, they would not arrive until that procession reached the walkway to deep water; and Kit, her limbs bound together with great stones for weights, would not be able to escape this time. "We'll have to go in after her," Locklear called into the wind.

"I cannot swim," cried Scarface, his eyes slitted.

"I can," said Locklear, taking great breaths to hoard oxygen. As he positioned himself for the leap, his friend began to fire his sidearm.

As the scooter swept lower and slower, one Kzin priest crumpled. The rest saw the scooter and exhorted the acolytes forward. The hapless Kit was flung without further ceremony into deep water but, as he was leaping feet-first off the scooter, Locklear saw that she had spotted him. As he slammed into deep water, he could hear the full-automatic thunder of Scarface's weapon.

Misjudging his leap, Locklear let inertia carry him before striking out forward and down. His left arm was only at half-strength but the weight of his weapons helped carry him to the sandy bottom. Eyes open, he struggled to the one darker mass looming ahead.

But it was only a small boulder. Feeling the prickles of oxygen starvation across his back and scalp, he swiveled, kicking hard—and felt one foot strike something like fur. He wheeled, ignoring the demands of his lungs, wresting his *wtsai* out with one hand as he felt for cordage with the other. Three ferocious slices, and those cords were severed. He dropped the knife— the same weapon Kit herself had once dulled, then resharpened for him—and pushed off from the bottom in desperation.

He broke the surface, gasped twice, and saw a wide-eyed priest fling a lance in his direction. By sheer dumb luck, it missed, and after a last deep inhalation Locklear kicked toward the bottom again.

The last thing a wise man would do is locate a drowning tigress in deep water, but that is what Locklear did. Kit, no swimmer, literally climbed up his sodden flightsuit, forcing him into an underwater somersault, fine sand stinging his eyes. The next moment he was struggling toward the light again, disoriented and panicky.

He broke the surface, swam to a piling at the end of the walkway, and tried to hyperventilate for another hopeless foray after Kit. Then, between gasps, he heard a spitting cough echo in the space between the water's surface and the underside of the walkway. "Kit!" He swam forward, seeing her frightened gaze and her formidable claws locked into those rough planks, and patted her shoulder. Above them, someone was raising Kzin hell. "Stay here," he commanded, and kicked off toward the shallows.

He waded with his sidearm drawn. What he saw on the walkway was abundant proof that the priesthood truly did not seem to learn very fast.

Five bodies sprawled where they had been shot, bleeding on the planks near deep water, but more of them lay curled on the planks within a few paces of the shore, piled atop one another. One last acolyte stood on the walkway, staring over the curled bodies. He was staring at Scarface, who stood on dry land with his own long *wtsai* held before him, snarling a challenge with eyes that held the light of madness. Then, despite what he had seen happen a half-dozen times in moments, the acolyte screamed and leaped.

Losing consciousness in midair, the acolyte fell heavily across his fellows and drew into a foetal crouch, as all the others had done when crossing the last six meters of planking toward shore. Those units Locklear had placed beneath the planks in darkness had kept three-ton herbivores in stasis, and worked even bet-

ter on Kzinti. They'd known damned well the priesthood would be using the walkway again sooner or
later; but they'd had no idea it would be *this* soon.

Scarface did not seem entirely sane again until he
saw Kit wading from the water. Then he clasped his
mate to him, ignoring the wetness he so despised.
Asked how he managed to trip the gangswitch,
Scarface replied, "You had told me it was on the
inside of that piling, and those idiots did not try to
stop me from wading to it."

"I noticed you were wet," said Locklear, smiling.
"Sorry about that."

"I shall be wetter with blood presently," Scarface
said with a grim look toward the pile of inert sleepers.

Locklear, aghast, opened his mouth.

But Kit placed her hand over it. "Rockear, I know
you, and I know my mate. It is not your way but this
is Kzersatz. Did you see what they did to the captive
they took last night?"

"Big man, short black hair? His name is Gomulka."

"His name is meat. What they left of him hangs
from a post yonder."

"Oh my God," Locklear mumbled, swallowing hard.
"But—look, just don't ask me to help execute anyone
in stasis."

"Indeed." Scarface stood, stretched, and walked
toward the piled bodies. "You may want to take a
brief walk, Locklear," he said, picking up a discarded
lance twice his length. "This is Kzin business, not
monkey business." But he did not understand why,
as Locklear strode away, the little man was laughing
ruefully at the choice of words.

Locklear's arm was well enough, after two days, to

let him dive for his *wtsai* while Kzinti villagers watched in curiosity—and perhaps in distaste. By that time they had buried their dead in a common plot and, with the help of Stalwart, begun to repair the pinnace's canopy holes and twisted hinges. The little hand-welder would have sped the job greatly but, Locklear promised, "We'll get it back. If we don't hit first, there'll be a stolen warship overhead with enough clout to fry us all."

Scarface had to agree. As the warrior who had overthrown the earlier regime, he now held not only the rights, but also the responsibilities of leading his people. Lounging on grassy beds in the village's meeting hut on the third night, they slurped hot stew and made plans. "Only the two of us can make that raid, you know," said the big Kzin.

"I was thinking of volunteers," said Locklear, who knew very well that Scarface would honor his wish if he made it a demand.

"If we had time to train them," Scarface replied. "But that ship could be searching for the pinnace at any moment. Only you and I can pilot the pinnace so, if we are lost in battle, those volunteers will be stranded forever among hostile monk— Hostiles," he amended. "Nor can they use modern weapons."

"Stalwart probably could, he's a natural mechanic. I know Kit can use a weapon—not that I want her along."

"For a better reason than you know," Scarface agreed, his ears winking across the fire at the somnolent Kit.

"He is trying to say I will soon bear his kittens, Rockear," Kit said. "And please do not take Boots's new mate away merely because he can work magics with his hands." She saw the surprise in Locklear's face. "How could you miss that? He fought those acolytes in the cave for Boots's sake."

"I, uh, guess I've been pretty busy," Locklear admitted.

"We will be busier if that warship strikes before we do," Scarface reminded him. "I suggest we go as soon as it is light."

Locklear sat bolt upright. "Damn! If they hadn't taken my wristcomp—I keep forgetting. The schedules of those little suns aren't in synch; It's probably daylight there now, and we can find out by idling the pinnace near the force walls. You can damned well see whether it's light there."

"I would rather go in darkness," Scarface complained, "if we could master those night-vision sensors in the pinnace."

"Maybe, in time. I flew the thing here to the village, didn't I?"

"In daylight, after a fashion," Scarface said in friendly insult, and flicked his sidearm from its holster to check its magazine. "Would you like to fly it again, right now?"

Kit saw the little man fill his hand as he checked his own weapon, and marveled at a creature with the courage to show such puny teeth in such a feral grin. "I know you must go," she said as they turned toward the door, and nuzzled the throat of her mate. "But what do we do if you fail?"

"You expect enemies with the biggest ship you ever saw," Locklear said. "And you know how those stasis traps work. Just remember, those people have night sensors and they can burn you from a distance."

Scarface patted her firm belly once. "Take great care," he said, and strode into darkness.

The pinnace's controls were simple, and Locklear's only worry was the thin chorus of whistles: air, escaping from a canopy that was not quite perfectly sealed. He briefed Scarface yet again as their craft carried them over Newduvai, and piloted the pinnace so that its re-entry thunder would roll gently, as far as possible from the *Anthony Wayne*.

It was late morning on Newduvai, and they could see the gleam of the *Wayne*'s hull from afar. Locklear slid the pinnace at a furtive pace, brushing spiny shrubs for the last few kilometers before landing in a small desert wadi. They pulled hinge pins from the canopy and hid them in the pinnace to make its theft tedious. Then, stuffing a roll of binder tape into his pocket, Locklear began to trot toward his clearing.

"I am a kitten again," Scarface rejoiced, fairly floating along in the reduced gravity of Newduvai. Then he slowed, nose twitching. "Not far," he warned.

Locklear nodded, moved cautiously ahead, and then sat behind a green thicket. Ahead lay the clearing with the warship and cabin, seeming little changed—but a heavy limb held the door shut as if to keep things in, not out. And Scarface noticed two mansized craters just outside the cabin's foundation logs. After ten minutes without sound or movement from the clearing, Scarface was ready to employ what he called the monkey ruse; not quite a lie, but certainly a misdirection.

"Patience," Locklear counseled. "I thought you tabbies were hunters."

"Hunters, yes; not skulkers."

"No wonder you lose wars," Locklear muttered. But after another half-hour in which they ghosted in deep cover around the clearing, he too was ready to move.

The massive Kzin sighed, slid his *wtsai* to the rear and handed over his sidearm, then dutifully held his big pawlike hands out. Locklear wrapped the thin, bright red binder tape around his friend's wrists many times, then severed it with its special stylus. Scarface was certain he could bite it through until he tried. Then he was happy to let Locklear draw the stylus, with its chemical enabler, across the tape where the slit could not be seen. Then, hailing the clearing as he went, the little man drew his own *wtsai* and prodded his "prisoner" toward the cabin.

His neck crawling with premonition, Locklear stood five paces from the door and called again: "Hello, the cabin!"

From inside, several female voices and then only one, which he knew very well: "Locklear go soon soon!"

"Ruth says that many times," he replied, half amused, though he knew somehow that this time she feared for him. "New people keep gentles inside?"

Scarface, standing uneasily, had his ear umbrellas moving fore and aft. He mumbled something as, from inside, Ruth said, "Ruth teach new talk to gentles, get food. No teach, no food," she explained with vast economy.

"I'll see about that," he called and then, in Kzin, "what was that, Scarface?"

Low but urgent: "Behind us, fool."

Locklear turned. Not twenty paces away, Anse Parker was moving forward as silently as he could and now the hatchway of the *Anthony Wayne* yawned open. Parker's rifle hung from its sling but his service parabellum was leveled, and he was smirking. "If this don't beat all: my prisoner has a prisoner," he drawled.

For a frozen instant, Locklear feared the deserter had spied the *wtsai* hanging above Scarface's backside—but the Kzin's tail was erect, hiding the weapon. "Where are the others?" Locklear asked.

"Around. Pacifyin' the natives in that tabby lifeboat," Parker replied. "I'll ask you the same question, asshole."

The parabellum was not wavering. Locklear stepped away from his friend, who faced Parker so that the wrist tape was obvious. "Gomulka's boys are in trouble. Promised me amnesty if I'd come for help, and I brought a hostage," Locklear said.

Parker's movements were not fast, but so casual that Locklear was taken by surprise. The parabellum's short barrel whipped across his face, splitting his lip, bowling him over. Parker stood over him, sneering. "Buncha shit. If that happened, you'd hide out. You can tell a better one than that."

Locklear privately realized that Parker was right. And then Parker himself, who had turned half away from Scarface, made a discovery of his own. He discovered that, without moving one step, a Kzin could reach out a long way to stick the point of a *wtsai* against a man's throat. Parker froze.

"If you shoot me, you are deader than chivalry," Locklear said, propping himself up on an elbow. "Toss the pistol away."

Parker, cursing, did so, looking at Scarface, finding his chance as the Kzin glanced toward the weapon.

Parker shied away with a sidelong leap, snatching for his slung rifle. And ignoring the leg of Locklear who tripped him nicely.

As his rifle tumbled into grass, Parker rolled to his feet and began sprinting for the warship two hundred meters away. Scarface outran him easily, then stationed himself in front of the warship's hatch. Locklear could not hear Parker's words, but his gestures toward the *wtsai* were clear: there ain't no justice.

Scarface understood. With that Kzin grin that so many humans failed to understand, he tossed the *wtsai* near Parker's feet in pure contempt. Parker grabbed the knife and saw his enemy's face, howled in fear, then raced into the forest, Scarface bounding lazily behind.

Locklear knocked the limb away from his cabin door and found Ruth inside with three others, all young females. He embraced the homely Ruth with great joy. The other young Neanderthalers disappeared from the clearing in seconds but Ruth walked off with Locklear. He had already seen the spider grenades that lay with sensors outspread just outside the cabin's walls. Two gentles had already died trying to dig their way out, she said.

He tried to prepare Ruth for his ally's appearance but, when Scarface reappeared with his *wtsai*, she needed time to adjust. "I don't see any blood," was Locklear's comment.

"The blood of cowards is distasteful," was the Kzin's wry response. "I believe you have my sidearm, friend Locklear."

They should have counted, said Locklear, on Stockton learning to fly the Kzin lifeboat. But lacking heavy weapons, it might not complicate their capture strategy too much. As it happened, the capture was more absurd than complicated.

Stockton brought the lifeboat bumbling down in late afternoon almost in the same depressions the craft's jackpads had made previously, within fifty paces of the *Anthony Wayne*. He and the lissome Grace wore holstered pistols, stretching out their muscle kinks as they walked toward the bigger craft, unaware that they were being watched. "Anse; we're back," Stockton shouted. "Any word from Gomulka?"

Silence from the ship, though its hatch steps were down. Grace shrugged, then glanced at Locklear's cabin. "The door prop is down, Curt. He's trying to hump those animals again."

"Damn him," Stockton railed, and both turned toward the cabin. To Grace he complained, "If you were a better lay, he wouldn't always be—*good God!*"

The source of his alarm was a long blood-chilling, gut-wrenching scream. A Kzin scream, the kind featured in horror holovision productions; and very, very near. "Battle stations, red alert, up ship," Stockton cried, bolting for the hatch.

Briefly, he had his pistol ready but had to grip it in his teeth as he reached for the hatch rails of the *Anthony Wayne*. For that one moment he almost resembled a piratical man of action, and that was the moment when he stopped, one foot on the top step, and Grace bumped her head against his rump as she fled up those steps.

"I don't think so," said Locklear softly. To Curt Stockton, the muzzle of that alien sidearm so near must have looked like a torpedo launcher. His face drained of color, the commander allowed Locklear to take the pistol from his trembling lips. "And Grace," Locklear went on, because he could not see her past Stockton's bulk, "I doubt if it's your style anyway, but don't give your pistol a second thought. That Kzin you heard? Well, they're out there behind you, but they aren't in here. Toss your parabellum away and I'll let you in."

Late the next afternoon they finished walling up the crypt on Newduvai, with a small work force of willing hands recruited by Ruth. As the little group of gentles filed away down the hillside, Scarface nodded toward the rubble-choked entrance. "I still believe we should have executed those two, Locklear."

"I know you do. But they'll keep in stasis for as long as the war lasts, and on Newduvai— Well, Ruth's people agree with me that there's been enough killing." Locklear turned his back on the crypt and Ruth moved to his side, still wary of the huge alien whose speech sounded like the sizzle of fat on a skewer.

"Your ways are strange," said the Kzin, as they walked toward the nearby pinnace. "I know something of Interworld beauty standards. As long as you want that female lieutenant alive, it seems to me you would keep her, um, available."

"Grace Agostinho's beauty is all on the outside. And there's a girl hiding somewhere on Newduvai that those deserters never did catch. In a few years she'll be— Well, you'll meet her someday." Locklear put an arm around Ruth's waist and grinned. "The truth is, Ruth thinks *I'm* pretty funny-looking, but some things you can learn to overlook."

At the clearing, Ruth hopped from the pinnace

first. "Ruth will fix place nice, like before," she promised, and walked to the cabin.

"She's learning Interworld fast," Locklear said proudly. "Her telepathy helps—in a lot of ways. Scarface, do you realize that her people may be the most tremendous discovery of modern times? And the irony of it! The empathy these people share probably helped isolate them from the modern humans that came from their own gene pool. Yet their kind of empathy might be the only viable future for us." He sighed and stepped to the turf. "Sometimes I wonder whether I want to be found."

Standing beside the pinnace, they gazed at the *Anthony Wayne.* Scarface said, "With that warship, you could do the finding."

Locklear assessed the longing in the face of the big Kzin. "I know how you feel about piloting, Scarface. But you must accept that I can't let you have any craft more advanced than your scooter back on Kzersatz."

"But— Surely, the pinnace or my own lifeboat?"

"You see that?" Locklear pointed toward the forest.

Scarface looked dutifully away, then back, and when he saw the sidearm pointing at his breast, a look of terrible loss crossed his face. "I see that I will never understand you," he growled, clasping his hands behind his head. "And I see that you still doubt my honor."

Locklear forced him to lean against the pinnace, arms behind his back, and secured his hands with binder tape. "Sorry, but I have to do this," he said. "Now get back in the pinnace. I'm taking you to Kzersatz."

"But I would have—"

"Don't say it," Locklear demanded. "Don't tell me what you want, and don't remind me of your honor, goddammit! Look here, I *know* you don't lie. And what if the next ship here is another Kzin ship? You won't lie to them either, your bloody honor won't let you. They'll find you sitting pretty on Kzersatz, right?"

Teetering off-balance as he climbed into the pinnace without using his arms, Scarface still glowered. But after a moment he admitted, "Correct."

"They won't court-martial you, Scarface. Because a lying, sneaking monkey pulled a gun on you, tied you up, and sent you back to prison. I'm telling you here and now, I see Kzersatz as a prison and every tabby on this planet will be locked up there for the duration of the war!" With that, Locklear sealed the canopy and made a quick check of the console readouts. He reached across to adjust the inertia-reel harness of his companion, then shrugged into his own. "You have no choice, and no tabby telepath can ever claim you did. *Now* do you understand?"

The big Kzin was looking below as the forest dropped away, but Locklear could see his ears forming the Kzin equivalent of a smile. "No wonder you win wars," said Scarface.

Authors' Dedications:

Steve Stirling:

To Jan, with love

To Farrell McGovern, for lending me his computer when mine broke down—amici ex machina.

To Jerry Pournelle, for being a fascinating collaborator, an interesting conversationalist, a thoughtful host, and a thorough gentleman.

Jerry Pournelle:

To Steve Stirling, who seems determined to ruin my reputation for irrascibility.

THE CHILDREN'S HOUR

Jerry Pournelle & S.M. Stirling

Chapter I

"We want you to kill a Kzin."

The general didn't seem to be joking. Captain Jonah Matthieson frowned and reminded himself that flatlanders were odd. Damned odd. He ran his hand down the short-cropped black crest that was his concession to military dress codes. Even by Belter standards Jonah was tall, and if he'd stood straight he would have made a fine figure of a soldier, but he stood in the alert crouch Belters learn early. Matthieson's green slanted eyes showed little amusement as they flickered over General Buford Early's developing paunch. "Well . . . that's more or less what I've been doing."

The general's expression didn't change, but he took a box of cheroots from his desk, offered one perfunctorily, and lit his own with a lighter built into what looked to be a genuine Kzin skull. "Gracie. Display. A-7, schematic," Early said through a cloud of thick smoke.

The rear wall of the cubicle office lit with a display of hatchmarked columns. Jonah stared without comprehension.

"That's been boiled down to make it easier to see," the general said. "Ships, weapons, casualties, for both sides. Think of it as battle intensity and duration."

"Yes, sir?"

"Now look at it this way. Gracie: time sequence, phased." The screen changed to show four separate matts. "Captain, this is the record of the four fleets the Kzin have sent since they took Wunderland and the Alpha Centauri system, forty-two years ago. Notice anything?"

Jonah shrugged. "We're losing." The war with the felinoid aliens had been going on since before his birth—since humanity's first contact with them, sixty years before. Interstellar warfare at sublight speeds was a game for the patient.

"Fucking brilliant, Captain!" The general was short, black, and balding, and carried a mass of muscle that was almost obscene to someone raised in low gravity. He looked to be in early middle age, which depending on how much he cared about appearances, might mean anything up to a century and a half these days. "Yeah. We're losing. Their fleets are getting bigger and their weapons are getting better. We've made some improvements, too, but not as fast as they have."

Jonah nodded. There wasn't any need to say anything.

"What do you think I did before the war?" the general demanded.

"I have no idea, sir."

"Sure you do: ARM bureaucrat, like all the other generals," Early said. "Well, I was. But I also taught

military history in the ARM Academy. Damn near
the only Terran left who paid any attention to the
subject."

"Oh."

"Right. We weren't ready for wars, any of us.
Terrans didn't believe in them. Belters didn't either;
too damned independent. Well, the goddamn pussies do."

"Yes, sir."

"Right. Everyone knows that. Now *think* about it,
Captain. We're facing a race of carnivores with a
unified interstellar government of completely unknown
size, organized for war. They started ahead of us,
and now they've had Wunderland and its belt for
better than a generation. If nothing else, at this rate
they can eventually swamp us with numbers. Just
one set of multimegatonners getting through to
Earth—"

The general puffed on his cigar with short, vicious
breaths.

Jonah shivered inside himself at the thought: all
those people dependent on a single life-support system. He wondered how flatlanders had ever stood it.
Why, a single asteroid impact . . . The Belt was less
vulnerable. Too much delta vee need to match the
wildly varying vectors of its scores of thousands of
rocks; its targets were weaker individually, but vastly
more numerous and scattered.

He forced his mind back to the troll-like man
before him, gagging slightly on the smell of the
tobacco. *Even with his rank, how does he get away
with that on shipboard?* He had thought that even
on Earth, the filthy habit had died out. It must have

been revived since the pussies came, like so many archaic customs.

Like war and armies, the Belter thought sardonically. The branch-of-service insignias on the shoulder of the flatlander's coverall were not ones he recognized. Of course, there were 18 billion people in the solar system, and most of them seemed to be wearing some sort of uniform these days; flatlanders loved playing dress-up. *Comes of having nothing useful to do most of their lives*, he supposed.

"So every time it gets harder," Early said. "First time was bad enough, but they really underestimated us. Did the next time, too, but not so badly. They're getting better all the time. This last one— that was bad." General Early pointedly eyed the ribbons on Jonah's chest. Two Comets, and the unit citation his squadron of Darts had earned when they destroyed a Kzin fighter-base ship.

"As you know. You saw some of that. What you didn't see was the big picture—because we censored it, even from our military units. Captain, they nearly broke us. Because *we* underestimated *them*. This time they didn't just 'shriek and leap,' they came in tricky, fooled us completely when they looked like retreating . . . and we know why."

He spoke to the computer again, and the rear wall became a holo image. Centered in it was a woman wearing lieutenant's stripes and the same branch-badges as the general. Tall, slender, and paler-skinned than most, she was muscular in the fashion of low-gravity types who exercise. When she spoke it was in Belter dialect.

"The subject's name was Esteban Cheung Jagrannath," the woman said. The screen split, and a battered-looking individual appeared beside her. Jonah's eye picked out the glisten of sealant over artificial skin, the dying-rummy pattern of burst blood vessels from explosive decompression, the mangy look of someone given accelerated marrow treatments for radiation overdose. *That is one sorry-looking son of a bitch.* "He claims to have been born in Tiamat, in the Serpent Swarm of Wunderland, twenty-five subjective years ago."

Now I recognize the accent, Jonah thought. The lieutenant's English had a guttural quality despite the crisp Belter vowels; descendants of Belters who migrated to the asteroids of Alpha Centauri talked that way. Wunderlander influence.

"Subject is a power-systems specialist, drafted into the Kzin service as a crewman on a corvette tender—" the blue eyes looked down to a read-out below the pickup's line of sight "—called—" Something followed in the snarling hiss-spit of the Hero's Tongue.

"Roughly translated, the *Bounteous Mother's Teats*. Tits took a near-miss from a radiation-pulse bomb. The Kzin captain didn't have time to self-destruct; the bridge took most of the blast. She was a big mother—" the general blinked, snorted "—so a few of the repair crew survived, like this gonzo. All humans, as were most of the technical staff. We found a few nonhuman, nonKzin as well, but they were all killed. Pity."

Jonah and the flatlander nodded in unconscious unison. The Kzin empire was big, hostile, not interested in negotiation, and contained many subject species and planets; and that was about the limit of human knowledge. Not much background information had been included in the computers of the previous fleets, and very little of that survived; vessels too badly damaged for their crews to self-destruct before capture usually held little beyond wreckage.

The general spoke again. "Gracie, fast-forward to the main point." The holo-recording blurred ahead. "Captain, you can review at your leisure. It's all important background, but for now . . ." The general signed and the recording returned to normal speed.

". . . the new Kzin commander arrived three years before they left. His name's Chuut-Riit, which indicates a close relation to the . . . 'Patriarch,' that's as close as we've been able to get. Apparently, Chuut-Riit's first order was to delay the departure of the fleet." A thin smile. "Chuut-Riit's not just related to their panjumandrum; he's an author, of sorts. Two works on strategy: *Logistical Preparation As The Key to Victory In War*, and *Conquest Through The Defensive Offensive*."

Jonah shaped a soundless whistle. *Not your typical Kzin. If we have any idea of what a typical Kzin is like. We've only met their warriors, coming our way behind beams and bombs.*

The lieutenant's image was agreeing with him. "The pussies find him a little eccentric as well; according to the subject, gossip had it that he fought a whole series of duels, starting almost the moment he arrived and held a staff conference. The new directives included a massive increase in the fleet's support infrastructure, and he ordered and supervised a complete changeover in tactics, especially to ensure that accurate reports of the fighting got back to Wunderland."

The flatlander general cut off the scene with a wave. "So." He folded his hands and leaned forward, the yellowish whites of his eyes glittering in lights that must be kept deliberately low. "We are in trouble, Captain. So far we've beaten off the pussies because we're a lot closer to our main sources of supply, and because they're . . . predictable. Adequate tacticians, but with little strategic sense, less even than we had at first, despite the Long Peace. The analysts say that indicates they've never come across much in the way of significant opposition before. If they had they'd have learned from it like they are—damn it!—learning from us.

"And in fact, what little intelligence information we've got, a lot of it from prisoners taken with the Fourth Fleet, backs that up; the Kzin just don't have much experience of war."

Jonah blinked. "Not what you'd assume," he said carefully.

A choppy nod. "Yep. Surprises you, eh? Me, too."

General Early puffed delicately on his cigar. "Oh, they're aggressive enough. Almost insanely so, barely gregarious enough to maintain a civilization. Ritualized conflict to the death is a central institution of theirs. Some of the xenologists swear they must have gotten their technology from somebody else, that this culture they've got could barely have risen above the neolithic stage on its own.

"In any event, they're wedded to a style of attack that's almost pitifully straightforward." He looked thoughtfully at the wet, chewed cigar-end, discarded it and selected another from the humidor. "And as far as we can tell, they have only one society, one social system, one religion, and one state. That fits in with some other clues we've gotten; the entire Kzin species has a longer continuous history than any human culture. Maybe a *lot* longer." Another puff. "They're curiously genetically uniform, too; at least their fighters are. We know more about their biology than their beliefs—more corpses than live prisoners. Less variation than you'd expect, and large numbers of them seem to be siblings."

Jonah stirred. "Well, this is all very interesting, general, but—"

"—what's it got to do with you?" The flatlander leaned forward again, tapping paired thumbs together. "This Chuut-Riit is a first-class menace. You see, we're losing those advantages I mentioned. The Kzin have been shipping additional force into the Wunderland system in relays. Not so much weapons as knocked-down industrial plants and personnel. Furthermore, they've got the locals well organized. It's become a fully industrialized, system-wide economy, with an earth-type planet and an asteroid belt richer than Sol's. The population's much lower—hundreds of millions instead of nearly twenty billion—but that doesn't matter much."

Jonah nodded in his turn. With ample energy and raw materials, the geometric-increase potential of automated machinery could build a war-making capacity in a single generation. Faster than that, if a few crucial administrators and technicians were imported, too. Earth's witless hordes were of little help to Sol's military effort. Most of them were a mere drain on resources—not even useful as cannon fodder in a conflict largely fought in space.

"So now they're in a position to outproduce us. We have to keep our advantages in operational efficiency."

"You play Go with masters, you get good," the Belter said.

"No. It's academic whether the pussies are more or less intelligent than we. What's intelligence, anyway? But we've proven experimentally that they're culturally and genetically less flexible. Man, when this war started we were absolute pacifists—we hadn't had so much as a riot in three centuries. We even censored history so that the majority didn't know there had ever been wars! That was less than a century ago, less than a single lifetime, and look at what we've done since. The pussies are only just now starting to smarten up about us."

"This Chuut-Riit sounds as if he's . . . oh shit. Sir."

A wide white grin. "Exactly. An *exceptionally* able ratcat. The Kzinti are less prone to either genius or stupidity than we are; they don't tolerate eccentrics, duel them to death, usually. But here they've got a goddamn genius in a position to knock sense into their heads.

"He has to go."

The flatlander stood and began striding back and forth behind the desk, gesturing with the cigar. Something more than the stink made Jonah's stomach clench.

"Covert operations is another thing we've had to reinvent, just lately. We need somebody who's good with spacecraft . . . a Belter, because the ones who settled the Serpent Swarm belt of Wunderland have stayed closer to the ancestral stock than the Wunderlanders downside. A good combat man who's proved himself capable of taking on Kzin at close quarters. And someone who's good with computer systems, because our informants tell us that is the skill most in demand by the Kzin on Wunderland itself."

The general halted and stabbed toward Jonah with the hand that held the stub of burning weeds. "Last but not least, someone with contacts in the Alpha Centauri system."

Jonah felt a wave of relief. A little relief, because the general was still grinning at him.

"Sir, I've never left—"

An upraised hand halted him. "Gracie. Tell Lieutenant Raines we're ready for her."

A woman came in and saluted smartly, first the general and then Jonah; he recognized her from the holo. "I'd like you to meet Captain Matthieson."

"God, what have you done to her?" Jonah asked the tall lieutenant as they grabbed stanchions and halted by the viewport nearest his ship.

The observation corridor outside the central graving dock of the base-asteroid was a luxury, but then, with a multimegaton mass to work with and unlimited energy, the Sol-system military could afford that type of luxury. Take a nickel-iron rock. Drill a hole down the center with bomb-pumped lasers. Put a spin on the resulting tube, and rig large mirrors with the object at their focal points; the sun is dim beyond the orbit of Mars, but in zero-G you can build awfully big mirrors. The nickel-iron pipe heats, glows, turns soft as taffy, swells outward evenly, like cotton-candy at a fair. Cooling, it leaves a huge open space surrounded by a thick shell of metal-rich rock. Robots drill the tunnels and corridors. Humans and robots install the power sources, life-support, gravity polarizers. . . .

An enlisted crewman bounced by them horizontal to their plane of reference, sketching a sloppy salute as he twisted, hit the corner feet first and rebounded away. The air had the cool clean tang that Belters were used to, but with an industrial-tasting underlay of ozone and hot metal; the seals inside UNSN base Gibraltar were adequate for health but not up to Belt civilian standards. Even while he hung motionless and watched the technicians gutting his ship, some remote corner of Jonah's mind noted again that flat-landers had a nerve-wracking tendency to tolerate jury-rigged and barely adequate solutions. Simple self-respect demanded that the air one breathed be *clean*, damn it!

UNSN *Catskinner* hung in the vacuum chamber, surrounded by the flitting shapes of space-suited re-pair workers, compuwaldos and robots, torches that blinked blue-white, and a haze of detached fittings that hinted at the haste of the work. Beneath the mods and clutter the basic shape of the Dart-class attack boat still showed: massive fusion-power unit, tiny life-support bubble, asymmetric fringe of weap-ons and sensors designed for deep-space operation.

"What have you done to my ship?" Jonah asked again.

"Made some necessary modifications, Captain," Raines replied. "The basic drive and armament sys-tems are unaltered."

Jonah nodded grudgingly. He could see the clus-tered grips for the spike-pods, featureless egg-shaped ovoids, that were the basic weapon for light vessels, a one-megaton bomb pumping an X-ray laser. In battle they would spread out like the wings of a raptor, a pattern thousands of kilometers wide slaved to the computers in the control pod. The other weapons remained as well: fixed lasers, ball-bearing scatterers, railguns, particle-beam projectors, the antennae for stealthing and beam-deflection fields.

Unconsciously, the pilot's hands twitched; his reflexes and memory were back in the crashcouch, fingers moving infinitesimally in the lightfield gloves, holos feeding data into his eyes. Dodging with fusion-powered feet, striking with missile fists, his Darts locked with the Kzinti Vengeful Slashers in a dance of battle that was as much like zero-G ballet as anything else. . . .

"What modifications?" he asked.

"Grappling points for attachment to a ramscoop ship. Experimental. They're calling it the *Yamamoto*. The plan is that we ride piggyback until we reach the Wunderland system at high tau, having accelerated all the way. We drop off just this side of Alpha Centauri. They won't have much time to prepare for us at those speeds." The ship would be on the heels of the wave-front announcing its arrival.

"Great," he said sarcastically. "And just how are we supposed to stop?"

"Oh, that's simple," Raines said. For the first time in their brief acquaintance, she smiled. *Damn, she's good looking*, Jonah thought with mild surprise. *Better than good. How could I not notice?*

"We ram ourselves into the sun."

Several billion years before, there had been a species of sophonts with a peculiar ability. They called themselves (as nearly as humans could reproduce the sound) the Thrint; others knew them as Slavers. The ability amounted to an absolutely irresistible form of telepathic hypnosis, evolved as a hunting aid in an ecosystem where most animals advanced enough to have a spinal cord were at least mildly telepathic. This was a low-probability development, but in a universe as large as ours anything possible will occur sooner or later. On their native world, Thrintun could give a subtle prod to a prey-animal, enough to tip its decision to come down to the waterhole. The Thrint evolved intelligence as an additional advantage. After all, their prey had millions of years to develop resistance.

Then a spaceship landed on the Thrint homeworld. Its crew immediately became slaves. Absolutely obedient, absolutely trustworthy, willing and enthusiastic slaves. Operating on nervous systems that had not evolved in an environment saturated with the Power, any Thrint could control dozens of sophonts. With the amplifiers that slave-technicians developed, a Thrint could control an entire planet. Slaves industrialized a culture in the hunting-band stage in a single generation; controlled by the Power, in a few generations more slaves built an interstellar empire covering most of a galaxy.

Slaves did everything, because the Thrint had never been a *very* intelligent species, and once loose with the Power they had no need to think. Eventually they met, and thought they had enslaved, a very clever race indeed, the tnuctipun. The revolt that eventually followed resulted in the extermination of every tool-using sentient in the Galaxy, but before it did the tnuctipun made some remarkable things. . . .

"A Slaver stasis field?" he said. Despite himself, awe showed in his voice. One such field had been discovered on Earth, then lost. Later, one more on a human-explored world. Three centuries of study had found no slightest clue concerning their operating principles; they were as incomprehensible as a molecular-distortion battery would have been to Thomas Edison. Monkey-see monkey-do copies had been made, each taking more time and expense than the *Gibraltar.* So far exactly two had functioned.

"Uh-mmm, give the captain a big cigar; right first time."

Jonah shuddered, remembering the flatlander's smoke. "No, thanks."

"Too right, Captain. Just a figure of speech."

"Call me Jonah, we're going to be cramped enough on this trip without poking rank-elbows in each other's ribs."

"Jonah. The *Yamamoto* skims through the system, throwing rocks." At .999 of C, missiles needed no warheads. The kinetic energies involved made the impacts as destructive as antimatter. "We go in as an offcourse rock. Course corrections, then on with the stasis field, go ballistic, use the outer layer of the sun for breaking down to orbital speeds."

Nothing outside its surface could affect the contents of a Slaver field; let the path of the *Catskinner* stray too far inward and they would spend the rest of the lifespan of the universe at the center of Alpha Centauri's sun, in a single instant of frozen time. For that matter, the stasis field would probably survive the re-contraction of the primal monobloc and its explosion into a new cosmic cycle . . . he forced his mind away from the prospect.

"And we're putting in a Class-VII computer system."

Jonah raised a brow. Class-VII systems were

consciousness-level; they also went irredeemably insane sometime between six months and a year after
activation, as did any artificial entity complex enough
to be aware of being aware.

"Our . . . mission won't take any longer than that,
and it's worth it." A shrug. "Look, why don't we hit a
cafeteria and talk some more—really talk. You're
going to have briefings running out of every orifice
before long, but that isn't the same."

Jonah sighed, and stopped thinking of ways out of
the role for which he had been "volunteered." This
was too big to be dodged, far and away too big. Two
stasis fields in the whole Sol system; one guarding
United Nations Space Navy H.Q., the other on his
ship. His ship, a Dart-Commander like ten thousand
or so others, until this week. How many Class-VII
computers? Nobody built consciousness-level systems
any more, except occasionally for research; it simply
wasn't cost-effective. And if you built them to be
more intelligent than genius humans they went
noncomp so quickly you couldn't prove they had
ever been aware. A human-level machine gave you a
sentient entity with a six-month lifespan that could
do arithmetic in its head. Ordinary computers could
do more—and for thinking people were much cheaper.
It was a dead-end technology, like direct interfacing
between human neural systems and computers. And
they had revived it, for a special-purpose mission.

"Shit," Jonah mumbled, as they came to a lock and
reoriented themselves feet-down. There was a gravity warning strobing beside it; they pushed through
the airscreen curtain and into the dragging acceleration of a one-G field. The crewfolk about them were

mostly flatlander now, relaxed in the murderous weight that crushed their frames lifelong.

"Naacht wh'r?" Ingrid asked. In Wunderlander, but the Sol-Belter did not have to know that bastard offspring of Danish and Plattdeutsch to sense the meaning.

"I just realized . . . hell, I just realized how important this must all be. If the high command were willing to put that much effort into this, willing to sacrifice half of our most precious military asset, throw in a computer that costs more than this base complete with crew . . . then they must have put at least equal effort into searching for just the right pilot. There's simply no point in trying to get out of it. Tanj. I need a drink."

"Take your grass-eater stink out of my air!" Chuut-Riit shrieked. He was standing, looking twice his size as his orange-red pelt bottled out, teeth exposed in what an uninformed human might have mistaken for a grin, naked pink tail lashing. The reference to smell was purely metaphorical, since the conversation was 'cast. Which was as well; he was pouring aggression-pheromones into the air at a rate that would have made a roomful of adult male Kzinti nervous to the point of lost control.

The holo images on the wall before him laid themselves belly-down on the decking of their ship and crinkled their ears, their fur lying flat in propitiation.

"Leave the recordings and flee, devourers of your own kittens!" screamed the Kzinti governor of the Alpha Centauri system. The Hero's Tongue is remarkably rich in expressive insults. *"Roll in your own shit and mate with sthondats!"* The wall blanked,

and a light blinked in one corner as the data was packed through the link into his private files.

Chuut-Riit's fur smoothed as he strode around the great chamber. It stood open to the sky, beneath a near-invisible dome that kept the scant rain of this area off the kudlotlin-hide rugs. They were priceless imports from the home world. The stuffed matched pair of Chunquen on a granite pedestal were souvenirs acquired during the pacification of that world. He looked at them, soothing his eyes with the memory-taste of a successful hunt, then at other mementos. Wild smells drifted in over thin walls that were crystal-enclosed sandwiches of circuitry. In the distance something squalled hungrily. The palace-preserve-fortress of a planetary governor, governor of the richest world to be conquered by Kzinti in living memory. Richest in wealth, richest in honor . . . if the next attack on the human homeworld was something more than a fifth disaster.

"Secretariat," he rasped. The wall lit.

A human looked up from a desk, stood and came to attention. "Henrietta," the Kzin began, "hold my calls for the rest of the day. I've just gotten the final download on the Fourth Fleet fiasco, and I'm a little upset. Run it against my projections, will you?"

"Yes, Chuut-Riit," he said—*no, God devour it, she, I've got to start remembering human females are sentient*. At least he could tell them apart without smelling them, now. Even distinguish between individuals of the same subspecies. *There are so many types of them!*

"I don't think you'll find major discrepancies."

"That bad?" the human said, with a closed curve of the lips; the locals had learned that barring their teeth at a Kzin was not a good idea. The expression was called a "smile," Chuut-Riit reminded himself. Betokening amusement, or friendliness, or submission. *Which is it feeling?* Born after the Conquest Fleet arrived here. Reared from a cub in the governor's palace, superbly efficient . . . *but what does it think inside that ugly little head?*

"Worse, the"—he lapsed into the Hero's Tongue, since no human language was sufficient—"couldn't apply the strategy properly in circumstances beyond the calculated range of probable response." It was impossible to set out too detailed a plan of campaign, when communication took over four years. His fur began to bristle again, and he controlled his reaction with a monumental effort of will. *I need to fight something,* he thought.

"Screen out all calls for the next sixteen hours, unless they're Code VI or above." A thought prompted at him. "Oh, it's your offspring's naming-day next week, isn't it?"

"Yes, Chuut-Riit." Henrietta had once told him that among pre-Conquest humans it had been a mark of deference to refer to a superior by title, and of familiarity to use names. His tail twitched. Extraordinary. Of course, humans all had names, without having to earn them. *In a sense, they're assigned names as we are rank-titles,* he thought.

"Well, I'll drop by at the celebration for an hour or so and bring one of my cubs." That would be safe enough if closely supervised.

"We are honored, Chuut-Riit!" The human bowed, and the Kzin waved a hand to break contact.

"Valuable," he muttered to himself rising and pacing once more. Humans were the most valuable subject-species the Kzin had yet acquired. *Or partially acquired*, he reminded himself. Most Kzin nobles on Wunderland had large numbers of human servants and technicians about their estates, but few had gone as far as he in using their administrative talents.

"Fools," he said in the same undertone; his Kzin peers knew his opinion of them, but it was still inadvisable to get into the habit of saying it aloud. "I am surrounded by fools." Humans fell into groups *naturally*; they thought in terms of organization. The remote ancestors of Kzin had hunted in small packs, the prehumans in much larger ones. *Stupidity to deny the evidence of senses and logic*, he thought with contempt. *These hairless monkeys have talents we lack*.

Most refused to admit that, as though it somehow diminished the Hero to grant that a servant could do what the master could not. Idiocy. Chuut-Riit yawned, revealing a pink-red-and-white expanse of ridged pallet, tongue and fangs, his species' equivalent of a dismissive shrug. *Is it beneath the Hero to admit that a sword extends his claws, or a computer his mind?* With human patience and organizational talent at the service of the Heroes, there was *nothing* they could not accomplish! Even monkey inquisitiveness was a trait not without merit, irritating though it could be.

He pulled his mind away from vistas of endless victory, a hunt ranging over whole spiral arms; that was a familiar vision, one that had driven him to intrigue and duel for this position. To use a tool effectively, you had to know its balance and heft, its strengths and weaknesses. Humans were more gregarious than Kzinti, more ready to identify with a leader-figure. But to elicit such cooperation, you had to know the symbol-systems that held power over them. *I must wear the mask they can see. Besides which, their young are . . . what is their word? Cute. I will select the cub carefully, one just weaned, and stuff it full of meat first. That will be safest.*

Chuut-Riit intended to take his offspring with him to earth, after the conquest, the best of them. Early exposure to humans would give them an intuitive grasp of the animals that he could only simulate through careful study. With a fully-domesticated human species at their disposal, his son's son's sons could even aspire to . . . no, unthinkable. And not necessary to think of, that was generations away.

Besides, it would take a great deal of time to properly tame the humans. They were useful already, but far too wild, too undependable, too various. A millennium of culling might be necessary before they were fully shaped to the purpose.

". . . didn't just bull in," Lieutenant Raines was saying, as she followed the third *akvavit* with a beer chaser. Jonah sipped more cautiously at his, thinking the asymmetry of nearly pure alcohol and laager was typically Wunderlander. "Only it wasn't caution, the pussies just didn't want to mess the place up and weren't expecting much resistance. Rightly so."

Jonah restrained himself from patting her hand as she scowled into her beer. It was dim in their nook, and the gravity was Wunderland-standard .61 Earth; the initial refugees from the Alpha Centauri system had been mostly planetsiders, and from the dominant Danish-Dutch-German-Balt ethnic group. They had grown even more clannish in the generation since, which showed in the tall ceramic steins along the walls, plastic wainscotting that made a valiant attempt to imitate fumed oak, and a human bartender in wooden shoes, lederhosen, and a beard clipped closer on one side than the other.

The drinks slipped up out of the center of the table, of course.

"That was, *teufel*, three years ago, my time. We'd had some warning, of course, once the UN started mastering what the crew of the *Angel's Pencil* found on the wreckage of that Kzin ship. Plenty of singleships, and any reaction drive's a weapon; couple of big boost-lasers. But," a shrug, "you know how it was back then."

"Before my time, Lieutenant," Jonah said, then cursed himself as he saw her wince. Raines had been born nearly three quarters of a century ago, even if her private duration included only two and a half decades of it.

"I'm Ingrid, if you're going to be Jonah instead of Captain Matthiesson. Time—I keep forgetting, my head remembers but my gut forgets . . . Well, we just weren't set up to think in terms of war; that was ancient history. We held them off for nearly six months, though. Long enough to refit the three slowships in orbit, and give them emergency boost. I think the pussies didn't catch up and blast us simply because they didn't give a damn; they couldn't decelerate us and get the ships back, so why bother? Arrogant sons of . . ." another of those broad urchin grins "well, bitches isn't quite appropriate, is it?"

Jonah laughed. "You were in Munchen when the Kzin arrived?"

"No, I'd been studying at the Scholarium there—software design philosophy—but I was on sabbatical in Vallburg with two friends of mine, working out some, ha, personal problems."

The bartender with the unevenly-forked beard was nearly as attenuated as a Belter, but he had the disturbingly mobile ears of a pure-bred Wunderland *Herrenmann*, and they were pricked forward. Alpha Centauri's only habitable planet has a thin atmosphere; the original settlers have adapted, and keen hearing is common among them. Jonah smiled at the man and stabbed a finger for a privacy screen. It flickered into the air across the outlet of the booth, and the refugee saloonkeeper went back to polishing a mug.

"That'd be, hmmm, Claude Montferrat-Palme and Harold Yarthkin-Schotmann?"

Raines nodded, moodily drawing a design on the tabletop with a forefinger dipped in the dark beer. "Yes . . . *teufel*, they're both of them in their fifties now, getting on for middle-aged." A sigh. "Look . . . Harold's a, hmmm, hard to explain to a Sol-Belter, or even someone from the Serpent Swarm who hasn't spent a lot of time dirtside. His father was a *Herrenmann*, one of the Nineteen Families, senior line. His mother wasn't married to him."

"Oh," Jonah said, racking his memory. History had never been an interest of his, and his generation had been brought up to the War, anyway. "Problems with wills and inheritances and suchlike?"

"You know what a bastard is?"

"Sure. Someone you don't like, such as for example that flatlander bastard who assigned me to this project." He raised his stein in salute. "Though I'm fast becoming resigned to it, Ingrid."

She half-smiled in absent-minded acknowledgment,
her mind 4.3 light-years and four decades away. "It
means he got an expensive education, a nice little
nest-egg settled on him . . . and that he'd never,
never be allowed past the front door of the Yarthkin-
Schotmann's family schloss. Lucky to be allowed to
use the name. An embarrassment."

"Might eat at a man," Jonah said.

"Like a little kzin in the guts. Especially when he
grew enough to realize why his father only came for
occasional visits; and then that his half-siblings didn't
have half his brains or drive and didn't need them
either. It drove him, he had to do everything twice
as fast and twice as good, take crazy risks . . . made
him a bit of a bastard in the Sol sense of the word,
too, spines like a pincodillo, sense of humor that
could flay a gruntfish."

"And Montferrat-Palme?"

"Claude? Now, *he* was *Herrenmann* all through;
younger son of a younger son, poor as an Amish dirt-
farmer, and . . ." A laugh. "You had to meet Claude
to understand him. I think he got serious about me
mostly because I kept turning him down, it was a
new experience and drove him crazy. And Harold he
halfway liked, and halfway enjoyed needling. . . ."

Municipal Director of Internal Affairs Claude
Montferrat-Palme adjusted his cape and looked up at
the luminous letters that floated disembodied ten
centimeters from the smooth brown brick of the
building in front of him.

Harold's Terran Bar, it read. *A World On Its
Own.* Below, in smaller letters: *humans only*.

Ah, Harold, he thought. Always the one for a

piece of useless melodrama. As if Kzin would be likely to frequent this section of Old Munchen, or wish to enter a human entertainment spot if they did, or could be stopped if by some fluke of probabilities they did end up down here.

His escort stirred, looking around nervously. The Karl-Jorge Avenue was dark, most of its glowstrips long ago stolen or simply spray-painted in the random vandalism that breeds in lives fueled by purposeless anger. It was fairly clean, because the Kzin insisted on that, and the four-story brick buildings were solid enough, because the early settlers had built well. Brick and concrete and cobbled streets glimmered faintly, still damp from the afternoon's rain, loud wailing music echoed from open windows, and there would have been groups of idle-looking youths loitering on the front steps of the tenements, if the car had not had Munchen Polizei plates.

Ba'hai, he thought, mentally snapping his fingers. He was tall, even for a *Herrenmann*, with one side of his face cleanshaven and the other a close-trimmed brown beard cut to a foppish point; the plain blue uniform and circular brimmed cap of the city police emphasized the deep-chested greyhound build. *This was a Ba'hai neighborhood.*

"You may go," he said to the guards. "I will call for the car."

"Sir," the sergeant said, the guide-cone of her stunner waving about uncertainly. Helmet and night-sight goggles made her eyes unreadable. " 'tis iz a rough district."

"I am aware of that, sergeant. Also that Harold's Place is a known underworld hangout. Assignment to my headquarters squad is a promotion; please do not

assume that it entitles you to doubt my judgment."
Or you may find yourself back walking a beat, without such opportunities for income-enhancement, went unspoken between them. He ignored her salute and walked up the two low stairs.

The door recognized him, read retinas and encephalograph patterns, slid open. The coal-black doorman was as tall as the police officer and twice as broad, with highly-illegal impact armor underneath the white coat and bowtie of Harold's Terran Bar. The impassive smoky eyes above the ritually-scarred cheeks gave him a polite once-over, an equally polite and empty bow.

"Pleased to see you here again, *Herrenmann* Montferrat-Palme," he said.

You grafting ratcat-loving collaborationist son of a bitch. Montferrat added the unspoken portion himself. *And I love you too.*

Harold's Terran Bar was a historical revival, and therefore less out of place on Wunderland than it would have been in the Sol system. Once through the vestibule's inner bead-curtain doorway Montferrat could see most of the smoke-hazed main room, a raised platform in a C around the sunken dance floor and the long bar. Strictly human service here, which was less of an affectation now than it had been when the place opened, twenty years ago. Machinery was dearer than it had been, and human labor much cheaper, particularly since refugees began pouring into Munchen from a countryside increasingly preempted for Kzin estates. Not to mention those displaced by strip-mining . . .

"Good evening, Claude."

He started. It was always disconcerting, how quietly Harold moved. There he was at his elbow now, blue eyes expressionless. Face that should have been ugly, big-nosed with a thick lower lip and drooping eyelids. He was . . . what, sixty-three now? Just going grizzled at the temples, which was an affectation, or a sign that his income didn't stretch to really thorough geriatric treatments. Short, barrel-chested . . . what sort of genetic mismatch had produced that build from a *Herrenmann* father and a Belter mother?

"Looking me over for signs of impending dissolution, Claude?" Harold said, steering him toward his usual table and snapping his fingers for a waiter. "It'll be a while yet."

Perhaps not so long, Montferrat thought, looking at the pouches beneath his eyes. That could be stress . . . or Harold could be *really* skimping on the geriatrics. *They become more expensive every year, the kzin don't care . . . There are people dying of old age at seventy, now, and not just Amish. Shut up, Claude, you hypocrite. Nothing you can do about it.*

"You will outlast me, old friend."

"A case of cynical apathy wearing better than cynical corruption?" Harold asked, seating himself across from the police chief.

Montferrat pulled a cigarette case from his jacket's inner pocket and snapped it open with a flick of the wrist. It was plain white gold, from Earth, with a Paris jeweller's initials inside the frame and a date two centuries old, one of his few inheritances from his parents . . . Harold took the proffered cigarette.

"You will join me in a schnapps?" Montferrat said.

"Claude, you've been asking that question for twenty years, and I've been saying no for twenty years. I don't drink with the paying customers."

Yarthkin leaned back, let smoke trickle through his nostrils. The liquor arrived, and a plateful of grilled things that resembled shrimps about as much as a lemur resembled a man, apart from being dark green and having far too many eyes. "Now, didn't my bribe arrive on time?"

Montferrat winced. "Harold, Harold, will you never learn to phrase these things politely?" He peeled the translucent shell back from one of the grumblies, snapped off the head between thumb and forefinger and dipped it in the sauce. "Exquisite . . ." he breathed, after the first bite, and chased it down with a swallow of schnapps. "Bribes? Merely a token recompense, when out of the goodness of my heart and in memory of old friendship, I secure licenses, produce permits, contacts with owners of estates and fishing boats—"

"—so you can have a first-rate place to guzzle—"

"—I allow this questionable establishment to flourish, risking my position, despite the, shall we say, *dubious* characters known to frequent it—"

"—because it makes a convenient listening post and you get a lot of, *shall we say*, lucrative contacts."

They looked at each other coolly for a moment, and then Montferrat laughed. "Harold, perhaps the real reason I allow this den of iniquity to continue is that you're the only person who still has the audacity to deflate my hypocrisies."

Yarthkin nodded calmly. "Comes of knowing you when you were an idealistic patriot, Director. Like being in hospital together . . . Will you be gambling tonight, or did you come to pump me about the rumors?"

"Rumors?" Montferrat said mildly, shelling another grumbly.

"Of another kzin defeat. Two shiploads of our esteemed ratcat masters coming back with their fur
singed."

"For *god's* sake!" Montferrat hissed, looking around.

"No bugs," Yarthkin continued. "Not even by your
ambitious assistants. They offered a hefty sweetener,
but I wouldn't want to see them in your office. They
don't stay bought."

Montferrat smoothed his mustache. "Well, the kzin
do seem to have a rather lax attitude toward security
at times," he said. *Mostly, they don't realize how
strong the human desire to get together and chatter
is*, he mused.

"Then there's the rumor about a flatlander counter-
strike," Yarthkin continued.

Montferrat raised a brow and cocked his mobile
Herrenmann ears forward. "Not becoming a believer
in the myth of Liberation, I hope," he drawled.

Yarthkin waved the hand that held the cigarette,
leaving a trail of blue smoke. "I did my bit for
liberation. Got left at the altar, as I recall, and took
the amnesty." His face had become even more blank,
merely the slightest hint of a sardonic curve to the
lips. "Now I'm just an innkeeper. What goes on
outside these walls is no business of mine." A pause.
"It is yours, of course, Director. People know the
ratcats got their whiskers pasted back, for the fourth
time. They're encouraged . . . also desperate. The
kzin will be stepping up the war effort, which means
they'll be putting more pressure on us. Not to mention that they're breeding faster than ever."

Montferrat nodded with a frown. Battle casualties
made little difference to a kzin population; their
nonsentient females were held in harems by a small

minority of males, in any event. Heavy losses meant the lands and mates of the dead passing to the survivors . . . and more young males thrown out of the nest, looking for lands and a Name of their own. And kzin took up a *lot* of space; they weighed in at a quarter-ton each, and they were pure carnivores. Nor would they eat synthesized meat except on board a military spaceship. There were still fewer than a hundred thousand in the Wunderland system, and more than twenty times that many humans; it was getting crowded.

"More 'flighters crowding into Munchen every day," Yarthkin continued in that carefully neutral tone.

Refugees. Munchen had been a small town within their own lifetimes; the original settlers of Wunderland had been a close-knit coterie of plutocrats, looking for elbow-room. They had allowed only limited industrialization, even in the Serpent Swarm, and very little indeed on the planetary surface. Huge domains staked out by the Nineteen Families and their descendants; later immigrants had fitted into the cracks of the pattern, as tenants or carving out smallholdings on the fringes of the settled zone, many of them were ethnic or religious separatists anyway. Until the Kzin came. Kzin nobles expected vast territories for their own polygamous households, and naturally seized the best and ready-developed acreages. Some of the human landworkers stayed to labor for new masters, but many more were displaced. Or eaten.

One of the first effects of the new ownership had been forced-draft industrialization in Munchen and the other towns; kzin did not live in cities, and cared little for the social consequences. Their planets had always been sparsely settled, and they had developed the gravity polarizer early in their history, hence they mined their asteroid belts but put little industry in space. The refugees flooding in worked in industries that produced war materiel for the kzin fleets, not housing or consumer-goods for human use . . .

"It must be a bonanza for you, selling exit-permits to the Swarm," Harold continued. Outside the base-asteroid of Tiamat, the Belters were much more loosely controlled than the groundside population. "And exemptions from military call-up."

Montferrat smiled and leaned back, following the schnapps with laager. "There must be regulations," he said reasonably. "The Swarm cannot absorb all the would-be immigrants. Nor can Wunderland afford to lose the labor of all who would like to leave. The kzin demand technicians, and we cannot refuse, the burden must be allocated."

"Nor can you afford to pass up the palm-greasing and the, ach, *romantic* possibilities—" Yarthkin began.

"*Alert! Alert! Emergency broadcast!*" The mirror behind the long bar flashed from reflective to broadcast, and the smoky gloom of the bar's main hall erupted in shouted questions and screams.

The strobing pattern of light settled into the civil-defense blazon, and the unmistakable precision of an artificial voice. "All civilians are to remain in their residences. Emergency and security personnel to their duty stations, repeat, emergency and security personnel to their—"

A blast of static and white noise loud enough to send hands to ears, before the system's emergency overrides cut in. When reception returned the broadcast was two-dimensional, a space-armored figure reading from a screenprompt over the receiver. The noise

in Harold's Terran Bar sank to shocked silence at the
sight of the human shape of the combat armor, the
blue-and-white UN sigil on its chest.

"—o all citizens of the Alpha Centauri system,"
the Terran was saying. In Wunderlander, but with a
thick accent that could not handle the gutturals.
"Evacuate areas of military or industrial importance
immediately. Repeat, *immediately*. The United Nations Space Command is attacking kzin military and
industrial targets in the Alpha Centauri system. Evacuate areas—" The screen split to scroll the same
message in English and two more of the planet's
principal languages. The door burst open and a squad
of Munchen Polizei burst through.

"*Scheisse!*" Montferrat shouted, rising. He froze as
the receiver in his uniform cap began a hissing and
snarling override-transmission in the Hero's Tongue.
Yarthkin relaxed and smiled as the policeman sprinted
for the exit. He cocked one eye towards the ceiling
and silently flourished Montferrat's last glass of
schnapps before sending it down with a snap of his wrist.

"Weird," Jonah Matthieson muttered, looking at
the redshifted cone of light ahead of them. *Better
this way*. This way he didn't have to think of what
they were going to do when they arrived. He had
been a singleship pilot before doing his military service. You could do software design anywhere there
was a computer system, of course, and miners had a
lot of spare time. But his reflexes were a pilot's, and
they included a strong inhibition against high-speed
intercept trajectories.

This was going to be the highest speed intercept of
all time . . .

The forward end of the pilot's cabin was very simple, a hemisphere of smooth synthetic. For that matter, the rest of the cabin was quite basic as well; two padded crashcouches, which was one more than normal, an autodoc, an autochef, and rather basic sanitary facilities. That left just enough room to move . . . in zero gravity. Right now they were under one-G acceleration, crushingly uncomfortable. They had been under one-G for weeks, subjective time; the *Yamamoto* was being run to flatlander specifications.

"Compensate," Ingrid said. The view swam back, the blue stars ahead and the dim red behind turning to the normal variation of colors. The dual-sun Centauri system was dead "ahead," looking uncomfortably close. "We're making good time. It took thirty years coming back on the slowboat, but the *Yamamoto*'s going to put us near Wunderland in five. Five objective, that is. Probably right on the heels of the pussy scouts."

Jonah nodded, looking ahead at the innocuous twinned stars. His hands were on the control-gloves of his couch, but the pressure-sensors and lightfields were off, of course. There had been very little to do in the month-subjective since they left the orbit of Pluto other than accelerated learning with RNA boosters. He could now speak as much of the Hero's Tongue as Ingrid. Enough to understand it, kzin evidently didn't like their slaves to speak much of it; slaves weren't worthy. He could also talk Belter-English with the accent of the Serpent Swarm, Wunderland's dominant language, and the five or six other tongues prevalent in the many ethnic enclaves . . . sometimes he found himself dreaming in Pahlavi or Croat or Amish *pletterdeisz*. Thank God it wasn't going to be a long trip; with the gravity polarizer and the big orbital lasers to push them up to ramscoop speeds, and no limit on the acceleration their compensators could handle . . .

We must be at a high fraction of the speed of a photon by now, he thought. Speeds only robot ships had achieved before, with experimental fields supposedly keeping the killing torrent of secondary radiation out. . . .

"Tell me some more about Wunderland," he said. Neither of them were fidgeting, Belters didn't; this sort of cramped environment had been normal for their people since the settlement of the Sol-system Belt three centuries before. It was the thought of how they were going to *stop* that had his nerves twisting.

"I've already briefed you twenty times," she replied, with something of a snap in her tone. Military formality wore thin pretty quickly in close quarters like this. "All the first-hand stuff is fifty-six years out of date, and the nine-year-old material's all in the computer if you really want it. You're just bored."

No, I'm just scared shitless. "Well, talking would be better than nothing. Spending a month strapped to this thing has been even more monotonous than being a rockjack. You were right, I'm bored."

"And scared."

He looked around. She was lying with her hands behind her head, grinning at him.

"Okay, I'm scared, too. Among other reasons because we will start this mission utterly dependent on the intervention of outside forces; the offswitch is exterior to the surface of the effect." It had to be; time did not pass inside a stasis field.

"The designers were pretty sure it'd work."

"I'm sure of only two things, Jonah."

"Which are?"

"Well, the *first* one is that the designers aren't going to be diving into the photosphere of a sun at .99 lights."

"Oh." That had occurred to him, too. On the other hand, it really was easier to be objective when your life wasn't on the line . . . and in any case, it would be quick. "What's the other thing?"

Her smile grew wider, and she undid the collar-catch of her uniform. "Even if it has to be in a gravity field, there's *one* thing I want to experience again before possible death."

Much later, they commanded the front screen to stop mimicking a control board. Now the upper half was an unmodified view of the Alpha Centauri system. The lower was a battle-schematic, dots and graphs and probability-curves like bundles of fuzzy sticks.

The *Yamamoto* was going to cross the disk of the Wunderland system in subjective minutes, mere hours even by outside clocks. With her ramscoop fields spreading a corona around her deadly to any lifeform with a nervous system, and the fusion flare a sword behind her half a parsec long; nothing could stop her and only beam-weapons stood a chance of catching her, even messages were going to take prodigies of computing power to unscramble. Her own weapons were quite simple; quarter-ton iron eggs. When they intercepted their targets at .99+ C, the results would be in the gigaton-yield range.

Jonah's teeth skinned back from his teeth and the

hair struggled to raise itself along his spine. *Plains-ape reflex*, he thought, smelling the rank odor of fight-flight sweat trickling down his flanks. *Your genes think you're about to tackle a Cape buffalo with a thighbone club*. His fingers pressed the inside of the chairseat in a complex pattern.

"Responding," said the computer in its usual husky contralto.

Was it imagination that there was already more inflection in its voice? And what did that really signify? Consciousness in a computer was *not* human consciousness, even though memory and drives were designed by humans . . . it possessed free will, unless he or Ingrid used the override keys, and unless the high command had left sleeper drives. Perhaps not so much free will; a computer would see the path most likely to succeed and follow it. Still, he supposed, he did the same, usually.

How would it be to know that you were a made thing, and doomed to encysted madness in six months or less?

Nobody had ever been able to learn why. He had speculated to himself that it was a matter of time; to a consciousness that could think in nanoseconds, that could govern its own sensory input, what would be the point of remaining linked to a refractory cosmos? It could make its own universe, and have it last forever in a few milliseconds. Perhaps that was why humans who linked directly to a computer system of any size went irretrievably catatonic as well. . . .

"Detection. Neutronic and electromagnetic-range sensors." The ship's system was linked to the hugely powerful but sub-conscious level machines of the *Yamamoto*. "Point sources."

Rubies sprang out across the battle map, moving as he watched, swelling up on either side and pivoting in relation to each other. The fire-bright point source of Alpha Centauri in the upper screen became a perceptible and growing disk. Jonah's skin crawled at the sight.

This was like ancient history, air and sea battles out of Earth's past. He was used to maneuvers that lasted hours or days, ships and fleets matching relative velocities while the planets moved *slowly* and the sun might as well be a fixed point at the center of the universe . . . Perhaps when gravity polarizers were small and cheap enough to fit in Dart-class boats it would all be like this.

"The pussies have the system pretty well covered," he said.

"And the Swarm's Belters," Ingrid replied. Jonah turned his head, slowly, at the sound of her voice. Shocked, he saw a glistening in her eyes.

"Home . . ." she whispered. Then more decisively: "Identification. Human-range sensors. Discrete."

Half the rubies flickered for a few seconds. Ingrid continued to Jonah: "This is a messy system; more of its mass is in asteroids and assorted junk than yours. Belters use more deep-radar and don't rely on telescopes as much. The pussies couldn't have changed that. They'd cripple the Swarm's economy and destroy its value." Slowly. "That's the big station on Tiamat. They've got a garrison there, it's a major shipbuilding center, was even," she swallowed, "fifty years ago. Those others are bubbleworlds . . . More detectors on Wunderland than there used to be, and in close orbit. At the poles, and that looks like a military-geosynchronous setup."

Jonah thought briefly what it would be like to return to the Sol-Belt after fifty years. Nearly a third of the average lifetime, longer than he had been alive—if he ever got home. The *Yamamoto* could expect to see Sol again in twenty years objective, allowing time to pass through the Alpha Centauri system, decelerate and work back up to a respectable Tau value. The plan-in-theory was for him and Ingrid to accomplish their mission, rejoin the *Catskinner*, boost her out in the direction of Sol, turn on the stasis field again—and wait to be picked up by UNSN craft. *About as likely as getting back by putting our heads between our knees and spitting hard.*

"Ships," the computer said in its dispassionate tone. "Movement. Status, probable class and dispersal cones."

Color-coded lines blinked over the tactical map. Columns of print scrolled down one margin: coded velocities and key-data. Hypnotic training triggered bursts into their minds, crystalline shards of fact, faster than conscious recall. Jonah whistled.

"Loaded for bandersnatch," he said. There were a *lot* of warships spraying out from bases and holding-orbits, and that was not counting those too small for the *Yamamoto*'s detection systems; their own speed would be degrading signal drastically. Between the ramscoop fields, their velocity, and normal shielding there was very little that could touch them, but the kzin were certainly going to try.

"Aggressive bastards," he said, keeping his eyes firmly fixed on the tactical display. It took courage, individually and on the part of their commander to put themselves in the way of the *Yamamoto*. Nobody had used a ramscoop ship like this before;

the kzin had never developed a Bussard-type drive, they had had the gravity polarizer for a long time, and it had aborted work on reaction jet systems. But they must have made staff studies, and they would know what they were facing. Which was something more in the nature of a large-scale cosmic event than a ship. Mass increases with velocity: by now moving only fractionally slower than a laser beam, the *Yamamoto* had the effective bulk of a medium-sized moon.

That reminded him of what the *Catskinner* would be doing shortly, and the Dart did not have anything *like* the scale of protection the ramscoop warship did. Even a micrometeorite . . . Alpha Centauri was a black disk edged by fire in the upper half of the screen.

"Projectiles away," the computer said. Nothing physical, but an inverted cone of trajectories splayed out from the path of the *Yamamoto*. Highly-polished chrome-tungsten-steel alloy slugs, that had spent the trip from Sol riding grapnel-fields in the *Yamamoto*'s wake. Wildly varying albedos, from fully-stealthed to deliberately reflective; the *Catskinner* was going to be rather conspicuous when the Slaver stasis field's impenetrable surface went on. Now the warship's magnetics were twitching the slugs out in sprays and clusters, at velocities that would send them across the Wunderland system in mere hours. It would take the firepower of a heavy cruiser to significantly damage one, and there were a *lot* of slugs. Iron was cheap, and the *Yamamoto* grossly overpowered.

"You know, we ought to have done this before," Jonah said. The sun-disk filled the upper screen, then snapped down several sizes as the computer reduced the field. A sphere, floating in the wild arching discharges and coronas of a G-type sun. "We could have used ramrobots. Or the pussies could have copied our designs and done it to us."

"Nope," Ingrid said. She coughed, and he wondered if her eyes were locking on the sphere again as it clicked down to a size that would fit the upper screen. "Ramscoop fields. Think about it."

"Oh." When you put it that way, he could think of about a half-dozen ways to destabilize one; drop, oh, ultracompressed radon into it. Countermeasures . . . luckily, nothing the kzin were likely to have right on hand.

"For that matter," she continued, "throwing relativistic weapons around inside a solar system is a bad idea. If you want to keep it."

"Impact," the computer said helpfully. An asteroid winked, the tactical screen's way of showing an expanding sphere of plasma. Nickel-iron, oxygen, nitrogen, carbon-compounds, some of the latter kzin and humans and children and their pet budgies.

"You have to aim at stationary targets," Ingrid was saying. "The very things that war is supposed to be about seizing. Blowing them up is as insane as fighting a planetside war with fusion weapons and no effective defense. Only possible once."

"Once would be enough, if we knew where the kzin home system was." For a vengeful moment he imagined robot ships falling into a sun from infinite distances, scores of lightyears of acceleration at hundreds of G's, their own masses raised to near-stellar proportions. "No. Then again, no."

"I'm glad you said that," Ingrid replied. Softly: "I wonder what it's like, for them out there."

"Interesting," Jonah said tightly. "At the very least, interesting."

Chapter II

"Please, keep calm," Harold Yarthkin-Schotmann said, for the fourth time. "For Finagle's sake, *sit down and shut up!*"

This one seemed to sink in, or perhaps the remaining patrons were getting tired of running around in circles and shouting. The staff were all at their posts, or preventing the paying customers from hitting each other or breaking anything expensive. Several of them had police-model stunners under their dinner jackets, like his; hideously illegal, hence quite difficult to square. Not through Claude—he was quite conscientious about avoiding things that would seriously annoy the ratcats—but there were plenty lower down the totem pole who lacked his gentlemanly sense of their own long-term interests.

Everyone was watching the screen behind the bar again; the UNSN announcement was off the air, but the Munchen news service was slapping in random readouts from all over the planet. For once the collaborationist government was too busy to follow their natural instincts and keep everyone in the dark, and the kzin had never given much of a damn, the only thing *they* cared about was behavior. Propaganda be damned.

The flatlander warship was still headed insystem; from the look of things they were going to use the sun for a whip-round. He could feel rusty spaceman's reflexes creaking into action. That was a perfectly sensible ploy; ramscoop ships were *not* easy to turn. Even at relativistic speeds you couldn't use the interstellar medium to bank. Turning meant applying lateral thrust; it would be easier to decelerate, turn and work back up to high Tau—unless you could use a gravitational sling, like a kid on roller-skates going hell-for-leather down a street and then slapping a hand on a lamppost.

He raised his glass to the sometime mirror behind the bar. It was showing a scene from the south polar zone with its abundance of ratcat installations; kzin were stuck with Wunderland's light gravity, but they preferred a cooler, drier climate than humans. The first impact had looked like a line of light drawn down from heaven to earth, and the shockwave flipped the robot camera into a spin that had probably ended on hard, cold ground.

Yarthkin grinned, and snapped his fingers for the waitress. He ordered coffee, black, and a sandwich.

"Heavy on the mustard, sweetheart," he told the waitress. He loosened his tie and watched flickershots of boiling dust-clouds crawling with networks of purple-white lightning. Closer, into canyons of night seething up out of red-shot blackness, that must be molten rock . . .

"Sam." The man at the musicomp looked up from trailing his fingers across the keyboard. It was configured for piano tonight—an archaism, like the whole setup. Popular, as more and more fled in fantasy what could not be avoided in reality, back into a history that was at least human. Of course, Wunderlanders were prone to that, the planet had been a patchwork of refugees from an increasingly homogenized and technophile Earth anyway. *I've spent a generation cashing in on a nostalgia boom,* Yarthkin thought wryly. *Was that because I had foresight, or was I one of the first victims?*

"Sir?" Sam was Krio, like McAndrews the doorman, although he had never gone the whole route and taken warrior scars. Many of the descendants of the refugees from Sierra Leone were traditionalists to a fault. Just as tough in a fight, though. He'd been enrolled in the Sensor-Effector program at the Scholarium, been a gunner with Yarthkin in the brief war in space, and they had been together in the hills. And he had come along when Yarthkin took the amnesty, too. Even more of a wizard with the keys than he had been with a jizzer or a strakaker or a ratchet knife.

"Play something appropriate, Sam. *Stormy Weather.*"

The musician's face lit with a vast white grin, and he launched into the ancient tune with a will, even singing his own version translated into Wunderlander. Yarthkin murmured into his lapel to turn down the hysterical commentary from the screen, still babbling about dastardly attacks and massive casualties.

It took a man back. Humans were dying out there, but so were ratcats . . . *Here's looking at you*, he thought to the hypothetical crew of the *Yamamoto*. Possibly nothing more than A.I. and sensor-effector mechanisms, but he doubted it.

"Stormy weather for sure," he said softly to himself. Megatons of dust and water vapor were being pumped into the atmosphere. "Bad for the crops." Though there would be a harvest from this, yes indeed. *I could have been on that ship*, he thought to himself, with a sudden flare of murderous anger. *I was good enough. There are probably Wunderlanders aboard her; those slowships got through. If I hadn't been left sucking vacuum at the airlock, it could have been me out there!*

"But not Ingrid," he whispered to himself. "The bitch wouldn't have the guts." Sam was looking at him; it had been a long time since the memory of the last days came back. With a practiced effort of will he shoved it deeper below the threshold of consciousness and produced the same mocking smile with which he had faced the world for most of his adult life.

"I wonder how our esteemed ratcat masters are taking it," he said. "Been a while since the ones here've had to lap out of the same saucer as us lowlife monkey-boys. I'd like to see it, I truly would."

". . . estimate probability of successful interception at less than one-fifth," the figure on the screen said. "*Vengeance Fang* and *Rampant Slayer* do not respond to signals; *Lurker at Waterholes* continues to accelerate at right angles to the elliptic. We must assume they were struck by the ramscoop fields."

The governor watched closely; the slight bristle of

whiskers and rapid open-shut flare of wet black nostrils was a sign of intense frustration.

"You have leapt well, Traat-Admiral," Chuut-Riit said formally. "Break off pursuit." A good tactician, Traat-Admiral; if he had come from a better family, he would have a double name by now. And he *would* have a double name, when Earth was conquered, a name and vast wealth. One percent of all the product of the new conquest, since he was to be in supreme military command of the Fifth Fleet. That would make him founder of a Noble Line, his bones in a worship shrine for a thousand generations. Chuut-Riit had hinted that he would send several of his daughters to the admiral's harem, letting him mingle his blood with that of the Patriarch.

"Chuut-Riit, are we to let the . . . the . . . omnivores escape unscathed?" The admiral's ears were quivering.

A rumble came from the space-armored figures that bulked in the dim orange light behind the flotilla commandant. *Good*, the planetary governor thought. *They are not daunted.*

"Your bloodlust is commendable, Traat-Admiral, but the fact remains that the human ship is traveling at velocities which render it . . . it is at a different point on the energy gradient, Traat-Admiral."

"We can pursue as it leaves the system!"

"In ships designed to travel at .8 lightspeed? From behind? Remember the Human Lesson. That is a *very* effective reaction drive they are using."

A deep ticking sound came from his throat and Traat-Admiral's ears laid back instinctively. The thought of trying to maneuver past that planetary-length sword of nuclear fire . . . .

Chuut-Riit paused to let the thought sink home before continuing: "This has been a startling tactic. We assumed that possession of the gravity polarizer would lead the humans to neglect reaction drives, as we had done, *hr'rrearow t'chssseee mearowet'aatrurrre*, this-does-not-follow. We must prepare countermeasures, investigate the possibility of ramscoop interstellar missiles . . . at least they did not strike at this system's sun, or drop a really large mass into the planetary gravity well."

The fur of the kzin on the battlewagon's bridge laid flat, sculpting the bone-and-muscle planes of their faces.

"Indeed, Chuut-Riit," Traat-Admiral said fervently.

"It was only surprise that made the tactic so effective. Counters come readily to mind: a series of polarizer-driven missiles, with laser-cannon boost, deployed ready to destabilize ramscoop fields. In any case, you are ordered to break off action, assist with emergency efforts, detach two units with interstellar capacity to shadow the intruder until it leaves the immediate vicinity. Waste no more Heroes in futility; instead, we must repair the damage, redouble our preparations for the next attack on Sol."

"As you command, Chuut-Riit, although it shaves my mane to let the leaf-eating monkeys escape, when the Fifth Fleet is so near completion."

The governor rose, letting his weight forward on hands whose claws slid free. He restrained any further display of impatience. *I must teach him to think. To learn to think correctly he must be allowed to make errors.* "Its departure has already been delayed. Will losing further units in fruitless pursuit speed the repairs and modifications which must be made? Attend to your orders!"

"At once, Chuut-Riit!"

The governor held himself impressively immobile until the screen blanked. Then he turned and leaped with a tearing shriek over the nearest wall, out into the unnatural storm and darkness. A half-hour later he returned, meditatively picking bits of hide and bone from between his teeth with a thumb-claw. His pelt was plastered flat with mud, leaves, and blood, and a thorned branch had cut a bleeding trough across his sloping forehead. The screens were still flicking between various disasters, each one worse than the last.

"Any emergency calls?" he asked mildly.

"None at the priority levels you established," the computer replied.

"Murmeroumph," he said, opening his mouth wide into the killing gape to get at an irritating fragment between two of the back shearing teeth. "Staff."

One wall turned to the ordered bustle of the household's management centrum. "Ah, Henrietta," he said in Wunderlander. "You have that preliminary summary ready?"

The human swallowed and averted her eyes from the bits of *something* that the kzin was flicking from his fangs and muzzle. The others behind her were looking drawn and tense as well, but displayed no signs of panic. *If I could recognize such signs*, the kzin thought. *They panic differently*. A Hero overcome with terror either fled, striking out at anything in his path, or went into mindless berserker frenzy.

Berserker, he mused thoughtfully. The concept was fascinating; reading of it had convinced him that kzin and human kind were enough alike to cooperate effectively.

"Yes, Chuut-Riit," she was saying. "Installations Seven, Three, and Twelve in the north polar zone have been effectively destroyed, loss of industrial function in the 75-80% range. Over 90% at Six, the main fusion generator destabilized in the pulse from a near-miss." Ionization effects had been quite spectacular. "Casualties in the range of five thousand Heroes, thirty thousand humans. Four major orbital facilities hit, but there was less collateral damage there, of course, and more near-misses." No air to transmit blast in space. "Reports from the asteroid belt still coming in."

"*Merrower*," he said, meditatively. Kzin government was heavily decentralized; the average Hero did not make a good bureaucrat, that was work for slaves and computers. A governor was expected to confine himself to policy decisions. Still . . . "Have my personal spaceship prepared for lift, I will be doing a tour."

Henrietta hesitated. "Ah, noble Chuut-Riit, the feral humans will be active, with defense functions thrown out of order."

She was far too experienced to mistake Chuut-Riit's expression for a smile.

"Markham and his gang? I hope they do, Henrietta, I sincerely hope they do." He relaxed. "I'll view the reports from here. Send in the groomers, my pelt must be fit to be seen." A pause. "And replacements for one of the bull buffaloes in the holding pen."

The kzin threw himself down on the pillow behind his desk, massive head propped with its chin on the stone surface of the workspace. Grooming would help him think, humans were so good at grooming . . . and blowdryers, blowdryers alone were worth the trouble of conquering them.

"Prepare for separation," the computer said. The upper field of the *Catskinner*'s screen was a crawling slow-motion curve of orange and yellow and darker spots; the battle schematic showed the last few slugs dropping away from the *Yamamoto*, using the gravity of the sun to whip around and curve out toward targets in a different quarter of the elliptic plane. More than a few were deliberately misaimed, headed for catastrophic destruction in Alpha Centauri's photosphere as camouflage.

It can't be getting hotter, he thought.

"Gottdamn, it's hot," Ingrid said. "I'm swine-sweating."

Thanks, he thought, refraining from speaking aloud with a savage effort. "Purely psychosomatic," he grated.

"There's one thing I regret," Ingrid continued.

"What's that?"

"That we're not going to be able to see what happens when the *Catskinner* and those slugs make a high-Tau transit of the sun's outer envelope," she said.

Jonah felt a smile crease the rigid sweat-slick muscles of his face. The consequences had been extrapolated, but only roughly. At the very least, there would be solar-flare effects like nothing this system had ever witnessed before, enough to foul up every receptor pointed this way. "It would be interesting, at that."

"Prepare for separation," the computer continued. "Five seconds and counting."

One. Ingrid had crossed herself just before the field went on. Astonishing. There were worse people to be crammed into a Dart with for a month, even among the more interesting half of the human race.

Two. They were probably going to be closer to an active star than any other human beings had ever been and survived to tell the tale. Provided they survived, of course.

Three. His grandparents had considered emigrating to the Wunderland system; he remembered them complaining about how the Belt had been then, everything regulated and taxed to death, and psychists hovering to resanitize your mind as soon as you came in from a prospecting trip. If they'd done it, *he* might have ended up as a conscript technician with the Fourth Fleet.

Four. Or a guerrilla, the prisoners had mentioned activity by "feral humans." Jonah barred his teeth in an expression a kzin would have had no trouble at all understanding. *I intend to remain very feral indeed. The kzin may have done us a favor; we were well on the way to turning ourselves into sheep when they arrived. If I'm going to be a monkey, I'll be a big, mean baboon, by choice.*

Five. Ingrid was right, it was a pity they wouldn't be able to see—

-discontinuity-

"Greow-Captain, there is an anomaly in the last projectile!"

"They are all anomalies, Sensor Operator!" The

commander did not move his eyes from the schematic before his face, but his tone held conviction that the humans had used irritatingly nonstandard weapons solely to annoy and humiliate him. Behind his back, the other two kzin exchanged glances and moved expressive ears.

The *Slasher*-class armed scout held three crewkzin in its delta-shaped control chamber, the commander forward and the Sensor and Weapons Operators behind him to either side; three small screens instead of the single larger divisible one a human boat of the same size would have had, and many more manually-activated controls. Kzin had broader-range senses than humans, faster reflexes, and they trusted cybernetic systems rather less. They had also had gravity control almost from the beginning of spaceflight; a failure serious enough to immobilize the crew usually destroyed the vessel.

"Simply tell me," the kzin commander said, "if our particle-beam is driving it down." The cooling system was whining audibly as it pumped energy into its central tank of degenerate matter, and still the cabin was furnace hot and dry, full of the wild odors of fear and blood that the habitation-system poured out in combat conditions. The ship shuddered and banged as it plunged in a curve that was not quite suicidally close to the outer envelope of the sun.

Before Greow-Captain a stepped-down image showed the darkened curve of the gas envelope, and the gouting coriolis-driven plumes as the human ship's projectiles ploughed their way through plasma. Shocks of discharge arched between them as they drew away from the kzin craft above, away from the beams that sought to tumble them down into denser layers where even their velocity would not protect them. Or at least throw them enough off course that they would recede harmlessly into interstellar space. The light from the holo-screen crawled in iridescent streamers across the flared scarlet synthetic of the kzin's helmet and the huge lambent eyes; the whole corona of Alpha Centauri was writhing, flowers of nuclear fire, a thunder of forces beyond the understanding of human- or kzinkind.

The two Operators were uneasily conscious that Greow-Captain felt neither awe nor the slightest hint of fear. Not because he was more than normally courageous for a young male kzin, but because he was utterly indifferent to everything but how this would look on his record. Another glance went between them; younger sons of nobles were notoriously anxious to earn full Names at record ages, and Greow-Captain had complained long and bitterly when their squadron was not assigned to the Fourth Fleet. He was so intent on looking good that operational efficiency might suffer.

They knew better than to complain openly, of course. Whatever the state of his wits, there was *nothing* wrong with Greow-Captain's reflexes, and he already had an imposing collection of kzin-ear dueling trophies.

"Greow-Captain, the anomaly is greater than a variance in reflectivity," the Sensor Operator yowled. Half his instruments were useless in the flux of energetic particles that were sheeting off the *Slasher*'s screens. He *hoped* they were being deflected; as a lowly Sensor Operator he had not had a chance to breed. Not so much as a sniff of kzinrret fur since they carried him mewling from the teats of his mother to the training creche. "The projectile is not absorbing the quanta of our beam as the previous one did, nor is its surface ablating. And its trajectory is incompatible with the shape of the others; this is larger, less dense, and moving . . ."—a pause of less than a second to query the computer—". . . moving as if its outer shell were absolutely frictionless and reflective, Greow-Captain. Should this not be reported?"

Reporting would mean retreat, out to where a message-maser could punch through the chaotic broad-spectrum noise of an injured star's bellow.

"Do my Heroes refuse to follow into danger?" Greow-Captain snarled.

"Lead us, Greow-Captain!" Put that way, they had no choice; which was why a sensible officer would never have put it that way. Both Operators silently cursed the better diet and personal-combat training available to offspring of a noble's household. It had been a *long* time since kzin had met an enemy capable of exercising greater selective pressure than their own social system.

"Weapons Operator, shift your aim to the region of compressed gasses directly ahead of our target, all energy weapons. I am taking us down and accelerating past redline." With a little luck, he could ignite the superheated and compressed monatomic hydrogen directly ahead of the projectile, and let the multimegaton explosion flip it up or down off the ballistic trajectory the humans had launched it on.

Muffled howls and spitting sounds came from the workstations behind him; the thin black lips wrinkled back more fully from his fangs, and slender lines of saliva drooled down past the open neckring of his suit. *Warren-dwellers*, he thought, as the *Slasher* lurched and swooped.

His hands darted over the controls, prompting the machinery that was throwing it about at hundreds of accelerations. *Vatach hunters*. The little quasi-rodents were all lower-caste kzin could get in the way of live meat. Although the anomaly was interesting, and he would report noticing it to Khurut-SquadronCaptain. *I will show them how a true hunter—*

The input from the kzin boat's weapons was barely a fraction of the kinetic energy the *Catskinner* was shedding into the gasses that slowed it, but that was just enough. Enough to set off chain-reaction fusion in a sizable volume around the invulnerably-protected human vessel. The kzin craft was far enough away for the wave-front to arrive before the killing blow:

"—shield overload, loss of directional *hhnrrreaw*—"

The Sensor Operator shrieked and burned as induction-arcs crashed through his position. Weapons Operator was screaming the hiss of a nursing kitten as his claws slashed at the useless controls.

Greow-Captain's last fractional second was spent in a cry as well, but his was of pure rage. The *Slasher*'s fusion-bottle destabilized at almost the same nanosecond as her shields went down and the gravity control vanished; an imperceptible instant later only a mass-spectroscope could have told the location as atoms of carbon and iron scattered through the hot plasma of the inner solar wind.

-discontinuity-

"*Shit*," Jonah said, with quiet conviction. "Report. *And stabilize that view.*" The streaking pinwheel in the exterior-view screen slowed and halted, but the control surface beside it continued to show the *Catskinner* twirling end-over-end at a rate that would have pasted them both as a thin reddish film over the interior without the compensation fields.

The screen split down the middle as Ingrid began establishing their possible paths.

"We are," the computer said, "traveling at twice our velocity at switchoff, and on a path twenty-five degrees further to the solar north." A pause. "We are still, you will note, in the plane of the elliptic."

"Thank Finagle for small favors," Jonah muttered, working his hands in the control gloves. The *Catskinner* was running on her accumulators, the fusion reactor, and its so-detectable neutrino flux shut down.

"Jonah," Ingrid said. "Take a look." A corner of the screen lit, showing the surface of the sun and a gigantic pillar of flare reaching out in their wake like the tongue of a hungry fire-elemental. "The pussies are burning up the communications spectra, yowling about losing scoutboats. They had them down low and dirty, trying to throw the slugs that went into the photosphere with us offcourse."

"Lovely," the man muttered. *So much for quietly matching velocities with Wunderland while the commnet is still down.* To the computer: "What's ahead of us?"

"For approximately twenty-three point six lightyears, nothing.."

"What do you mean, nothing?"

"Hard vacuum, micrometeorites, interstellar dust, possible spacecraft, bodies too small or nonradiating to be detected from our position, superstrings, shadowmatter—"

"Shut up!" he snarled. "Can we brake?"

"Yes. Unfortunately, this will require several hours of thrust and exhaust our onboard fuel reserves."

"And put up a fucking great sign, 'Hurrah, we're back' for every pussy in the system," he grated. Ingrid touched him on the arm.

"Wait, I have an idea . . . is there anything substantial in our way, that we could reach with less of a burn?"

"Several asteroids, Lieutenant Raines. Uninhabited."

"What's the status of our stasis-controller."

A pause. "Still . . . I must confess, I am surprised." The computer sounded surprised that it could be. "Still functional, Lieutenant Raines."

Jonah winced. "Are you thinking what I think you're thinking?" he said plaintively. "*Another* collision?"

Ingrid shrugged. "Right now, it'll be less noticeable than a long burn. Computer, will it work?"

"97% chance of achieving a stable Swarm orbit. The risk of emitting infrared and visible-light signals is unquantifiable. The field switch will *probably* continue to function, Lieutenant Raines."

"It should, it's covered in neutronium." She turned her head to Jonah. "Well?"

He sighed. "Offhand, I can't think of a better solution. When you can't think of a better solution than a high-speed collision with a rock, something's wrong with your thinking, but I can't think of what would be better to think . . . What do *you* think?"

"That an *unshielded* collision with a rock might be better than another month imprisoned with your sense of humor . . . *Gott*, all those fish puns . . ."

"Computer, prepare for minimal burn. Any distinguishing characteristics of those rocks?"

"One largely silicate, one 83% nickel-iron with traces of—"

"Spare me. The nickel-iron, it's denser and less likely to break up. Prepare for minimal burn."

"I have so prepared, on the orders of Lieutenant Raines."

Jonah opened his mouth, then frowned. "Wait a minute. Why is it always *Lieutenant Raines?* You're a damned sight more respectful of *her*."

Ingrid buffed her fingernails. "While you were briefing up on Wunderland and the Swarm . . . I was helping the team that programmed our tin friend."

"Are you sure?"

The radar operator held her temper in check with an effort. She had not been part of the *Nietzsche*'s crew long, but more than long enough to learn that you did not backtalk *Herrenmann* Ulf Reichstein-Markham. *Bastard's as arrogant as a kzin,* she thought resentfully.

"Yes, sir. It's definitely heading our way since that microburn. Overpowered thruster, usual spectrum, and unless it's unmanned they have a gravity polarizer. 200 G's, they pulled."

The guerrilla commander nodded thoughtfully. "Then it is either kzin, which is unlikely in the extreme since they do not use reaction drives on any of their standard vessels, or . . ."

"And, sir, it's cool. Hardly radiating at all, when the fusion plant's off. If we weren't close and didn't know where to look . . . granted this isn't a military sensor, but I doubt the ratcats have seen him."

Markham's long face drew into an expression of disapproval. "They are called kzin, soldier. I will tolerate no vulgarities in my command."

Bastard. "Yessir."

The man was tugging at his asymmetric beard. "Evacuate the asteroid. It will be interesting to see how they decelerate, perhaps some gravitic effect . . . And even more interesting to find out what those fat cowards in the Sol system think they are doing."

"Prepare for stasis," the computer said.

"How?" Ingrid and Jonah asked in unison. The rock came closer, tumbling, half a kilometer on a side, falling forever in a slow silent spiral. Closer. . . .

"Interesting," the computer said. "There is a ship adjacent."

"*What?*" Jonah said. His fingers slid into the control gloves like snakes fleeing a mongoose, then froze. It was too late; they were committed.

"Very well stealthed." A pause, and the asteroid grew in the wall before them, filling it from end to end.

Tin-brained idiot's a sadist, Jonah thought.

"And the asteroid is an artifact. Well hidden as well, but at this range my semi-passive systems can pick up a tunnel complex and shut-down power system. Lifesupport on maintenance. Twelve seconds to impact."

"*Is anybody there?*" Jonah barked.

"Negative, Jonah. The ship is occupied; I scan twinned fusion drives, and hull-mounted weaponry. Concealed as part of the grappling apparatus. X-ray lasers, possible railguns. Two of the cargo bays have dropslots that would be of appropriate size for kzin light seeker missiles. Eight seconds to impact."

"Put us into combat mode," the Sol-Belter snapped. "Prepare for emergency stabilization as soon as the stasis field is off. Warm for boost. Ingrid, if we're going to talk you'll probably be better able to convince them of our—

-discontinuity-

"—bona fides."

The ripping-cloth sound of the gravity polarizer hummed louder and louder, and there was a wobble felt more as a subliminal tugging at the inner ear as the system strained to stop a spin as rapid as a gyroscope's. The asteroid was fragments glowing a dull orange-red streaked with dark slag, receding; the *Catskinner* was backing under twenty G's, her laser-pods starfishing out and railguns humming with maximum charge.

"Alive again," Jonah breathed, feeling the response under his fingertips. The wall ahead had divided into a dozen panels, schematics of information, stresses, possibilities; the central was the exterior view. "Tightbeam signal, identify yourselves."

"Sent. Receiving signal, also tightbeam." A pause. "Obsolete hailing pattern. Requesting identification."

"Request video, same pattern."

The screen flickered twice, and an offright panel lit with a furious bearded face. Tightly contained fury, in a face no older than his own, less than thirty. Beard close-shaven on one side, pointed on the right. Yellow-blond and wiry, like the close-cropped matt on the narrow skull; pale narrow eyes, mobile ears, long-nosed with a prominent boney chin beneath the carefully cultivated goatee. Behind him a control-chamber that was like the Belter museum back at Ceres, an early-model independent miner. But modified, crammed with jury-rigged systems of which many were marked in the squiggles-and-angles kzin script; crammed with people as well, some of them in armored spacesuits. An improvised warship, then. Most of the crew were in neatly tailored gray skinsuits, with a design of a phoenix on their chests.

"Explain yourzelfs," the man said, with a slight guttural overtone to his Belter-English, enough to mark him as one born speaking Wunderlander.

"UNSN *Catskinner*, Captain Jonah Matthieson commanding, Lieutenant Raines as second. Presently," he added dryly, "on detached duty. As representative of the human armed forces, I require your cooperation."

"Cooperation!" That was one of the spacesuited figures behind the Wunderlander. A tall man with hair cut in the Belter crest, and adorned with small silver bells. "You fucker, you just missiled my bloody base and a year's takings!"

"We didn't missile it, we just rammed into it," Jonah said. "Takings? What are these people, pirates?"

"Calm yourzelf, McAllistaire," the Wunderlander said. His eyes had narrowed slightly at the Sol-Belter's words, and his ears cocked forward. "Permit self-introduction, Haupmann Matthieson. Commandant Ulf Reichstein-Markham, at your zerfice. Commandant in the Free Wunderland navy, zat is. My, ahh, coworker here is an independent entrepreneur who iss pleazed to cooperate wit' the Naval forces."

"Goddam you, Markham, that was a year's profit,

yours and mine both. Shop the bastard to the ratcats, *now*. We could get a pardon out of it, easy. Hell, you could get that piece of dirt back on Wunderland you're always on about."

The self-proclaimed commandant held up a hand palm-forward to Jonah and turned to speak to the owner of the ex-asteroid. "You try my patience, McAllistaire. Zilence."

"Silence yourself, dirtsider. I—"

"Am now dispensible." Markham's finger tapped the console. Stunners hummed in the guerrilla ship, and the figures not in gray crumpled.

The commandant turned to a figure offscreen. "Strip zem of all useful equipment and space zem," he said casually. Turning to the screen again, with a slight smile. "It is true, you haff cost us valuable materiel . . . you will understant, a clandestine war requires unortodox measures, Captain. Ve are forced sometimes to requisition goods, as the Free Wunderland government cannot levy ordinary taxes, and it iss necessary to exchange these for vital supplies vit t'ose not of our cause." A more genuine smile. "As an officer ant a chentelman, you vill appreciate the relief of no lonker having to deal vit this schweinerie."

Ingrid spoke softly to the computer, and another portion of the screen switched to an exterior view of the Free Wunderland ship. An airlock door swung open, and figures spewed out into vacuum with a puff of vapor; some struggled and thrashed for nearly a minute. Another murmur, and a green line drew itself around the figure of Markham. *Stress-reading,* Jonah reminded himself. *Pupil-dilation monitoring. I should have thought of that. Interesting, he thinks he's telling the truth.*

One of the gray-clad figures gave a dry retch at her console. "Control yourzelf, soldier," Markham snapped. To the screen: "Wit all the troubles, the kzin are unlikely to have noticed your, ah, sudden deceleration." The green line remained. "Still, ve should establish vectors to a less conspicuous spot. Then I can offer you the hozpitality of the *Nietzsche*, and we can discuss your mission and how I may assist you at leisure."

The green line flickered, shaded to green-blue. Mental reservations. *Not on board your ship, that's for sure*, Jonah thought, smiling into the steely fanatic's gaze in the screen. "By all means," he murmured.

". . . Zo, as you can imagine, we are anxious to take advantage of your actions," Markham was saying. The control chamber of the *Catskinner* was crowded with him and the three "advisors" he had insisted on; all three looked wirecord-tough, and all had stripped to usefully lumpy coveralls. And they all had something of the outer-orbit chill of Markham's expression.

"To raid kzin outposts while they're off-balance?" Ingrid said. Markham gave her a quick glance down the eagle sweep of his nose.

"You vill understand, wit improvised equipment it is not always possible to attack the kzin directly," he said to Jonah, pointedly ignoring the junior officer. "As the great military tinker Clausewitz said, the role of a guerrilla is to avoid strength and attack weakness. Ve undertake to sabotage their operations by disrupting commerce, and to aid ze groundside partisans wit intelligence and supplies as often as pozzible."

Translated, you hijack ships and bung the crews

*out the airlock when it isn't an unmanned cargo pod,
all for the Greater Good. Finagle's ghost, this is one
scary bastard. Luckily, I know some things he doesn't.*

"And the late unlamented McAllistaire?"

A frown. "Vell, unfortunately, not all are as devoted to the Cause as might be hoped. In terms of
realpolitik, it iss to be eggspected, particularly of the
common folk when so many of deir superiors haff
decided that collaboration wit the kzin is an unavoid-
able necessity." The faded blue eyes blinked at him.
"Not an unreasonable supposition, when Earth has
abandoned us . . . until now . . . zo, of the ones
willing to help, many are merely the lawless and
corrupt. Motivated by money; vell, if one must shovel
manure, one uses a pitchfork."

Jonah smiled and nodded, grasping the meaning if
not the agricultural metaphor. *And the end justifies
the means. My cheeks are starting to hurt.* "Well, I
have my mission to perform. On a need-to-know
basis, let's just say that Lieutenant Raines and I have
to get to Wunderland, preferably to a city. With
cover identities, currency, and instructions to the
underground there to assist us, if it's safe enough to
contact."

"Vell." Markham seemed lost in thought for moments. "I do not believe ve can expect a fleet from
Earth. They would have followed on the heels of the
so-effective attack, and such would be impossible to
hide. You are an afterthought." Decision, and a mouth
drawn into a cold line. "You must tell me of this
mission before scarce resources are devoted to it."

"Impossible. This whole attack was to get Ingri—
the lieutenant and me to Wunderland." Jonah cursed
himself for the slip, saw Markham's ears twitch slightly.

His mouth was dry, and he could feel his vision focusing and narrowing, bringing the aquiline features of the guerrilla chieftain into closer view.

"Zo. This I seriously doubt. But we haff become adept at finding answers, even some kzin haff ve persuaded." The three "aides" drew their weapons, smooth and fast; two stunners and some sort of home-made dart-thrower. "You will answer. Pozzibley, if the answers come quickly and wizzout our having to damage you, I will let you proceed and giff you the help you require. This ship vill be of extreme use to the Cause, vahtever the bankers and merchants of Earth, who have done for us nothing in fifty years of fighting, intended. Ve who haff fought the kzin vit our bare hands, while Earth did nothing, nothing . . ."

Markham pulled himself back to self-command. "If it is inadvisable to assist you, you may join my crew or die." His eyes, flatly dispassionate, turned to Ingrid. "You are from zis system. You also will speak, and then join or . . . no, there is always a market for workable bodies, if the mind is first removed. Search them thoroughly and take them across to the *Nietzsche* in a bubble." A sign to his followers. "The first thing you must learn, is that I am not to be lied to."

"I don't doubt it," Jonah drawled, lying back in his crashcouch. "But you can't take this ship."

"Ah." Markham smiled again. "Codes. You vill furnish them."

"The ship," Ingrid said, considering her fingertips, "has a mind of its own. You may test it."

The Wunderlander snorted. "A self-aware computer? Impossible. Laboratory curiosities."

"Now that," the computer said, "could be considered an insult, Landholder Ulf Reichstein-Markham."

The weapons of Markham's companions were suddenly thrown away with stifled curses and cries of pain. "Induction fields . . . your error, sir. Spaceships in this benighted vicinity may be metal shells with various systems tacked on, but *I* am an organism. *And you are in my intestines.*"

Markham crossed his arms. "You are two to our four, and in the same environment, so no gasses or other such may be used. You vill tell me the control codes for this machine eventually; it is easy to make such a device mimic certain functions of sentience. Better for you if you come quietly."

"Landholder Markham, I grow annoyed with you," the computer said. "Furthermore, consider that your knowledge of cybernetics is fifty years out of date, and that the kzin are a technologically conservative people with no particular gift for information systems. Watch."

A railgun yapped through the hull, and there was a bright flare on the flank of the stubby toroid of Markham's ship. A voice babbled from the handset at his belt, and the view in the screen swooped crazily as the *Catskinner* dodged.

"That was your main screen generator," the computer continued. "You are now open to energy weapons. Need I remind you that this ship carries more than thirty parasite-rider X-ray lasers, pumped by one-megaton bombs? Do we need to alert the kzin to our presence?"

There was a sheen of sweat on Markham's face. "I haff perhaps been somewhat hasty," he said flatly. No nonsentient computer could have been given this degree of initiative. "A fault of youth, as mein mutter is saying." His accent had become thicker. "As chentlemen, we may come to some agreement."

"Or we can barter like merchants," Jonah said, with malice aforethought. Out of the corner of his eye, he saw Ingrid flash an "o" with her fingers. "Is he telling the truth?"

"To within 97% of probability," the computer said. "From pupil, skin-conductivity, encephalographic and other evidence." Markham hid his start quite well. "I suggest the bargaining commence. Commandant Reichstein-Markham, you would also be well advised not to . . . engage in falsehoods."

Chuut-Riit always enjoyed visiting the quarters of his male offspring.

"What will it be this time?" he wondered, as he passed the outer guards.

The household troopers drew claws before their eyes in salute, faceless in impact-armor and goggled helmets, the beam-rifles ready in their hands. He paced past the surveillance cameras, the detector pods, the death-casters and the mines; then past the inner guards at their consoles, humans raised in the household under the supervision of his personal retainers.

The retainers were males grown old in the Riit family's service. There had always been those willing to exchange the uncertain rewards of competition for a secure place, maintenance, and the odd female. Ordinary kzin were not to be trusted in so sensitive a position, of course, but these were families which had served the Riit clan for generation after generation. There was a natural culling effect; those too ambitious left for the Patriarchy's military and the slim chance of advancement, those too timid were not given opportunity to breed.

Perhaps a pity that such cannot be used outside the household, Chuut-Riit thought. Competition for rank was far too intense and personal for that, of course.

He walked past the modern sections, and into an area that was pure Old Kzin; maze-walls of reddish sandstone with twisted spines of wrought-iron on their tops, the tips glistening razor-edged. Fortress-architecture from a world older than this, more massive, colder and drier; from a planet harsh enough that a plains carnivore had changed its ways, put to different use an upright posture designed to place its head above savanna grass, grasping paws evolved to climb rock. Here the modern features were reclusive, hidden in wall and buttress. The door was a hammered slab graven with the faces of night-hunting beasts, between towers five times the height of a kzin. The air smelled of wet rock and the raked sand of the gardens.

Chuut-Riit put his hand on the black metal of the outer portal, stopped. His ears pivoted, and he blinked; out of the corner of his eye he saw a pair of tufted eyebrows glancing through the thick twisted metal on the rim of the ten-meter battlement. *Why, the little sthondats*, he thought affectionately. *They managed to put it together out of reach of the holo pickups.*

The adult put his hand to the door again, keying the locking sequence, then bounded backward four times his own length from a standing start. Even under the lighter gravity of Wunderland, it was a creditable feat. And necessary, for the massive panels rang and toppled as the rope-swung boulder slammed forward. The children had hung two cables from either tower, with the rock at the point of the V and a third rope to draw it back. As the doors bounced wide he saw the blade they had driven into the apex of the egg-shaped granite rock, long and barbed and polished to a wicked point.

Kittens, he thought. *Always going for the dramatic.* If that thing had struck him, or the doors under its impetus had, there would have been no need of a blade.*Watching too many historical adventure holos.*

"*Errorowwww!*" he shrieked in mock-rage, bounding through the shattered portal and into the interior court, halting atop the kzin-high boulder. A round dozen of his older sons were grouped behind the rock, standing in a defensive clump and glaring at him; the crackly scent of their excitement and fear made the fur bristle along his spine. He glared until they dropped their eyes, continued it until they went down on their stomachs, rubbed their chins along the ground and then rolled over for a symbolic exposure of the stomach.

"Congratulations," he said. "That was the closest you've gotten. Who was in charge?"

More guilty sidelong glances among the adolescent males crouching among their discarded pull-rope, and then a lanky youngster with platter-sized feet and hands came squatting-erect. His fur was in the proper flat posture, but the naked pink of his tail still twitched stiffly.

"I was," he said, keeping his eyes formally down. "Honored Sire Chuut-Riit," he added, at the adult's warning rumble.

"Now, youngling, what did you learn from your first attempt?"

"That no one among us is your match, Honored Sire Chuut-Riit," the kitten said. Uneasy ripples went over the black-striped orange of his pelt.

"And what have you learned from this attempt?"

"That all of us together are no match for you, Honored Sire Chuut-Riit," the striped youth said.

"That we didn't locate all of the cameras," another muttered. "You idiot, Spotty." That to one of his siblings; they snarled at each other from their crouches, hissing past barred fangs and making striking motions with unsheathed claws.

"No, you did locate them all, cubs," Chuut-Riit said. "I presume you stole the ropes and tools from the workshop, prepared the boulder in the ravine in the next courtyard, then rushed to set it all up between the time I cleared the last gatehouse and my arrival?"

Uneasy nods. He held his ears and tail stiffly, letting his whiskers quiver slightly and holding in the rush of love and pride he felt, more delicious than milk heated with bourbon. *Look at them!* he thought. At the age when most young kzin were helpless prisoners of instinct and hormone, wasting their strength ripping each other up or making fruitless direct attacks on their sires, or demanding to be allowed to join the Patriarchy's service *at once* to win a Name and household of their own . . . *His* get had learned to *cooperate* and use their minds!

"Ah, Honored Sire Chuut-Riit, we set the ropes up beforehand, but made it look as if we were using them for tumbling practice," the one the others called

Spotty said. Some of them glared at him, and the adult raised his hand again.

"No, no, I am *moderately* pleased." A pause. "You did not hope to take over my official position if you had disposed of me?"

"No, Honored Sire Chuut-Riit," the tall leader said. There had been a time when any kzin's holdings were the prize of the victor in a duel, and the dueling rules were interpreted more leniently for a young subadult. Everyone had a sentimental streak for a successful youngster; every male kzin remembered the intolerable stress of being physically mature but remaining under dominance as a child.

Still, these days affairs were handled in a more civilized manner. Only the Patriarchy could award military and political office. And this mass assassination attempt was . . . unorthodox, to say the least. Outside the rules more because of its rarity than because of formal disapproval. . . .

A vigorous toss of the head. "Oh, no, Honored Sire Chuut-Riit. We had an agreement to divide the private possessions. The lands and the, ah, females." Passing their own mothers to half-siblings, of course. "Then we wouldn't each have so much we'd get too many challenges, and we'd agreed to help each other against outsiders," the leader of the plot finished virtuously.

"Fatuous young scoundrels," Chuut-Riit said. His eyes narrowed dangerously. "You haven't been communicating outside the household, have you?" he snarled.

"Oh, *no*, Honored Sire Chuut-Riit!"

"Word of honor! May we die nameless if we should do such a thing!"

The adult nodded, satisfied that good family feeling had prevailed. "Well, as I said, I am somewhat pleased. If you have been keeping up with your lessons. Is there anything you wish?"

"Fresh meat, Honored Sire Chuut-Riit," the spotted one said. The adult could have told him by the scent, of course, a kzin never forgot another's personal odor, that was one reason why names were less necessary among their species. "The reconstituted stuff from the dispensers is always . . . so . . . *quiet*."

Chuut-Riit hid his amusement. Young Heroes-to-be were always kept on an inadequate diet, to increase their aggressiveness. A matter for careful gauging, since too much hunger would drive them into mindless cannibalistic frenzy.

"And couldn't we have the human servants back? They were nice." Vigorous gestures of assent. Another added: "They told good stories. I miss my Clothilda-human."

"Silence!" Chuut-Riit roared. The youngsters flattened stomach and chin to the ground again. "Not until you can be trusted not to injure them; how many times do I have to tell you, it's dishonorable to attack household servants! Until you learn self-control, you will have to make do with machines."

This time all of them turned and glared at a mottled youngster in the rear of their group; there were half-healed scars over his head and shoulders. "It bared its *teeth* at me," he said sulkily. "All I did was swipe at it, how was I supposed to know it would die?" A chorus of rumbles, and this time several of the covert kicks and clawstrikes landed.

"Enough," Chuut-Riit said after a moment. *Good, they have even learned how to discipline each other*

as a unit. "I will consider it, when all of you can pass
a test on the interpretation of human expressions and
body-language." He drew himself up. "In the mean-
time, within the next two eight-days, there will be a
formal hunt and meeting in the Patriarch's Preserve;
kzinti homeworld game, the best Earth animals, and
even some feral-human outlaws, perhaps!"

He could smell their excitement increase, a mane-
crinkling musky odor not unmixed with the sour
whiff of fear. Such a hunt was not without danger for
adolescents, being a good opportunity for hostile adults
to cull a few of a hated rival's offspring with no
possibility of blame. *They will be in less danger than
most,* Chuut-Riit thought judiciously. *In fact, they
may run across a few of my subordinates' get and
mob them. Good.*

"And if we do well, afterwards a feast and a visit to
the Sterile Ones." That had them all quiveringly
alert, their tails held rigid and tongues lolling; non-
bearing females were kept as a rare privilege for
Heroes whose accomplishments were not *quite* de-
serving of a mate of their own. Very rare for kits still
in the household to be granted such, but Chuut-Riit
thought it past time to admit that modern society
demanded a prolonged adolescence. The day when a
male kit could be given a spear, a knife, a rope, and a
bag of salt and kicked out the front gate at puberty
were long gone. Those were the wild, wandering
years in the old days, when survival challenges used
up the superabundant energies. Now they must be
spent learning history, technology, xenology, none of
which burned off the gland-juices saturating flesh
and brain.

He jumped down amid his sons, and they pressed

around him, purring throatily with adoration and fear and respect; his presence and the failure of their plot had reestablished his personal dominance unambiguously, and there was no danger from them for now. Chuut-Riit basked in their worship, feeling the rough caress of their tongues on his fur and scratching behind his ears. *Together,* he thought. *Together we will do wonders.*

Chapter III

Interesting, Chuut-Riit thought, standing on the verandah of his staff-secretary's house and lapping at the gallon tub of half-melted vanilla ice cream in his hands. *Quite comely, in its way.*

In a very un-kzin fashion. The senior staff quarters of his estate were laid out in a section of rolling hills, lawns and shrubs and eucalyptus trees, modest stone houses with high-pitched shingle roofs set among flowerbeds. A dozen or so of the adults who dwelt here were gathered at a discreet distance, down by the landingpad; he could smell their colognes and perfumes, the slightly mealy odor of human flesh beneath, a mechanical tang overlaid with alien greenness and animals and . . . yes, the children were coming back. Preceded by the usual blast of sound. The kzin's ears folded themselves away at the jumbled high-pitched squealing, one of the less attractive qualities of young humans. Although there was a very kzinlike warbling mixed in among the monkey sounds . . .

209

The giant ball of yarn bounced around the corner of the house and across the close-clipped grass of the lawn, bounding from side to side with the slight drifting wobble of .61 gravities, trailing floppy ends. A peacock fled shrieking from the toy and the shouting mob of youngsters that followed it; the bird's head was parallel to the ground and its feet pumped madly. Chuut-Riit sighed, finished the ice cream and began licking his muzzle and fingers clean. Alpha Centauri was setting, casting bronze shadows over the creeper-grown stone around him, and it was time to go.

"Like this!" the young kzin leading the pack screamed, and leaped in a soaring arch that landed spreadeagled on the soft fuzzy surface of the ball. He was a youngster of five, all head and hands and feet, the fur of his pelt an electric orange with fading black spots, the infant mottling that a very few kzin kept into early youth. Several of the human youngsters made a valiant attempt to follow, but only one landed and clutched the strands, screaming delightedly. The others fell, one skinning a knee and bawling.

Chuut-Riit rose smoothly to his feet and bounced forward, scooping the crying infant up and stopping the ball with his other hand.

"*You should be more careful, my son,*" he said to the Kzin child in the Hero's tongue. To the human: "Are you injured?"

"Mama!" the child wailed, twining its fists into his fur and burying its tear-and-snot streaked face in his side.

"*Errruumm,*" Chuut-Riit rumbled helplessly. *They are so fragile*. His nostrils flared as he bent over the tiny form, taking in the milky-sweat smell of distress and the slight metallic-salt odor of blood from its knee.

"Here is your mother," he continued, as the human female scuttled up and began apologetically untwining the child.

"Here, take it," he rumbled, as she cuddled the infant. The woman gave it a brief inspection and looked up at the eight-foot height of the kzin.

"No harm done, just over-excited, honored Chuut-Riit," she said. The kzin rumbled again, looked up at the guards standing by his flitter in the driveway and laid back his ears; they became elaborately casual, examining the sky or the ground and controlling their expressions. He switched his glare back to his own offspring on top of the ball. The cub flattened itself apologetically, then whipped its head to one side as the human child clinging to the slope of the ball threw a loose length of yarn. Chuut-Riit wrenched his eyes from the fascinating thing and plucked his son into the air by the loose skin at the back of his neck.

"It is time to depart," he said. The young kzin had gone into an instinctive half-curl. He cast a hopeful glance over his shoulder at his father, sighed and wrapped the limber pink length of his tail around the adult's massive forearm.

"Yes, Honored Sire Chuut-Riit," he said meekly, then brightened and waved at the clump of estate-worker children standing by the ball. "Goodbye," he called, waving a hand that seemed too large for his arm, and adding a cheerful parting yowl in the Hero's Tongue. Literally translated it meant roughly *drink blood and tear cattle into gobbets*, but the adult trusted the sentiment would carry over the wording.

The human children jumped and waved in reply as Chuut-Riit carried his son over to the car and the group of parents waiting there; Henrietta in the center with her offspring by her side. *I think her posture indicates contentment,* he thought. *This visit confers much prestige among the other human servants.* Which was excellent, a good executive secretary being a treasure beyond price. Besides . . .

"That was fun, father," the cub said. "Could I have another piece of cake?"

"Certainly not, you will be sick as it is," Chuut-Riit said decisively. Kzin were not quite the pure meat-eaters they claimed to be, and their normal diet contained the occasional sweet, but stuffing that much sugar-coated confection down on top of a stomach already full of good raw *ztirgor* was something the cub would regret soon. Ice cream, though . . . why had nobody told him about ice cream before? Even better than bourbon-and-milk; he must begin to order in bulk.

"I must be leaving, Henrietta," Chuut-Riit said. "And young Ilge," he added, looking down at the offspring. It was an odd-looking specimen, only slightly over knee-high to him and with long braided head-pelt of an almost kzinlike orange. The bare skin of its face was dotted with markings of almost the same color. Remarkable; the one standing next to it was *black*. There was no end to their variety.

The cub wiggled in his grasp and looked down. "I hope you like your armadillo, Ilge," he said. Ilge looked down at the creature she had not released since the gift-giving ceremony and patted it again; the beasts had adapted well to Wunderland, but they were less common since the Kzinti arrived. A snout and beady eye appeared for a second, caught the scent of kzin and disappeared back into an armored ball with a snap.

"They're lots of fun." Kzin children adored armadillos and Chuut-Riit provided his with a steady supply, even if the shells made a mess once the cubs finally got them peeled.

"It's nice," she said solemnly.

"The ball of fiber was an excellent idea," Chuut-Riit added to Henrietta. "I must procure one for my other offspring."

"I thought it would be, honored Chuut-Riit," the human replied, and the kzin blinked in bafflement at her amusement.

One of the guards was too obviously entertained by his commander's eccentricity. "Here," Chuut-Riit called as he walked through the small crowd of bowing humans. "Guard Trooper. Care for this infant as we fly, in the forward compartment. Care for him well."

The soldier blinked dubiously at the small bundle of chocolate-and-mud stained fur that looked with eager interest at the fascinating complexities of his equipment, then slung his beam rifle and accepted it with an unconscious bristling. Chuut-Riit gave the ear-and tail twitch that was the kzin equivalent of sly amusement as he stepped into the passenger compartment and threw himself down on the cushions. There was a slight internal wobble as the car lifted, an expected retching sound, and a yowl of protest from the forward compartment.

The ventilators will be overloaded, the governor thought happily. *Now, about that report. . . .*

* * *

Tiamat was shabby. Coming in to dock on the rockjacker prospecting craft Markham had found for them it had looked the same as it had half a century before—a little busier and more exterior lights; but basically the same spinning ironrock tube twenty kilometers across and sixty long, with ships of every description clustered at the docking yards at either end. More smelters and robofabricators hanging outside, more giant baggies of water ice and volatiles. But inside it was shabby, run-down.

That was Ingrid Raines's first thought. Shabby. The handgrips were worn, the vivid murals that covered the walls just in from the poles of the giant cylinder fading and grease-spotted. The constant subliminal rumble from the freighter docks was louder, nobody was bothering with the sonic baffles that damped the vibration of megatons of powdered ore, liquid metal, vacuum-separated refinates pouring into the network of pumptubes. Styles were more garish than she remembered, face-paint and tiger-striped oversuits. There were a quartet of police hanging spaced evenly around the entry corridor, toes hooked into rails and heads in toward the center. Obstructing traffic, but nobody was going to object, not when the goldskins wore impact armor and powdered endoskeletons, not when shockrods dangled negligently in their hands.

"Transfer booths closed down," Jonah murmured as they made flipover and went feet first into the stickyfield at the inward end of the passage. There was a familiar subjective click behind their eyes, and the corridor became a half-kilometer of hollow tower over their heads, filled with the up-and-down drift of people.

"Shut up," Ingrid muttered back. That had been no surprise, instantaneous transportation would foul up security too much. They went through the emergency pressure curtains, into the glare and blare of the inner corridors. Zero-G, here near the core of Tiamat, one-G at the rims. *Tigertown* was at one-G, she thought. The resident kzin were low-status engineers and supervisors, or navy types; they liked heavy gravity, the pussies had never lived in space without gravity control. *Tigers*, she reminded herself. That was the official slang term. Ratcat if you wanted to be a little dangerous.

They turned into a narrow side corridor that had been a residential section the last time she was here, transients' quarters around the lowgrav manufacturing sections of the core. Now it was lined on three sides by shops and small businesses, with the fourth, spinward, side acting as the "downward" direction. Not that there was enough gravity to matter this close to the center of the spin, but it was convenient. They slowed to a stroll, two more figures in plain rockjack innersuits, the form-fitting coverall everyone wore under vacuum armor. Conservative Belter stripcuts, backpacks with printseal locks to discourage pickpockets, and the black plastic hilts of humm-knives.

Ingrid looked around her, acutely conscious of the hard shape nestling butt-down on her collarbone. Distortion battery, and a blade-shaped loop of wire; switch it on, and the magnetic field made it vibrate, very fast. Very sharp. She had been shocked when Markham's Intelligence Officer pushed them across the table to the UNSN operatives.

"Things are *that* bad?"

"The ratcats don't care," the officer had said. "Humans are forbidden any weapon that can kill at a distance. Only the collabo police can carry stunners, and the only thing the ratcats care about is that production keeps up. What sort of people do you think join the collabo goldskins? Social altruists? The only ordinary criminals they go after are the ones too poor or stupid to pay them off. When things get bad enough to foul up war production, they have a big sweep, and maybe catch some of the middling-level gangrunners and feed them to the ratcats. The big boys? The big boys *are* the police, or vice versa. That's the way it is, sweetheart."

Ingrid shivered, and Jonah put an arm around her waist as they walked in the glide-lift-glide of a stickyfield. "Changed a lot, hey?" he said.

She nodded. The boots were for the sort of small-scale industry that bigger firms contracted out; filing, hardcopy, genetic engineering of bacteria for process production of organics, all mixed in with cookshops and handicrafts and service trades of a thousand types. Holo displays flashed and glittered, strobing with all shades of the visible spectrum; music pounded and blared and crooned, styles she remembered and styles utterly strange and others that were revivals of modes six centuries old; Baroque and Classical and Jazz and Dojin-Go Punk and Meddlehoffer. People crowded the 'way, on the rimside and wall-hopping between shops. Half the shops had private guards. The passers-by were mostly planetsiders, some so recent you could see they had trouble handling low-G movement.

Many were ragged, openly dirty. *How can that happen?* she thought. Fusion-distilled water was usually cheap in a closed system. *Oh. Probably a monopoly.* And there were beggars, actual beggars with open sores on their skins or hands twisted with arthritis, things she had only seen in historical flats so old they had been shot two-dimensional.

"Here it is," Jonah grunted. The eating-shop was directly above them; they switched off their shoes, waited for a clear space and flipped up and over, slapping their hands onto the catch net outside the door. Inside the place was clean, at least, with a globular freefall kitchen and a human chef, and customers in dark pajama-like clothing floating with their knees crossed under sticktables. Not Belters—too stocky and muscular—they seemed almost purely Oriental by bloodline, which was rare in the genetic stew of the Sol system but more common here.

Icy stares greeted them as they swung to a vacant booth and slid themselves in, their long legs tangling under the synthetic pineboard of the stick table.

"It must be harder for you," Jonah said. "Your home."

She looked up at him with quick surprise; he was usually the archetypical rockjack, the stereotype asteroid prospector; quiet, bookish, self-sufficient, a man without twitches or mannerisms but capable of cutting loose on furlough . . . but perceptive—and rockjacks were not supposed to be good at people.

Well, he was a successful officer, too, she thought. *And they* do *have to be good at people.*

A waitress in some many-folded garment of black silk floated up to the privacy screen of their cubicle and reached a hand through to scratch at the post. Ingrid keyed the screen, and the woman's features snapped clear.

"Sorry, so sorry," she said. "This special place, not Belter food." There was a sing-song accent to her English that Jonah did not recognize, but the underlying impatience and hostility came through the calm features.

He smiled at her and ran a hand over his crest. "But we were told the tekkamaki here is fine, the oyabun makes the best," he said. Ingrid could read the thought that followed: *Whatever the fuck that means*.

The frozen mask of the waitress' face could not alter, but the quick duck of her head was empty of the commonplace tension of a moment before. She returned quickly with bowls of soup and drinking straws; it was some sort of fish broth with onions and a strange musky undertaste. They drank in silence, waiting. *For what, the pussies to come and get us?* she thought. The *Catskinner*-computer had said Markham was on the level . . . but also that he was capable of utter treachery once he had convinced himself that Right was on his side, and that to Markham the only ultimate judge of Right was, guess who, the infallible Markham. *Gottdamned Herrenmann*, she mused: going on fifty years objective, everything else in the system had collapsed into shit, and the arrogant lop-sided bastards hadn't changed a bit. . . .

A man slid through the screen. Expensively nondescript dress, gray oversuit and bowl-cut black hair. Hint of an expensive natural cologne. Infocomp at his waist, and the silver button of a reader-bonephone behind his ear. This was Markham's "independent entrepreneur." Spoken with tones of deepest contempt, more than a *Herrenmann*'s usual disdain for business, so probably some type of criminal like

McAllistaire. She kept a calm smile on her face as she studied the man, walling off the remembered sickness as the kicking doll-figures tumbled into space, bleeding from every orifice. Oriental, definitely; there were Sina and Nipponjin enclaves down on Wunderland, but not in the Serpent Swarm Belt, not when she left. Things had changed.

The quiet man smiled and produced three small drinking-bulbs. "Rice wine," he said. "Heated. An affectation, to be sure, but we are very traditional these days." Pure Belter English, no hint of an accent. She called up training, looked for clues. In the hands, the skin around the eyes, the set of the mouth. Very little, no more than polite attention, this was a very calm man. Hard to tell even the age, if he was getting good geriatric care; anything from fifty minimum up to a hundred. *Teufel*, he could have been from Sol system himself, one of the last bunches of immigrants and wouldn't *that* be a joke to end them.

Silence stretched. The oriental sat and sipped at his hot sake and smiled; the two Belters followed suit, controlling their surprise at the vanish-in-the-throat taste. At the last, Jonah spoke:

"I'm Jonah. This is Ingrid. The man with gray eyes sent us for tekkamaki."

"Ah, our esteemed GVB," the man said. A deprecatory laugh and a slight wave of the fingers; the man had almost as few hand-gestures as a Belter. "*Gotz von Blerichgen*, a little joke. Yes, I know the one you speak of. My name is Shigehero Hirose, and as you will have guessed, I am a hardened criminal of the worst sort." He ducked his head in a polite bow. Ingrid noticed his hands then, the left missing the little finger, and the edges of vividly-colored tattoos under the cuffs of his suit.

"And you," he continued to Jonah, "are sent not by our so-Ayran friend, but by the UNSN." A slight frown. "Your charming companion is perhaps of the same provenance, but from the Serpent Swarm originally."

Jonah and Ingrid remained silent. Another shrug. "In any case, accordingly to our informants, you wish transportation to Wunderland, and well-documented cover identities."

"If you're wondering how we can pay . . ." Jonah began. They had the best and most compact source of valuata the UN military had been able to provide.

"No, please. From our own resources, we will be glad to do this."

"Why?" Ingrid said, curious. "Criminals seem to be doing better now than they ever did in the old days."

Hirose smiled again, that bland expression that revealed nothing and never touched his eyes. "The young lady is as perceptive as she is ornamental." He took up his sake bulb and considered it. "My . . . association is a very old one. You might call us predators; we would prefer to think of it as a symbiotic relationship. We have endured many changes, many social and technological revolutions. But something is common to each, the desire to have something and yet to forbid it.

"Consider drugs and alcohol . . . or wirehead drouds. All strictly forbidden at one time, legal another, but the demand continues. Instruction in martial arts, likewise. In our early days in *dai Nippon*, we performed services for feudal lords that their own code forbade. Later, the great corporations, the *zaibatsu*, found us convenient for dealing with recalcitrant shareholders and unions; we moved substances of various types across inconvenient national frontiers; liberated information selfishly stockpiled in closed data banks, recruited entertainers, provided banking services . . . Invested our wealth wisely, and moved outward with humanity to the planets and the stars. Sometimes so respectable that our affairs were beyond question; sometimes otherwise. A conservative fraction undertook to found our branch in the Alpha Centauri system, but I assure you the . . . family businesses, clans if you will, still flourish in Sol System as well. Inconspicuously."

"That doesn't answer Ingrid's question," Jonah said bluntly. "This setup looks like hog heaven for you."

"Only in the short term. Which is enough to satisfy mere thugs, mere bandits such as a certain rockholder known as McAllistaire . . . you met this person? But consider; we are doing well for the same reason bacteria flourish in a dead body. The human polity of this system is dying, its social defenses disorganized, but the carnival of the carrion-eaters will be shortlived. We speak of the free humans and those in the direct service of the kzin, but to our masters we of the 'free' are slaves of the Patriarchy who have not yet been assigned individual owners. We are squeezed, tighter and tighter; eventually, there will be nothing but the households of kzin nobles. My association could perhaps survive such a situation, and indeed we are making preparations." He shrugged. "We have survived much over the centuries. But perhaps this time it will not be. Better by far to restore a functioning human system; our

assets would be less in the short term, more secure
in the longer."

"And by helping us, you'll have a foot in both
camps and come up smelling of roses whoever wins."

Hirose spread his hands. "It is true, the kzin have
occasionally found themselves using our services."
His smile became more genuine, and sharklike. "Nor
are all, ah, Heroes, so incorruptible, so immune to
the temptations of vice and profit, as they would like
to believe.

"Enough." He produced two sealed packets and
slid them across the table to them. "This one con-
tains the names of criminals in Munchen who have
worked with us and have not betrayed us. You will
understand that this is no great endorsement. I cannot guarantee they will not sell you out to the authorities merely to win good will with them. However,
these are the only names I have.

"This one is more important. The documentation
and credit accounts are perfectly genuine. They will
stand even against kzin scrutiny; our influence reaches
far. I have no knowledge of what identities you have
been given, nor do I wish to. You in turn have
learned nothing from me that possible opponents do
not already know, and know that I know, and I know
that they know . . . but please, even if I cannot join
you, do stay and enjoy this excellent restaurant's
cuisine."

"Well . . ." Jonah palmed the folder. "It might be
out of character, rockjacks in a fancy live-service
place like this."

Shigehero Hirose halted, part-way through the privacy screen. "You would do well to study local conditions a little more carefully, man-from-far-away. It

has been a long time since autochefs and dispensers were cheaper than humans."

"The inefficiency of you leaf-eaters is becoming intolerable," the kzin said.

Claude Montferrat-Palme bowed his head. *Don't stare. Never, never stare at a ratca—at a kzin.* "We do our best, Ktriir-Supervisor-of-Animals," he said.

The kzin superintendent of Munchen stopped its restless striding and stood close, smiling, its tail held stiffly past one column-thick leg. Two and a half meters tall, a thickly padded cartoon-figure cat that might have looked funny in a holo. It grinned down at him, the direct gaze that was as much a threat display as the barred fangs.

"You play your monkey games of position and money while the enemies of the Patriarchy scurry and bite in the underbrush." Its head swiveled toward the police chief's desk. "Scroll!"

Data began to move across the suddenly transparent surface, accompanied by a moving schematic of the Serpent Swarm; colors and symbols indicated feral-human attacks. Ships lost, outposts raided, automatic cargo containers hijacked.

"Comparative!" the kzin snapped. Graphs replaced the schematic. "Distribution!

"See," he continued. "Raids of every description have sprouted like fungus since the sthondat-spawned Sol-monkeys made their coward's passage through this system. With no discernible pattern. And even the lurkers in the mountains are slipping out to trouble the estates again."

"With respect, Ktriir-Supervisor-of-Animals, my sphere of responsibility is the human population of this city. There has been little increase in feral activity here."

Claws rested centimeters from his eyes. "Because this city is the locus where feral-human packs dispose of their loot, exchange information and goods, meet and coordinate. Paying their percentage to you! Yes, yes, we have heard your arguments that it is better for this activity to take place where our minions may monitor it, and they are logical enough. While we lack the number of Heroes necessary to reduce this system to true order, and we are preoccupied with the renewed offensive against Sol."

He mumbled under his breath, and Montferrat caught an uncomplimentary reference to Chuut-Riit.

The human bowed again. "Ktriir-Supervisor-of-Animals, most of the groups operating against the righteous rule of the Patriarchy are motivated by material gain; this is a characteristic of my species. They cooperate with the genuine rebels, but it is an alliance plagued by mistrust and mutual contempt; furthermore, the rebels themselves are as much a grouping of bands as a unified whole." *And were slowly dying out, until the UN demonstrated its reach so spectacularly. Now they'll have recruits in plenty again, and the bandits will want to draw the cloak of respectable Resistance over themselves.*

His mind cautiously edged toward a consideration of whether it was time to begin hedging *his* bets, and he forced it back. The kzin used telepaths periodically to check the basic loyalties of their senior servants. That was one reason he had never tried to reach the upper policy levels of the collaborationist government, that and . . . A wash of non-thought buried the speculation.

"Accordingly, if their activity increases, our sources of information increase likewise. Once the confusion of the, ah, passing raid dies down, we will be in a position to make further gains. Perhaps to trap some of the greater leaders, Markham or Hirose."

"And you will take your percentage of all these transactions," Ktriir-Supervisor-of-Animals said with heavy irony. "Remember that a trained monkey that loses other values may always serve as monkeymeat. Remember where your loyalties ultimately lie, in this insect-web of betrayals you fashion, slave."

Yes, thought Montferrat, dabbing at his forehead as the kzin left. *I must remember that carefully.*

"Collation," he said to his desk. "Attack activity." The schematic returned. "Eliminate all post-*Yamamoto* raids that correlate to within 75% of the modus operandi of pre-*Yamamoto* attacks."

A scattering, mostly directed toward borderline targets that had been too heavily protected for the makeshift boats of the Free Wunderland space-guerrillas. Disconcertingly many of them on weapons-fabrication plants, with nearly as many seizing communications, stealthing, command-and-control components. Once those were passed along to the other asteroid lurkers all hell was going to break loose. And gravity polarization technology was becoming more and more widespread as well. The kzin had tried to keep it strictly for their own ships and for manufacturing use, but the principles were not too difficult and the methods the Patriarchy introduced were heavily dependent on it.

"Now, correlate filtered attacks with past ten year pattern for bandits Markham, McAllistaire, Finbogesson, Cheung, Latimer, Wu. Sequencing."

"*Scheisse*," he whispered. Markham, without a doubt, the man did everything by the book and you could rewrite the manuscript by watching him. Now equipped with something whose general capacities were equivalent to a kzin Stalker, and proceeding in a methodical amplification of the sort of thing he had been doing before . . . Markham was the sort for the Protracted Struggle, all right. He'd read his Mao and Styrikawsi and Laugidis, even if he gave Clausewitz all the credit.

"Code, *Till Eulenspiegel*. Lock previous analysis, non-redo, simulate other pattern if requested. Stop."

"Stop and locked," the desk said.

Montserrat relaxed. The Eulenspiegel file was supposedly secure. Certainly none of his subordinates had it, or they would have gone to the ratcats with it long ago; there had been more than enough in there to make him prime monkeymeat. He swallowed convulsively; as Police Chief of Munchen, he was obliged to screen the kzin hunts far too frequently. Straightening, he adjusted the lapels of his uniform and walked to the picture window that formed one wall of the office. Behind him stretched the sleek expanse of feathery downdropper-pelt rugs over marble tile, the settees and loungers of pebbled but butter-soft okkaran hide. A Matisse and two Vorenagles on the walls, and a priceless Pierneef . . . He stopped at the long oak bar and poured himself the single glass of Maivin that was permissible.

Interviews with the kzin Supervisor-of-Animals were always rather stressful. Montferrat sipped, looking down over the low-pitched tile roofs of Old Munchen. None of the sprawling shanty-suburbs and shoddy gimcrack factories of recent years, this ten-story view was almost as he had known it as a student: The curving tree-lined streets that curled through the hills beside the broad blue waters of the Donau, banked flowers beside the pedestrian ways, cafes, the honeygold quadrangles of the University, court-yarded homes built around expanses of greenery and fountains. Softly blooming frangipani and palms and gumblossom in the parks along the river; the Gothic flamboyance of the Ritterhuuse, where the Land-holders had met in council before the kzin came. And the bronze grouping in the great square before it; the Nineteen Founders.

Memory rose before him, turning the hard day-light of afternoon to a soft summer's night; he was young again, arm in arm with Ingrid and Harold and a dozen of their friends, the new student's caps on their head. They had come from the beercellar and hours of swaying song, the traditional graduation-night feast, and they were all a little merry. Not drunk, but happy and in love with all the world, a universe and a lifetime opening out before them. The three of them had lead the scrambling mob up the granite steps of the plinth, to put their white-and-gold caps on the three highest sculpted heads, and they had ridden the bronze shoulders and waved to the sea of dancing, laughing young faces below. Fire-works had burst overhead, yellow and green . . . *shut up*, he told himself. The present was what mat-tered. The UN raid had not been the simple smash-on-the wing affair it seemed, not at all.

"I knew it," he muttered. "It wasn't logical, they didn't do as much damage as they could have." The kzin had thought otherwise, but then, they had pred-ator's reflexes. They just did not think in terms of mass destruction; their approach to warfare was too pragmatic for that. Which was why their armament was lacking in planet-busting weapons: the thought of destroying valuable real estate did not occur to them. Montferrat had run his own projections, and with weapons like that ramship you could destabilize *stars*. "And humans *do* think that way."

So there must have been some other point to the raid, and not merely to get an effective ship to the Free Wunderlanders. Nothing overt, which left something clandestine. Intelligence work. Perhaps elsewhere in the system, pray *God* elsewhere in the system, not in his backyard. But it would be just as well . . .

He crossed to the desk. "Axelrod-Bauergartner," he said.

A holo of his second-in-command formed, seated at her desk. The meter-high image put down its coffee-cup and straightened. "Yes, Chief?"

"I want redoubled surveillance on all entry-exit movements in the Greater Munchen area. *Everything*, top priority. Activate all our contacts, call in favors, lean on everybody we can lean on. I'll be sending you some data on deep-hook threads I've been developing among the hardcore ferals." He saw her look of surprise; that was one of the hole-cards he used to keep his subordinates in order. *Poor Axelrod-Bauergartner*, he thought. *You want this job so much, and would do it so badly. I've held it for twenty years because I've got a sense of proportion; you'd be monkeymeat inside six months.*

"*Zum befehl*, Chief."

"Our esteemed superiors also wish evidence of our

zeal. Get them some monkeymeat for the next hunt, nobody too crucial."

"I'll round up the usual suspects, Chief."

The door retracted, and a white-coated steward came in with a covered wheeled tray. Montferrat looked up, checking . . . yes, the chilled Bloemvin 2337, the heart-of-palm salad, the paté . . .

"And for now, send in the exit-visa applicant, the one who was having the problems with the paperwork."

The projected figure grinned wickedly. "Oh, *her*. Right away, Chief." Montferrat flicked the transmission out of existence and rose, smoothing down his uniform jacket and flicking his mustache into shape with a deft forefinger. *This job isn't* all *grief*, he mused happily.

"Recode *Till Eulenspiegel*," Yarthkin said, leaning back. "Interesting speculation, Claude, old *kamerat*," he mused. The bucket chair creaked as he leaned back, putting his feet up on the cluttered desk. The remains of a cheese-and-mustard sandwich perched waveringly on a stack of printout at his elbow. The office around him was a similar clutter, bookcases and safe and a single glowlight, a narrow cubicle at the alley-wall of the bar. Shabby and rundown and smelling of beer and old socks, except for the extremely up-to-date infosystem built into the archaic wooden desk; one of the reasons the office was so shabby was that nobody but Yarthkin was allowed in, and he was an indifferent housekeeper at best.

He lit a cigarette and blew a smoke-ring at the ceiling. *Have to crank up my contacts*, he thought. *Activity's going to heat up system-wide, and there's no reason I shouldn't take advantage of it. Safety's sake, too:* arse to the wall, ratcats over all. *This wasn't all to get our heroic* Herrenmann *in the Swarm a new toy; that was just a side effect, somehow.*

"Sam," he said, keying an old-fashioned manual toggle. "Get me Suuomalisen."

"Finagle," Jonah muttered under his breath. The transfer booths were shut down at Munchenport as well, and the shuttle station had been moved out into open country. The station was a series of square extruded buildings and open spaces for the gravitic shuttles; mostly for freight, the passenger traffic was a sideline. "Security's tight."

Ingrid smiled at the guard and handed over their identicards.

The man smiled back and fed them into the reader, waiting a few seconds while the machine read the data, scanned the two Belters for congruence and consulted the central files.

"Clear," he said, and shifted into Wunderlander: "Enjoy your stay planetside. God knows, there are more trying to get off than on, what with casualties from the raid and all."

"Thank you," Jonah said; his command of the language was adequate, and his accent would pass among non-Belters. "It was pretty bad out in the Belt, too."

The lineup moving through the scanners in the opposite direction stretched hundreds of meters into the barnlike gloom of the terminal building. A few were obviously space-born returning home, but most were stockier, families with crying children and string-tied parcels, or ragged-looking laborers. They smelled of unwashed bodies and poverty, a peculiar sweet-sour odor blending with the machinery-and-synthetics smell of the building and the residual ozone of heavy powder release. More raw material for the industries of the Serpent Swarm, attracted by the higher wages and the lighter hand of the kzin offplanet.

"Watch it," Ingrid said. The milling crowds silenced and parted as a trio of the felinoids walked through trailed by human servants with baggage on maglifters; Jonah caught snatches of the Hero's tongue, technical jargon. They both wheeled at a sudden commotion. The guards were closing in on an emigrant at the head of the line, a man arguing furiously with the checker.

"It's right!" he screamed. "I paid good money for it, all we got for the farm, it's *right!*"

"Look, *scheisskopf*, the machine says there's no record of it. *Raus!* You're holding up the line."

"It's the right paper, let me through!" The man lunged, trying to vault the turnstile. The guard at the checker recoiled, shrieked as the would-be traveler slammed down his metal-edged carryall on her arm. The two agents could hear the wet crackle of broken bone even at five meters distance, and then the madman's body disappeared behind a circle of helmeted heads, marked by the rise and fall of shockrods. The others in the line drew back, as if afraid of infection, and the police dragged the man off by his arms; the injured one followed, holding her splinted arm and kicking the semiconscious form with every other step.

"Monkeymeat, you're *monkeymeat*, shithead," she shrilled, and kicked him again. There was solid force behind the blow, and she grunted with the effort and winced as it jarred her arm.

"Tanj," Jonah said softly. The old curse: *there ain't no justice*.

"No, there isn't," Ingrid answered. "Come on, the railcar's waiting."

"And the word from the Nippojen in Tiamat is that two important ferals will be coming through soon," Suuomalisen said.

Yarthkin leaned back, sipping at his coffee and considering him. Suuomalisen was fat, even by Wunderland standards, where the .61 standard gravity made it easy to carry extra tissue. His head was pink, egg-bald, a beak of a nose over a slit mouth and a double chin; the round body was expensively covered in a suit of white natural silk accented with a conservative black cravat and onyx ring. The owner of Harold's Terran Bar waited patiently while his companion tucked a linen handkerchief into his collar and began eating; scrambled eggs with scallions, grilled wurst, smoked *kopjfische*, biscuits.

"You set a marvelous table, my friend," the fat man said. They were alone in the dining nook; Harold's did not serve breakfast, except for the owner and staff. "Twice I have offered your cook a position in my *Suuomalisen's Sauna*, and twice he has refused. You must tell me your secret."

Acquaintance, not friend, Harold thought. *And my chef prefers to work for someone who lets his people quit if they want to*. Mildly: "From the Free Wunderland people? They've been doing better at getting through to the bands in the Jotunscarp recently."

"No, no, these are *special* somehow. Carrying special goods, something that will upset the ratcats very much. The tip was vague, I don't know if my source was not informed or whether the slant-eyed devils are just playing both ends against the middle again. It might be a power-struggle below the oyabun's level." A friendly leer. "If you could identify them for me, my friend, I'd be glad to share the police reward. Not from Montferrat, from lower down . . . strictly confidential, of course, I wouldn't want to cut into the income you get from those who think this is the safest place in town."

"Suuomalisen, has anyone ever told you what a toad you are?" Yarthkin said, butting out the cigarette in the cold remains of the coffee.

"Many times, many times! But a very *successful* toad." The shrewd little eyes blinked at him. "Harold, my friend, it is a grief to me that you take such little advantage of this excellent base of operations. A fine profit source, and you have wonderful contacts; think of the use you could make of them! You should diversify, my friend. Into contracting, it is a natural with the suppliers you have. Then, with your gambling, you could bid for the lottery contracts . . . perhaps even get into Guild work!"

"I'll leave that to you, Suuomalisen. Your Sauna is a good 'base of operations'; me, I run a bar and some games in the back, and I put people together sometimes. That's all. The tree that grows too high attracts the attention of people with axes."

The fat man shook his head. "You independent entrepreneurs must learn to move with the times, and the time of the little man is past . . . Ah, well, I must be going."

Yarthkin nodded. "Thanks for the tip. I'll have

Wendy send round a case of the *kirsch*. Good stuff, pre-War."

"Pre-War!" The fat man's eyes lit. "Generous, generous. Where do you get such stuff?"

From ex-affluent people who can't pay their gambling debts, Yarthkin thought. "You have to let me keep a few little secrets; little secrets for little men."

A laugh. "And again, any time you wish to join my organization . . . or even just to sell Harold's Terran Bar, my offer stands. I'll even promise to keep on all your people, they make the ambience of the place anyway."

"No deal, Suuomalisen. Thanks for the consideration, though."

Dripping, Jonah padded back out of the shower; at least here in Munchen, nobody was charging you a month's wages for hot water. Ingrid was standing at the window toweling her hair and letting the evening breeze dry the rest of her. The room was narrow, part of an old mansion split into the cubicles of a cheap transient's hotel; there were more luxurious places in easy walking distance, but they would be the haunt of the local elite. He joined her at the opening and put an arm around her shoulders. She sighed and looked down the sloping street to the rippled surface of the Donau and the traffic of sailboats and barges. A metal planter creaked on chains below the window. It smelled of damp earth and half-dead flowers.

"This is the oldest section of Munchen," she said slowly. "There wasn't much else, when I was a student here. Five years ago, my time . . . and the buildings I knew are old and shabby . . . There must be a hundred thousand people living here now!"

He nodded, remembering the sprawling squatter-camps that surrounded the town. "We're going to have to act quickly," he said. "Those passes the oyabun got us are only good for two weeks."

"Right," she said with another sigh, turning from the window. Jonah watched with appreciation as she rummaged in their bags for a series of parts, assembling them into a featureless box and snapping it onto the bedside datachannel. "There are probably blocks on the public channels . . ." She turned her head. "Instead of standing there making the passing girls sigh, why not get some of the other gear put together?"

"Right." Weapons first. The UN had dug deep into the ARM's old stores, confiscated technology that was the product of centuries of perverted ingenuity. Jonah grinned: like most Belters, he had always felt the ARMs tended to err on the side of caution in the role as technological police. Opening their archives had been like pulling teeth, from what he heard, even with the kzin bearing down on Sol system in all their carnivorous splendor. *I bleed for them,* he thought. *I won't say from where.*

The killing-tools were simple, two light-pencils of the sort engineers carried for sketching on screens. Which was actually what they were, and any examination would prove it, according to the ARMs. The only difference was that if you twisted the cap, *so,* pressed down on the clip that held the pen in a pocket and pointed it at an organism with a spinal cord, the pen emitted a sharp yawping sound whereupon said being went into *grand mal* seizure. Range of up to two hundred meters, cause of death, "he died." Jonah frowned. *On second thought, maybe the ARMs were right about this one.*

"Tanj," Ingrid said.

"Problem?"

"No, just that you have to input your ID and pay a whopping great fee to access the commercial net . . . even allowing for the way this fake *krona* they've got has depreciated."

"We've got money."

"Sure, but we don't want to call *too* much attention to ourselves." She continued to tap the keys. "There, I'm past the standard blocks . . . confirming . . . yah, it'd be a bad idea to ask about the security arrangements at you-know-who's place, it's probably flagged."

"Commercial services," Jonah said. "Want me to drive?"

"Not just yet. Right, I'll just look at the record of commercial subcontracts. Hmm. About what you'd expect." Ingrid frowned. "Standard goods delivered to a depot and picked up by kzin military transports, no joy there. Most of the services are provided by household servants, born on the estate . . . no joy there, either. Ahh, outside contractors, now that's interesting."

"What is?" Jonah said, stripping packets of what looked like hard candy out of the lining of a suitcase. Sonic grenades, but you had to spit them at the target.

"Our great and good Rin-Tin-Kzin has been buying infosystems and 'ware from human makers. And he's the only one who is; the ratcat armed forces order subcomponents to their own specs and assemble them in plants under their direct supervision. But not him." She paused in thought. "It fits . . . limited number of system types, like an ascending series, with each step up a set increment of increased capacity over the one below. Nothing like our wild and woolly jungle of manufacturers. They're not used to nonstandardized goods, it makes them uneasy."

"How does that 'fit'?"

"With what the xenologists were saying. The ratcats have an old, old civilization . . . very stable. Like what the UN would have become in Sol system, with the psychists 'adjusting' everybody into peacefulness and the ARMs suppressing dangerous technology . . . which is to say, *all* technology. A few hundred years down the road we'd be on if the kzin hadn't come along and upset the trajectory."

"Maybe they do some good after all." Jonah finished checking the wire garrotes that lay coiled in the seams of their clothing, the tiny repeating blowgun with the poisoned darts, and the harmless-looking fulgurite plastic frames of their backpacks that you twisted *so* and they went soft as putty, with the buckle acting as detonator-timer.

"It fits with what we know about you-know-who, as well." The room had been very carefully swept, but it didn't hurt to take some precautions. Not mentioning names, for one; a robobugger could be set to tag conversations with key words in them. "Unconventional. Wonder why he has human infosystems installed, though? Ours aren't *that* much better. Can't be." Infosystems were a mature technology, long since pushed to the physical limits of quantum indeterminacy.

"Well, they're more versatile, even the obsolete

stuff here on Wunderland. I think—" she tugged at an ear "—I think it may be the 'ware he's after, though. Ratcat 'ware is almost as stereotyped as their hardwiring."

Jonah nodded; software was a favorite cottage industry in human space, and there must be millions of hobbyists who spent their leisure time fiddling with one problem or another. "So we just set up in business and enter a bid?" he said, flopping back on the bed. He was muscular for a Belter, but even the .61 Wunderland gravity was tiring when there was no place to get away from it.

"Doubt it." Ingrid murmured to the system. "Finagle, no joy. It's handled through something called the Datamonger's Guild: 'A mutual benefit association of those involved in infosystem development and maintenance.' Gottknows what that is." A pause. "Whatever it is, there's no public info on how to join it. The contracts listed say you-know-who takes a random selection from their duty roster to do his maintenance work."

"Perhaps our Japanese friend."

"Perhaps." Ingrid sank back on one elbow. "But what we really need are some local contacts," she said slowly. "Jonah . . . we both know why Intelligence picked me as your partner. I was the only one remotely qualified who might know anyone here . . . and I do."

"Which one?" he asked.

She laughed bitterly. "I'd have thought Claude, but he's— Jonah, I wouldn't have believed it!"

Jonah shrugged. "There's an underground surrender movement on Earth. Lots of flatlander quislings;

and the pussies aren't even there yet. Why be surprised there are more here?"

"But Claude! Oh, well."

"So who else you got?"

She continued to tap at the console. "Not many.
None. No one from the old days, none I'd trust,
anyway. Except Harold."

"Can you trust him?"

"Look, we have two choices. Go to Harold, or try
the underworld contacts. The known-unreliable underworld contacts."

"One of whom is your friend Harold."

She sighed. "Yes, but—well, that's a good sign,
isn't it? That he's worked with the—with them, and
against—"

"Maybe."

"And a bar is a good place to meet people."

*And mostly you just can't wait to see him. A man
who'll be twice your age while you're still young. Do
you love him or hate him?* "I still say it's damned
iffy, but I guess it's the best chance we have. At least
we'll be able to get a drink."

Chapter IV

"This is supposed to be a *Terran* bar?" Jonah asked dubiously. He lifted one of the greenish shrimpoids from the platter and clumsily shelled it, getting a thin cut under his thumbnail in the process. He sucked on it, cursing. There was a holo of a stick-thin girl with body paint dancing in a cage over the bar, and dancing couples and groups beneath it. Most of the tables were cheek-to-jowl, and they had had to pay heavily for one with a shield, here overlooking the lower level of the club.

Ingrid ignored him, focusing on the knot in her stomach and the clammy feel of nervous sweat across her shoulders under the formal low-necked black jumpsuit. Harold's Terran Bar was crowded tonight, and the entrance-fee had been stiff. The *Verguuz* was excellent, however, and she sipped cautiously, welcoming the familiar mint-sweet-*wham* taste. The imitations in the Sol system never quite measured up. Shuddering, she noticed that two Swarm-Belter types at the next table were knocking back shot-glasses of it, and then following the liqueur with beer chasers, in a mixture of extravagance and reckless disregard for their digestions. The square-built Krio at the musicomp was tinkling out something old-sounding, piano with muted saxophone undertones.

Gottdamn, but that takes me back.

Claude had had an enormous collection of classical music, expensively enhanced stuff originally recorded on Earth, some of it on hardcopy or analog disks. His grandfather had acquired it; one of the eccentricities that had ruined the Montferrat-Palme fortunes. A silver-chased ebony box as big as a man's head, with a marvelous projection system. All the ancient greats, Brahms and Mozart and Jagger and Armstrong . . . they had all spent hours up in his miserable little attic, knocking back cheap Maivin and playing *Eine Kleine Nachtmusik* or *Sympathy for the Devil* loud enough to bring hammering broomstick protests from the people below . . .

Gottdamn, it is *him,* she thought, with a sudden flare of determination.

"Jonah," she said, laying a hand on his arm. "This is too public, and we can't just wait for him. It's . . . likely to be something of a shock, you know? That musician, I knew him back-when too. I'll get him to call through directly, it'll be faster."

The Sol-Belter nodded tightly; she squeezed the forearm before she rose. In space, or trying to penetrate an infosystem, both rank and skill made him the leader; here the mission and his life were both dependent on her. And on her contacts, decades old here, and severed in no friendly wise. Ingrid moistened her lips; Sam had been on the edge of their circle of friends, and confronting him would be difficult enough. She wiped palms down her slacks and walked over to the musicomp; it was a handsome floor model in Svarterwood, with a beautiful point resonator and a damper field to ensure that nothing came from the area around it but the product of the keyboard.

"*G'tag*, Sam," she said, standing by one side of the instrument. "Still picking them out, I see."

"*Fra?*" he said, looking up at her with the dignified politeness of a well-raised Krio country-boy. She saw for the first time that one side of Sam's face was immobile; she recognized the signs of a rushed reconstruction job of the type they did after severe nerve-damage in the surface tissues.

"Well, I haven't changed *that* much, Sam. Remember Graduation Night, and that singalong we all had by the Founders?"

His features changed, from the surface smoothness of a well-trained professional to a shock so profound that the living tissue went as rigid as the dead. "Fra Raines," he whispered. The skilled hands continued over the musicomp's surface, but the tune had changed without conscious intent. He winced and hesitated, but she put a hand on his shoulder.

"No, keep playing, Sam."

Remember me and you
And you and me
Together forever
I can't see me lovin' nobody but you—
For all my life

The musician shook his head. "The boss doesn't

like me to play that one, Fra Raines," he said. "It reminds him, well, you'd know."

"I know, Sam. But this is bigger than any of us, and it means we can't let the past sleep in its grave. Call him, tell him we're waiting."

"Mr. Yarthkin?" the voice asked.

He had been leaning a shoulder against one wall of the inner room, watching the roulette table. The smoke in here was even denser than by the front bar, and the ornamental fans made patterns and traceries through the blue mist. Walls were set for a space scene, a holo of Jupiter taken from near orbit on one side and Wunderland on the other. Beyond them the stars were hard glitters, pinpoints of colored light receding into infinity, infinitely out of reach. Yarthkin dropped his eyes to the table. The ventilation system was too good to carry the odor of the sweat that gleamed on the hungrily intent faces . . .

Another escape, he thought. Like the religious revivals and the nostalgia craze, even the feverish corruption and pursuit of wealth was but a distraction.

"*Herrenmann* Yarthkin-Schotmann?" the voice asked again, and a hand touched his elbow.

He looked down, into a girl's face framed in a black kerchief. Repurified Mennonite, by the long drab dress. Well-to-do, by the excellent material; many of that sect were. Wunderland had never relied much on synthetic foods, and the *Herrenmann* estates had used the Amish extensively as subtenants. They had flourished, particularly since the kzin came and agricultural machinery grew still scarcer . . . That was ending now, of course.

"No 'Herrenmann,' sweetheart," he said gently. She was obviously terrified, this would be a den of Satan by her folk's teaching. "Just Harold, or Mr. Yarthkin if you'd rather. What can I do for you?"

She clasped her gloved hands together, a frown on the delicately pretty features and a wisp of blond hair escaping from her scarf and bonnet. "Oh . . . I was wondering if you could give me some advice, please, Mr. Yarthkin, everyone says you know what goes on in Munchen." He heard the horror in her voice as she named the city, probably from a lifetime of hearing it from the pulpit followed by "Whore of Babylon" or some such.

"Advice I provide free," he said neutrally. *Shut up*, he added to his mind. *There's thousands more in trouble just as bad as hers. None of your business.*

"Wilhelm and I," she began, and then halted to search for words. Harold's eyes flickered up to a dark-clad young man with a fringe of beard around his face sitting at the roulette table. Sitting slumped, placing his chips with mechanical despair.

"Wilhelm and I, we lost the farm." She put a hand to her eyes. "It wasn't his fault, we both worked so hard . . . but the kzin, they took the estate where we were tenants and . . ."

Yarthkin nodded. Kzin took a *lot* of feeding, and they would not willingly eat grain-fed meat, they wanted lean range beasts. More kzin estates meant less work for humans, and what there was was in menial positions, not the big tenant holdings for mixed farming that the *Herrenmenn* had preferred. Farmholders reduced to beggary, or to an outlaw existence that ended in a kzin hunt.

"Your church wouldn't help?" he said. The Amish were a close-knit breed.

"They found new positions for our workers, but the bishop, the bishop said Wilhelm . . . that there was no money to buy him a new tenancy, that he should humble himself and take work as a foreman and pray for forgiveness." Repurified Mennonites thought that worldly failure was punishment for sin. "Wilhelm, Wilhelm is a good man, I told him to listen to the bishop but he cursed him to his face, and now we are shunned." She paused. "Things, things are very bad there now. It is no place to live or raise children, with food so scarce and many families crowded together."

"Sweetheart, this isn't a charitable institution," Yarthkin said warily.

"No, Mr. Yarthkin." She drew herself up and wrapped pride around herself like a cloak. "We had some money, we sold everything, the stock and tools. Swarm Agrobiotics offered Wilhelm and me a place, they are terraforming new farm-asteroids. With what they pay we could afford to buy a new tenancy after a few years." He nodded. The Swarm's population was growing by leaps and bounds, and it was cheaper to grow than synthesize, but skilled dirt-farmers were rare. "But we must be there soon, and there are so many difficulties with the papers."

Bribes, Yarthkin translated to himself.

"It takes so much more than we thought, and to live while we wait! Now we have not enough for the final clearance, and . . . and we know nothing but farming. The policeman told Wilhelm that we must have four thousand *krona* more, and we had less than a thousand. Nobody would lend more against his wages, not even the Sina moneylender, he just laughed and offered to . . . to sell me to . . . and Wilhelm hit him, and we had to pay more to the police. Now he gambles, it is the only way we might get the money, but of course he loses."

The house always wins, Yarthkin thought. The girl steeled herself and continued.

"The *Herrenmann* policeman—"

"Claude Montferrat-Palme?" Yarthkin inquired, nodding with his chin. The police chief was over at the baccarat tables with a glass of Verguuz at his elbow, playing his usual cautiously skillful game.

"Yes," she whispered. "He told me that there was a way the papers could be approved." A silence. "I said nothing to Wilhelm, he is . . . very young, younger than me in some ways." The china-blue eyes turned to him. "Is this *Herrenmann* one who keeps his word?"

"Claude?" Yarthkin said. "Yes. A direct promise, yes; he'll keep the letter of it."

She gripped her hands tighter. "I do not know what to do," she said softly. "I must think."

She nodded jerkily to herself and moved off. Yarthkin threw the butt of his cigarette down for the floor to absorb and moved over to the roulette table. A smile quirked the corner of his mouth, and he picked up a handful of hundred-*krona* chips from in front of the croupier. *Stupid,* he thought to himself. *Oh, well, a man has to make a fool of himself occasionally.*

The Amishman had dropped his last chip and was waiting to lose it; he gulped at the drink at his elbow and loosened the tight collar of his jacket. *Probably seeing the Welfare Office ahead of him,* Yarthkin thought. These days, that meant a labor camp where the room-and-board charges were twice the theoretical wages . . . They would find something else for his wife to do. Yarthkin dropped his counter beside the young farmer's.

"I'm feeling lucky tonight, Toni," he said to the croupier. "We'll play the black. Let's see it."

She raised one thin eyebrow, shrugged her shoulders under the sequins and spun the wheel. "Place your bets, gentlefolk, please." Impassively, she tossed the ball into the whirring circle of metal. "Number eight. Even, in the black."

The Amishman blinked down in astonishment as the croupier's ladle pushed his doubled stake toward him. Yarthkin reached out and gripped his wrist as the young man made an automatic motion towards the plaques. It was thick and springy with muscle, the arm of a man who had worked with his hands all his life, but Yarthkin had no difficulty stopping the motion.

"Let it ride," he said. "Play the black. I'll do the same."

Another spin, but the croupier's lips were compressed into a thin line; she was a professional, and hated a break in routine. "Place your bets . . . Black wins again, gentlefolk."

"Try twelve," Yarthkin said, shifting his own chip. "No, all of it."

"Place your bets . . . Twelve wins, gentlefolk."

Glancing up, Yarthkin caught Montferrat's coldly furious eye, and grinned with an equal lack of warmth. At the next spin of the wheel he snapped his finger for the waiter and urged the younger man at his side to his feet, piling the chips on an emptied drink tray.

"That's five thousand," Yarthkin said. "Why don't you cash them in and call it a night?"

Wilhelm paused, scrubbed his hands across his face, straightened his rumpled clothes. "Yes . . . yes, thank you, sir, perhaps I should." He looked down at the pile of chips, and Yarthkin could see his lips whiten with shock as the impact hit home. "I . . ."

The girl came to meet him, and gave Yarthkin a single glance through tear-starred lashes before the two left, clinging to each other. The owner of Harold's shrugged and pushed his own counters back to the pile before the croupier.

"How are we doing tonight, Toni?" he asked.

"About five thousand *krona* less well than we could have," she said sharply.

"We'll none of us starve," Yarthkin added mildly, and strolled over to the baccarat table.

Montferrat raised an eyebrow and smiled thinly. His anger had faded. "You're a sentimental idiot, Harry."

"Probably true, Claude," Yarthkin said, and took a plain unlogoed credit chip from the inside pocket of his jacket. "The usual."

Montferrat palmed it and smoothed back his mustache with a finger. "Sometimes I think you indulge in these little quixotic gestures just to annoy me," he added, and dropped three cards from his hand. "Banco," he continued.

"Probably right there, too, Claude," he said. "I'm relying on the fact that you're not an unmitigated scoundrel."

"Now I'm an honest man?"

"No, a scoundrel with mitigating factors . . . and I'm a sentimental idiot, as you mentioned." He

stopped, listened abstractedly. "See you later, somebody wants to see me. Sam says it's important, and
he isn't given to exaggeration."

The doors slid open and Yarthkin stepped into the
main room, beside the north end of the long bar.
The music was the first thing he heard, the jaunty
remembered beat. Cold flushed over his skin, and the
man he had been smiling and waving to flinched.
That brought the owner of Harold's Place back to his
duties; they were self-imposed, and limited to this
building, but that did not mean they could be shirked.
He moved with swift grace through the throng, shouting an occasional greeting over the surf-roar of voices,
slapping a shoulder, shaking a hand, smiling. The
smile was still on his face as he stepped up off the
dance floor and through the muting field around the
musicomp, but he could taste the acid and copper of
his own rage at the back of his throat.

"*I told you never to play that song again,*" he said
coldly. "*We've been together a long time, Samuel
Ogun, it'd be a pity to end a beautiful friendship this
way.*"

The musician keyed the instrument to continue
without him and swiveled to face his employer. "Boss
. . . Mr. Yarthkin, once you've talked to those two
over at Table Three, you'll understand. Believe me."

Yarthkin nodded curtly and turned to the table.
The two Belters were sitting close to the musicomp,
with the shimmer of a privacy field around them,
shrouding features as well as dulling voices. Yarthkin
smoothed the lapels of his jacket and wove deftly
between tables and servers as he approached, forcing his anger down into an inner cesspit where dis-

carded emotions went. Sam was no fool, he must mean *something* by violating a standing order that old. He did not shake easy, either, and that he had been was plain to see on him. This should be interesting, at least; it would be good to have a straightforward bargaining session after the embarrassing exhilaration of the incident in the gambling room. Money was a relaxing game to play, the rules were clear, victory and defeat a matter of counting the score, and no embarrassing emotions; and these *might* be the ones with the special load that the rumors had told of. More profit and more enjoyment if they were . . . more danger, too, but a man had to take an occasional calculated risk. Otherwise, you might as well put a droud in your head and be done with it.

The man looked thirty and might be anything between that and seventy: tough-looking, without the physical softness that so many rockjacks got from a life spent in cramped zero-G spaceships. A conservative dark innersuit, much less gaudy than what most successful Swarmers wore these days, and an indefinably foreign look about the eyes. Yarthkin sat, pulled out a chair and looked over to study the woman's face. The world went black.

"Boss, are you all right?" There was a sharp hiss against his neck, and the sudden sharp-edged alertness of a stimshot. "Are you all right?"

"You," Yarthkin whispered, shaking the Krio's hand off his shoulder with a shrug. Ingrid's face hovered before him, unchanged, no, a little thinner, more tanned. But the *same*, not forty years different, the *same*. He could feel things moving in his head, like a mountain river he had seen on a spring hunting trip once. Cracks running across black ice, and the rock beneath his feet toning with the dark water's hidden power. "You." His voice went guttural, and his right hand went inside the dress jacket.

"Jonah, no!" Ingrid's hand shot out and slapped her companion's to the table. Yarthkin felt his mind stagger and broach back toward reality as the danger-prickle ran over his skin; that was probably *not* an engineer's light-pencil in the younger man's hand. He struggled for self-command, dropped his gun-hand back to the table.

"Well." What was there to say? "Long time, no see. Glad you could make it. The last time, you seemed to have a pressing appointment elsewhere. *I* showed up on time—and there the 'boat was, boosting like hell a couple of million klicks Solward. Me in a singleship with half a dozen kzin Slashers sniffing around."

Ingrid's face went chalk-white. "Let me explain—"

"Don't bother. Closed account." He paused, lit a cigarette, astonished at the steadiness of his own hands.

"Claude know you're here?"

"No, and it's best he doesn't."

"Sure. Let me guess. Now you're back, and Mr. Quick-Draw here with you, on some sort of UN skullbuggery, and need my help." He looked thoughtful. "Come to that, how did you get here?"

"Jonah Matthieson," the Sol-Belter said. "How we got here isn't important. But we do need your help. Damned little we've gotten in this system that hasn't been bought and paid for, and half the time we've been sold out to the pussies even so."

"Pussies? Oh, the ratcats." He laughed, a little

wildly. "So you haven't found legions of eager, idealistic volunteers ready to throw themselves into the jaws of the kzin to help you on your sacred mission, whatever it is. How *can* that be?"

"We can pay."

"Pay. Well, well, the UN has money." Yarthkin's finger touched behind one ear, and the mirror behind the bar went screenmode. It showed an overgrown park, flicking between micropickups scattered wholesale through the vegetation. There had been lawns here once; now there was waist-high grass, Earth trees grown to scores of meters in the light gravity, native Wunderlander growths soaring on spidery trunks. The sound of panting breath, and a naked human came stumbling through the undergrowth. His legs and flanks were lashed and scratched by thorns and burrs. He reeled with exhaustion, feet pounding with careless heaviness; the eyes were flat and blank in the stubbled face, mouth dribbling. Behind him there was a flash of orange-red, alien among the cool greens of Earth, the tawny olives of Wunderland. A flash, two hundred kilos of sentient carnivore charging on all fours in a hunching rush that parted the long grass in an arrow of rippling wind. Not so much like a cat as a giant weasel, blurring, looming up behind the fleeing human in a wall of flesh, a wall that fell tipped with bright teeth and black claws.

The screaming began at once, sank to a bubbling sound and the wet tearing noises of feeding. Shouts of protest rose from the dance floor and the other tables, and the sound of someone vomiting into an expensive meal. Yarthkin touched the spot behind his ear and the screen switched back to mirror. The protests lasted longer, and the staff of Harold's went among the patrons to soothe with free drinks and apologies, murmurs. *Technical mistake, government override, here, let me fix that for you, gentlefolk. . . .*

"And that," Yarthkin said, "is a *good* reason why you're not going to be finding hordes beating down your door to volunteer. For glory or for money. We've been living with that for *forty years*, you fool. While you in the Sol system sat fat and happy and safe."

Jonah leaned forward. "I'm here now, aren't I? Neither fat, nor very happy, and not at all safe right now. I was in two fleet actions, Mr. Yarthkin. Out of four. Earth's been fighting the kzin since I was old enough to vote. We haven't lost so far. Been close a couple of times, but we haven't lost. We could have stayed home. Note we didn't. Ingrid and I are considerably less safe than you."

Ingrid and I, Yarthkin thought, looking at the faces, side by side. The *young* faces. Sol-Belter. *Hotshot pilot. Secret agent. All-round romantic hero, come to save us worthless pussy-whipped peons.* Tonight seemed to be a night for powerful emotions, something he had been trying to unlearn. Now he felt hatred strong and thick, worse than anything he had ever felt for the kzin. Worse even than he had felt for himself, for a long time.

"So what do you need?"

"A way into the Datamonger's Guild for a start."

Yarthkin looked thoughtful. "That's easy enough." He realized that Ingrid had been holding her breath. *Bad. She wants this bad. How bad?*

"And any other access to the—to networks."

"Networks. Sure. Networks. Any old networks,

right? Want into Claude's system? Want to see his
private files? What else would you like?"

"Harry—"

"I can do that, you know. Networks."

She didn't say anything.

"Help. You want help," he said slowly. "Well, that
leaves only one question." He poured himself a drink
in Jonah's water-glass, tossed it back. "What will you
pay?"

"Anything we have. Anything you want."

"*Anything?*"

"Of course. When do you want me?"

"Ingrid—"

"Not your conversation, Belter. Get lost."

The club was dim, with the distinctive stale chill
smell of tobacco and absent people that came in the
hours just before dawn. Yarthkin sat at the table and
sipped methodically at the Verguuz; it was a shame
to waste it on just getting drunk, but owning a bar
did have *some* advantages. He took another swallow,
letting the smooth sweet minty taste flow over his
tongue, then breathing out as the cold fire ran back
up his throat. A pull at the cigarette, one of the
clove-scented ones well-to-do Ba'hai smoked, *my aren't
we wallowing in sensual indulgence tonight*.

"Play," he said to the man at the musicomp. The
Krio started and ran his fingers over the surface
of the instrument, and the brassy complexities of
Meddlehoffer lilted out into the deserted silence
of the room.

"Not that," Yarthkin said, and knocked back the
rest of the Verguuz. "You know what I want."

"No, you don't," Sam said. "That's a *manti-manti*

mara," he continued, dropping back into his native tongue: a great stupidity. "What you want is to get drunk and *manyamanya*, smash something up. Go ahead, it's your bar."

"I said, *play it*." The musician shrugged, and began the ancient melody. The husky voice followed:

". . . no matter what we say or do—"

A contralto joined it: *"so happy together."*

They both looked up with a start. Ingrid dropped into a chair across from Yarthkin, reached for the bottle and poured herself a glass.

"Isn't there enough for two?" she asked, raising a brow in response to his scowl. The musician rose, and Yarthkin waved him back.

"You don't have to leave, Sam."

"Do I have to stay? No? Then it's late, boss, and I'm going for bed. See you tomorrow."

"Where's the Sol-Belter?" Yarthkin asked. His voice was thickened but not slurred, and his hand was steady as he poured.

"In the belly of the whale . . . Still working in your office." *And trying not to think about what we're doing. Or will be doing in a minute, if you're sober enough.* "That's a pretty impressive system you have there."

"Yeah. And I'm taking a hell of a chance letting you two use it."

"So are we."

"So are we all. Honorable men, all, all honorable men. And women. Honorable."

"Hari—"

"That's *Herr* Yarthkin to you, Lieutenant."

"If you let me explain—"

"Explain what?"

"Hari, the rendezvous time was fixed, and you didn't make it! We *had* to boost, there were hundreds of lives riding on it."

"Oh, no, Lieutenant Raines. The *ships* had to boost, and we had to keep the kzin off your backs as long as we could. Not every pilot had to go with them."

"Angers was dying, radiation sickness, puking her guts out. Flambard's nerve had gone, Finagle's sake, Hari, I was the best they had, and—" she stopped, looking at his face, slumped. "Long ago, long ago."

Not so long for you as for me, he thought. Her face was the same, not even noticeably aged. What was different, where did the memory lie? *Unformed*, he thought. *She looks . . . younger than I remember. Not as much behind the eyes.*

"Long ago, kid. How'd you get here?"

"You wouldn't believe me if I told you."

"Probably I wouldn't. That raid—"

She nodded. "That raid. The whole reason for that raid was to get us here."

"For God's sake, why?"

"I can't tell you."

"It's part of the price, sweetheart."

"Literally, I can't," Ingrid said. "Post-hypnotic. Reinforced with—the psychists have some new tricks. Har', I would literally die before I told you, or anyone else."

"Even if they're taking you apart?"

She nodded.

Harold thought about that for a moment and shuddered. "OK. It was a long time ago, and maybe—maybe you saw things I didn't see. You always were bigger on romantic causes than the rest of us." He stood.

She got to her feet and stood expectantly. "Where?"

"There's a bedroom upstairs."

She nodded. "I've—I've thought about this a lot."

"Not as much as I have. You haven't had as long."

She laughed. "That's right."

"So now I'm old—"

"No. Not old, Hari. Not old. Which way? The stairs over there?"

"Just a minute, kid. So. Assuming it works, whatever you and the Belter have planned, what afterward?"

"Once that's done it doesn't matter."

"Sure it does."

"Well, we brought a ship with us. Nice boat, the best the UN's making these days. Markham's keeping her for us, and then we'll do the guerrilla circuit afterwards."

"Markham? Ulf *Reichstein*-Markham?" An old enmity sharpened his tone, one less personal. "A legitimate bastard of a long line of bastards, who does his best to out-bastard them all. He'd cut your throat for six rounds of pistol ammunition, if he needed them."

"Didn't strike me as a bandit."

"Worse. True Believer . . . and you can whistle in the wind for that ship."

She smiled. "That ship, you might say she has a mind of her own. Really; we've got a hold on it."

Then you'll be off to the Swarm, Yarthkin thought. *Playing dodgem with the ratcats, you and that Jonah. Flirting with danger and living proud.* There was a taste of bile at the back of his mouth. Remembering the long slow years of defeat, strength crumbling away as one after another of them despaired; until nothing was left but the fanatics and the outlaws, a nuisance to the enemy and a deadly danger to their own people. What was the honor in going on with the killing when it had all turned pointless and rancid? No more than in taking the amnesty and picking up the pieces of life. *But not for you. You and Jonah, you'll win or go out in a blaze of glory. No dirty alliances and dirtier compromises and decisions with no good choices. The two of you have stolen my life.*

"Get out," he said. "Get the hell out."

"No." She took his hand and led him toward the stairs.

Chapter V

"They've accepted our bid, Captain."

Jonah nodded stiffly. "Thank you, Lieutenant. Not that I'm surprised."

"No, sir."

Back in Sol System a thousand hackers had labored to produce advanced software they thought might be salable on Wunderland. Most of it had been too advanced; they'd predicted a higher state of the art than Wunderland had retained, and the stuff wouldn't work on the ancient hardware. Even so, there was plenty that did work. It had only taken fifty days to make Jan Hardman and Lucy van den Berg moderately big names in the Datamonger's Guild. The computer records showed them as old timers, with a scattering of previous individual sales. They told everyone on the net that they owed their big success to teaming up.

Teaming up. A damned tough fifty days . . . Jonah looked unashamedly at Ingrid. "I admit you've improved *Herr* Yarthkin's disposition one whole hell of a lot, but do you have to look so tanjhappy?"

"Capt—Jonah, I *am* happy."

"Yeah."

"I—Jonah, I'm sorry if it hurts you."

"Yeah. All right, Lieutenant. We've got work to do."

"These are the same monkeys as before." The guards spoke in the Hero's Tongue. "The computer says they have access."

The kzin tapped a large button on the console, and the door lifted.

Jonah and Ingrid cringed and waited. The kzin sniffed, then led the way outside. Another kzin warrior followed, and two more fell in on either side. The routine had been the same the other two times they had been there.

This will be different. Maybe. Jonah pushed the thoughts away. Kzin weren't really telepathic but they could sense excitement and smell fear. *Of course the fear's natural. They probably like that scent.*

Sunlight was failing behind evening clouds, and the air held a dank chill and the wild odors of storm-swept grassland. The two humans crossed the landing field between forms a third again their height, living walls of orange-red fur; claws slid out in unconscious reflex on the stocks of their heavy beam rifles. Jonah kept his eyes carefully down. It would be an unbearable irony if they were killed by reflex, victims of some overzealous kzin spooked by the upsurge in guerrilla activity. The attack of the *Yamamoto* had created the chaos that let them into Wunderland, but that same chaos just might kill them. Doors slid aside, and they descended into chill corridors like a dreadnought's, surfaces laced with armored data conduits and the superconducting coil-complexes of field generators.

One of the kzin followed. "This way," he said, prodding Jonah's shoulder with the muzzle of his weapon. The light down here was reddish, frequencies adjusted to the alien's convenience; the air was drier, colder than humans would have wished. And everything was too *big*, grips and stairs and doors adapted to a thick-bodied, short-legged race with the bulk of terrestrial gorillas.

They went through a chamber filled with computer consoles. This was as far as they'd been allowed the last two times. "Honored Governor Chuut-Riit is pleased with your work," the kzin officer said.

"We are honored," Ingrid said.

"This way." The kzin led them through another door. They stepped into an outsized transfer booth, were instantly elsewhere. Gravity increased to the kzin homeworld standard, sagging their knees, and they stepped through into another checkzone. The desire to gawk around was intolerable, but the gingery smell of kzin was enough to restrain them as they walked through a thick sliding door. The transfer booth was inside an armored box, and he recognized the snouts of heavy remote-waldoed weapons up along the edges of the roof. Outside was another control room, a dozen kzin operators lying recumbent on spaceship-style swiveling couches before semicircular consoles. Their helmets were not the featureless wraparounds humans would have used; these had thin crystal facepieces, adjustable audio pickups and cutouts for the ears. Not as efficient, but probably a psychological necessity. Kzin have keener senses than man, but are more vulnerable to claustrophobia, any sort of confinement that cuts off the flow of scent, sound, light.

Patience comes harder to them, too, Jonah thought, as they penetrated another set of armored doors to the ultimate sanctum. *At last!*

"Accomplish your work," the kzin said. "The inspector will arrive in six hours. Sanitary facilities are there."

Jonah exhaled a long breath as the alien left. Now there was only the featureless four-meter box of the control room; the walls were a neutral pearly white, ready to transmit visual data. The only consol was a standup model in the centre, with both human and kzin seating arrangements before it. Ingrid and he exchanged a wordless glance as they walked to it and began unpacking their own gear, snapping out the support tripod and sliding home the thin black lines of the data jacks.

A long pause, while their fingers played over the small black rectangles of their portable interfacing units; the only sound was a subliminal sough of ventilators and the faint natural chorus that the kzin always broadcast through the speakers of a closed installation: insects and the rustle of vegetation. Jonah felt a familiar narrowing, a focus of concentration more intense than sex or even combat, as the lines of a program-schematic sprang out on his unit.

"Finagle, talk about paranoids," he muttered. "See this freeze-function here?"

Ingrid's face was similarly intent, and the rushing flicker of the scroll-display on her unit gave her face a momentary look as of light through stained glass. "Got it. Freeze."

"We're bypassed?"

"This is under our authorized codes. All right, these are the four major subsystems. See the physical channeling? The hardware won't accept config commands of more than 10k except through this channel we're at."

"Slow response, for a major system like this," he mused. The security locks were massive and complex, but a little cumbrous.

"It's the man-kzin hardware interfacing," Ingrid said. "I think. Their basic architecture's more synchronic. Betcha they never had an industrial-espionage problem . . . Hey, notice that?"

"Ahhhh. Interesting." Jonah kept his voice carefully phlegmatic. *Tricky kitty. Tricky indeed.* "Odd. This would be much harder to access through the original Hero system."

"Tanj, you're right," Ingrid said. She looked up with an urchin grin that blossomed with the pure delight of solving a software problem.

Jonah gave her a cautioning look.

Her face went back to a mask of concentration. "Clearly this was designed with security against *kzin* in mind. See, here and here? That's why they've deliberately preserved the original human operating system on this—two of them, and used this spatchcocked integral translation chip here, see?"

"Right!" His fingers flew. "In fact, if analyzed with the original system as an integrating node and catchpoint . . . see?"

"Right. Murphy, but you'd have more luck wandering through a minefield than trying to get at this from an exterior connection! There's nothing in the original stem system *but* censor programs; by the

time you got by them, the human additions would have
alarmed and frozen. Catches you on the interface
transitions, see? That's why they haven't tried to
bring the core system up to the subsystem operating
speeds. Sure slows things down, though."

"We'll just have to live with it," Jonah said for the
benefit of any hidden listeners. It seemed unlikely.
There weren't many kzin programmers, and all of
them were working for the navy or the government.
This was the strictly personal system of Governor
Chuut-Riit.

"Wheels within wheels," Ingrid muttered.

"Right." Jonah shook his head; there was a certain
perverse beauty in using a cobbled-up rig's own lack
of functional integration as a screening mechanism.
*But all designed against kzinti. Not against us. Ye
gods, it would be easy enough for Chuut-Riit's rivals
to work through humans—*

*Only none of them would think of that. This is the
only estate that uses outside contractors. And the
Heroes don't think that way to begin with.*

His fingers flew. Ingrid—Lieutenant Raines—would
be busy installing the new data management system
they were supposed to be working at. What he was
doing was far beyond her. Jonah let his awareness
and fingers work together, almost bypassing his conscious mind. Absently he reached for a squeeze-bulb
before he remembered that the nearest Jolt Cola was
four lightyears away.

*Now. Bypass the kzin core system. Move into the
back door.* He keyed in the ancient passwords embedded into the Wunderland computer system by
Earth hackers almost a hundred years before. Terran
corporate managers had been concerned about com-

petition, and they'd built backdoors into every operating system destined for Wunderland. A built-in
industrial espionage system. And the kzin attack and
occupation should have kept the Wunderlanders from
finding them . . .

"/ Murphy Magic. The SeCrEt of the UnIvErSe is
43, NOT 42."

"$"

"There is justice," Jonah muttered.

"Joy?"

"Yeah." He typed furiously.

She caught her breath. "All right."

*By the time the core realizes what's going on, we'll
all be dead.* "May take a while. Here we go."

Two hours later he was done. He looked over at
Ingrid. She had long finished, except for sending the
final signals that would tell the system they were
done. "About ready," he said.

She caught her breath. "All right."

For a moment he was shocked at the dark half-
moons below her eyes, the lank hair sweat-plastered
to her cheeks, and then concentration dropped enough
for him to feel his own reaction. Pain clamped at his
stomach, and the muscles of his lower back screamed
protest at the posture he had been frozen in for long
hours of extra gravity.

He raised his hand to his mouth and extended the
little finger back to the rear molars. Precisely ma-
chined surfaces slipped into nanospaced fittings in
the vat-cultured substitute that had been serving
him as a fingernail; anything else would have wiped
the coded data. He took a deep breath and pulled;
there was a flash of pain before the embedded duller

drugs kicked in, and then it settled to a tearing ache. The raw surface of the stripped finger was before him, the wrist clenched in the opposite hand. Ingrid moved forward swiftly to bandage it, and he spat the translucent oblong into his palm.

"Tanj," he said resentfully. *Those sadistic flat-lander morons could have used a nervepinch.*

Ingrid picked the biochip up between thumb and forefinger. She licked her lips nervously. "Will it work?"

"It's supposed to." The sound of his own pulse in his ears was louder than the background noise the kzin used to fool their subconscious into comfort. Pain receded, irrelevant, as he looked at the tiny oblong of modified claw. Scores of highly-skilled men and women, thousands of hours of computer time on machines whose price-tags ran in the billions of stars, all for this. No, for the *information* contained in this . . . nearly as much information as was required to make a complete human body, it was amazing what they could do these days with quantum-well storage. Although the complete specs for a man were in a packet considerably smaller, if it came to that.

"Give it here." *It ought to be quick. Milliseconds quick. A lot better than being hunted down by the ratcats.* She handed over the nail, and he slipped it into his own interface unit. "As your boyfriend likes to say, here's viewing, *kinder.*"

She nodded tightly. He raised a thumb, pressed it down on one of the outlined squares of the schematic that occupied his interfacer. "Ram dam," he said. The words came from nowhere, and an eerie memory of old Mukeriji speaking flitted through his mind. *Dreadful Bride, spare us: ram dam ram dam ram—*

The walls pulsed, flickered green, flashed into an intricate strobing pattern and froze. Jonah closed his eyes for a second and felt an enormous thankfulness. They might still be only seconds away from death, but at least it wouldn't be for *nothing*.

"Finagle!" Jonah said bitterly. "How could even a kzin be this paranoid?" He kicked the pillar-console; it hurt through the light slipper. There were weapons and self-destruct systems in plenty, enough to leave nothing but a very large crater with magma at its core where Chuut-Riit's palace-estate had stood . . . but it wasn't clear how any of them could be triggered from here. "Who ever heard of . . . wheels within wheels!" Jonah said disbelievingly. "Am I imagining things, or are these systems completely separated?"

Ingrid shook her head slowly. "I'm afraid that's a long way past me. Can't you do anything with it?"

"Maybe. There's a chance. Worth a try, anyway." He touched icons on the screen surface, then tapped in new commands. "Nope. All right, what does this do? Nothing. Hmm. But if— Yeah, this may work. Not immediately, though. You about through?"

"Hours ago. We don't have much longer."

"Right. I do want to look at a couple of things, though." Jonah's eyes narrowed. "Call," he said to the computer. "Weekly schedule for user-CR, regression, six months, common elements." His finger flicked out to a sequence on the wall ahead of them. "Got it! Got it, by Murphy's asshole; that's the single common element outside going to his office! What is it?"

Ingrid's fingers were busy. "No joy, Jonah. That's

his visit to his kiddies. The males. They're in an isolation facility."

"Oh. Bat puckey. Here, let me look—"

A warning light blazed on the console.

"They're coming," Ingrid hissed. "Hurry."

"Right. Plan B. Only—" Jonah stared at the files in wonder. "I will be dipped in shit."

"We have positive identification," Axelrod-Bauer-gartner said. The staff conference rustled, ten men and women grouped around a table of black ebony. It was an elegant room, walls of white stone fretwork and floor of tile, a sideboard with refreshments. No sound but the gentle rush of water in the courtyard outside; this had been the *Herrenhaus*, the legislature, before the kzin came.

Claude Montferrat leaned forward slightly and looked down the table to his second in command. How alike we all are, he thought. Not physical appearance, but something about the eyes . . . She was a pallid woman, with a beginning potbelly disgusting on someone her age, hair cropped close on the left and in a braided ponytail on the other.

"Oh?" he drawled. It was important to crack this case and quickly, Supervisor-of-Animals was on his track. Unwise to have a subordinate take too much credit for it, particularly this one, she had been using her own dossier files to build influence in the higher echelons of human government. Two can play at that game, he thought. And I do it better, since relying on blackmail alone is a crudity I've grown beyond. She doesn't know I've penetrated her files, either . . . of course, she may have done likewise . . .

No. He would be dead if she had.

"From their hotel room. No correlation on finger-prints, of course." Alterations to fingerprints and retina patterns were an old story; you never caught anyone with access to underworld tailoring shops that way. "But they evidently whiled away their spare time with the old in-and-out, and they don't clean the mattresses there very well. DNA analysis.

"Case A, display," she continued. Sections of the ebony before each of the staff officers turned transpar-ent, a molecular analysis. "This is the male, what forensic could make of it. Young, not more than thirty. Sol-Belter, to 93%. Here's a graphic of his face, projection from the genes and descriptions by hotel staff."

A portrait overlaid the lines and curves of the analysis, a hard-lined blocky face with a short Belter strip. "This doesn't include any scars or birthmarks, of course."

"Very interesting," Montferrat drawled. "But as you're no doubt aware, chance recombination could easily reproduce a Sol-Belter genetic profile; the Ser-pent Swarm was only colonized three centuries ago, and there has been immigration since. Our records from the Belt are not complete, you know the trou-ble we've been having getting them to tighten up on registration."

Axelrod-Bauergartner shook her head, smiling thinly. "Less than a 3% chance, when you correlate with the probability of that configuration, then elimi-nate the high percentage of Swarmers we do have full records on. Beautiful job on the false idents, by the way. If we hadn't been tipped we'd never have found them.

"And this," she said, calling up another analysis,

"is the female. Also young, ten years post-maturity, and a Swarmer for sure. No contemporary record."

Montferrat raised a brow and lit his cigarette, looking indifferently down at the abstract. "We'll have to pick them both up on suspicion," he said, "and ream their memories. But I'd scarcely call this a positive ID; nothing I'd like to go to the kzin with, for certain." A pause, and a delicate smile. "Of course, if you'd like to take the responsibility yourself . . ."

"I may just take you up on that . . . sir," Axelrod-Bauergartner said, and a cold bell began ringing at the back of Montferrat's mind. "You see, we did find a perfect correlate for the female's DNA pattern. Not in any census registry, but in an old research file at the Scholarium, a genetics survey. Pre-War. Dead data, but I had the central system do a universal sweep, damn the expense, and there were no locks on the data. Just stored out of the way . . ."

"This doesn't make sense," Grimbardsun said. He was Economic Regulation, older than Axelrod-Bauergartner and fatter; less ambitious, except for the bank account he was so excellently placed to feed. Complications with the kzin made him sweat, and there were dark patches under the armpits of his uniform tunic. "You said she was young."

"Biological," Axelrod-Bauergartner said triumphantly. "The forensics people counted how many ticks she had on her biological clock. But the Scholarium file records her as . . ."

A picture flashed across the data, and Montferrat coughed to hide his reaction. He was grateful for the beard and the tan that hid the cold waxy pallor of his skin as the capillaries shrank and sent the blood back to the veins and heart. It felt as if a huge hand had grasped his innards and was squeezing.

"Ingrid Raines," Axelrod-Bauergartner said. "Chron-ological age, better than sixty. Qualified pilot and software wizard, and a possible alternate slotter on one of the slowboats that was launched just before the end."

"I was a possible alternate myself, if I hadn't been taken prisoner," Montferrat said, and even then felt a slight pleasure at Axelrod-Bauergartner's wince. She hadn't been born then, and it was a reminder that at least he had fought the kzin once, not spent his adolescence scheming to enter their service. "There were thousands of us, and most didn't make it any-where near the collection points. It was all pretty chaotic, toward the end." His hand did not tremble as he laid the cigarette in the ashtray, and his eyes were not fixed on the oval face with its long Belter strip that turned into an auburn fountain at the back.

"Which was why the ordinary student files were lost," Axelrod-Bauergartner said, nodding so that her incipient jowls swayed. "Yah. All we got from the genetics survey was a name and a student number that doesn't correlate to anything existing. But the DNA's a one-to-one, no doubt about it at all. Raines went out on that slowboat, and somehow Raines came back, still young."

Still young, Montferrat thought. *Still young . . . and I sit here, my soul older than Satan's.* "Came back. Dropped off from a ship going .999 lightspeed?"

A shrug. "The genes don't lie."

"Computer," Montferrat said steadily. "All points, maximum priority. Pictures and idents to be distri-buted to all sources; capture alive at all costs, we need the information they have."

To his second. "My congratulations, *Herrenfrau*

Axelrod-Bauergartner, on a job well done. We'll catch these revenants, and when we do all the summer soldiers who've been flocking to those Resistance idiots since the attack will feel a distinct chill. I think that's all for today?"

They rose with the usual round of handshakes, Grimbardsun's hand wet, Axelrod-Bauergartner's soft and cold as her eyes. Montferrat felt like someone smiling with his face, talking with his mouth. Impeccable, until he was in the privacy of his office, and staring down at the holo in his desk. Matching it with the one from his locked and sealed files, matching the reality with forensic's projection. Feeling the moisture spilling from his eyes, down onto the imperishable synthetic, into the face he had seen with the eye of the mind every day for the last forty years. The face he would arrest and turn over to the interrogators and the kzin, along with the last of his soul.

"Why did you come back?" he whispered. "Why did you come back, to torment us here in hell?"

"Right, now download," Jonah said. The interfacer bleeped quietly and opened to extrude the biochip.

"Well, *this* ought to be useful, if we can get the information back," Ingrid said dully, handing him the piece of curved transparent quasi-tissue.

He unwrapped his hand gingerly and slid the fingernail home, into the implanted flexible gasket beneath the cuticle. "Provided we can get ourselves, this, or a datalink to the ship."

Useful was an understatement; intelligence-gathering was not their primary job, but this was a priceless load. The complete specs on the most important infosystem on Wunderland, and strategic sampling of

the data in its banks. Ships, deployments, capacities
Kzin psychology and history and politics, command-
profiles, strategic planning and *kriegspiel*—wargames—
played by the pussy General Staff for decades. All
the back doors, from the human systems, then,
through them, into the kzin system. UN Naval Intelligence would willingly sacrifice half a fleet for
this. . . .

"That's it, then," Jonah said. "It's not what we
came for, but it can make a difference. And there—"

Ingrid was not listening. "Hold on! Look!"

"Eh?"

"An alert subroutine." Her fingers moved across
her interfacer. "Gottdamn, that is an alert! Murphy,
it's about us, those are our cover-idents it's broadcast-
ing. We're blown."

"Block it, quick." They worked in silence for a
moment. Jonah scrubbed a hand across his face.
"That'll hold it for a half-hour."

"We'll never make it back to Munchen before the
next call gets through," she said. "Not without putting up a holosign that this system's been subverted
down to the config."

"We don't have to," Jonah said. He squeezed eyes
shut, pressed his fingers to his forehead. "Finagle,
why now . . . the transfer booth. Computer," he
continued. "Is the civilian system still online? Slaved
to the core-system here?"

"Affirmative, to both."

"That's it, then. What's the closest functional booth
to the Ba'hai quarter? Right. Key the internal link to
that one. Code, full-wipe after execution, purge. Ingrid, let's go."

*   *   *

"Is the system compromised?" Chuut-Riit asked. He paced through the central control room of his estate. His nostrils flared: yes, the scent of two of the monkeys, a male and . . . He snuffled further. Yes, the female was bearing. Grimly, he filed the smell away, for possible future reference. It was unlikely that he would ever encounter either of them in person, but one could hope.

One of the kzin technicians was so involved with following the symbols scrolling by on the walls that he swept his hand behind him with claws extended in an exasperated protest at being interrupted. The governor bristled and then relaxed; it helped that he came from the hunt. Had killed and fed well, mated and washed his glands and tissues clear of hormones freeing the reasoning brain. Even more that he had spent most of his lifespan cooling a temper that had originally been hasty even by kzin standards. He controlled breath and motion, the desire to lash his tail and pace; it ran through him that perhaps it was his temper that had set him on the road to mastery, that never-to-be-forgotten moment in the nursery so many years ago. The realization that his rage could kill, and in time would kill *him* as dead as the sibling beneath his claws.

The guards behind him had snarled at the infotech's insolence, a low subliminal rumbling and the dry-spicy scent of anger. An expressive ripple of Chuut-Riit's fur, ears, tail quieted them.

"These specialists are all mad," he whispered aside. "One must humor them, like a cub that bites your ears." They were sorry specimens in truth: one scrubby and undersized, with knots in his fur; the other a giant, but clumsy, slow, actually *fat*. Heroes, indeed!

Any Hero seeing them would know their brilliance, since such disgusting examples of bad inheritance would only be kept alive for the most pressing of needs.

The governor schooled himself to wait, shifting only enough to keep his heated muscles from stiffening. The big technician mumbled to himself, occasionally taking out a brick of dull-red dried meat from his equipment apron and stuffing it into his mouth. Chuut-Riit caught a wiff of it and gagged, as much at the thought of someone eating infantry rations for *pleasure* as at the well-remembered smell. The other one muttered as well, but he chewed on the ends of his claws. Those on his right hand were actually frayed at the tips, useless for anything but scratching its doubtless completely ungroomed and verminous pelt.

"Is the system compromised?" Chuut-Riit asked again, patiently. Infosystems specialists were as bad as telepaths.

"*Hrrwweo?*" muttered the small one, blinking back to a consciousness somewhat more in congruence with the others'. "Well, we couldn't know that, could we? Honored Chuut-Riit," he added hastily, as he caught the governor's expression and scent.

"What–do–you–mean?" he said.

"Well, Honored Governor Chuut-Riit, a successful clandestine insertion is undetectable by definition, *hrrr?* We're *pretty sure* we've found their tracks. Computer, isolate-alpha, linear schematic, level three." A complex webbing sprang up all around the room, blue lines with a few sections picked out in green. "See, dominant one, where the picks were inserted? So that the config elements could be accessed and altered from an external source without detection. We've neutralized them, of course."

The claws went back into his mouth, and he mumbled around them. "This was humans, wasn't it? It was their scent. Very three-dimensional, I suppose it comes of their being monkeys. They do some wonderful gaming programs, very ingeniou— I abase myself in apology, Chuut-Riit." He flattened to the ground and covered his dry granular-looking nose. "We are as sure as we can be that all the unauthorized elements have been purged." To his companion: "Wake up, suckling!"

"*Whirrr?*" the fat giant chirruped, stopped his continuous nervous purring and then started. "Oh, yes. Lovely system you have here, Honored Governor Chuut-Riit. Yes, I think we've got it. I would like to meet the monkeys who did the alterations, very subtle work."

"You may go," he said, and crouched brooding, scratching moodily behind one ear. The internal-security team were in now, with the sniffer-machines to isolate the scent molecules of the intruders.

"I would like to meet them, too," he said, and a line of saliva spun itself down from one thin black lip. He snapped it back with a wet *chop* and licked his nose with a broad wash of pink tongue. "I would like that very much."

Chapter VI

"Somehow I think it's *too* quiet," Ingrid said. When Jonah cast a blankly puzzled look over his shoulder, she shrugged. "Aren't you interested in *anything* cultural?"

"I'm interested in staying alive," Jonah said.

They were strolling quietly down one of the riverside walks. The Donau rolled beside them, two kilometers across; it sparkled blue and green-gray, little waves showing white. A bridge soared from bank to bank, and sailboats heeled far over under the stiff warm breeze. Away from the shrilling poverty of the residential quarters, the air smelled of silty water, grass, flowers.

"Of course, staying alive from now on jeopardizes the mission," Jonah continued.

"No." Ingrid shook her head. "You have to get back."

"I do? Why?"

"You just do." *Murphy's Balls! Those ARM psychists*

really do know their stuff. He's forgotten already. What have I forgotten? It's no fun, holes in your memory. Even if they're deliberate.

"The plan doesn't matter," Jonah said. "If it were going to blow, it would have done it. And we'd have heard the bang." Something itched at the back of his mind. "Unless—"

"Jonah?"

"Nothing." *I don't want to remember. Or maybe there's nothing to remember.* "My hand hurts. Wonder what I did to it?"

"You don't need to know that, either." It was the tenth time he'd asked. Clearly the psychists had done some powerful voodoo on Jonah.

They hailed a pedicab and climbed into the twin-passenger back seat. They had both been surprised to see the little vehicles skittering about the streets; surely machinery could not have become *that* expensive. The man hunched over the pedals was thin, all wire and leather, dressed only in a pair of ragged shorts. It was not that machines were so dear, but that labor was so cheap, labor of a certain kind. For those with skills needed by the kzinti war economy, there was enough capital to support reasonable productivity. For the increasing number of those without, there was only what unaided brute labor would buy: starvation wages.

Get your mind off the troubles of Wunderland and on to the more urgent matter of saving your own ass, she told herself as they turned into the Ba'hai quarter. Back to Harold's Place . . . she winced. Then out to the Swarm. *Catskinner* would be waiting, and Markham would simply have to accept them; that was one of the virtues of a ship with a will of its own.

Then a straight boost out of the system, a Dart usually didn't have anything approaching interstellar capacity, but the stasis field changed things. Boost out, tightbeam the precious data, and wait for the fleet to scoop them up. Nothing could affect them within a stasis field, but the field as a whole could still be manipulated with a gravity polarizer. . . .

The chances of coming through this with a whole skin had seemed so remote that it wasn't even worth the trouble of thinking about. Now . . .

The ship will hold three. Hari, this time I won't leave you.

They turned into the street that fronted Harold's Place. Ingrid had just time enough to see Hari standing beside Claude at the entrance. Then police vomited forth, dark in their turtle helmets and goggles, and aircars rose silently over the roofs all about. Giant ginger-red shapes behind them—

She rolled out of her side of the pedicab as Jonah did on his, a motion so smooth they might have rehearsed it. The light-pen was in her hand, and it made its yawping sound. A policeman died, dropping like a puppet with the strings cut, and she dove forward, rolling, trying for an angle at the kzin and—

Blackness.

"The interrogation is complete?" Chuut-Riit reclined again at ease on the bubblecouch behind his desk; a censor was sending up aromatic smoke.

The holo on the far wall showed a room beneath the Munchen police headquarters; a combination of human and kzin talents had long proven most effective for such work. Ktriir-Supervisor-of-Animals was there, and a nameless shabby-looking telepath. The mind-reader's fur was matted and his hands twitched. Chuut-Riit could see spatters of vomit down the front of his pelt, and hear his mumble:

". . . salad, no, no, ak, ak, pftht, no please *boiled carrots* ak, pfffth . . ."

He shuddered slightly in sympathy, thinking of what it must be like to enter the mind of a human free-associating under drugs and pain. Telepathy was not like speech; it was a sharing that extended to sensations and memory as well. Food was a very fundamental drive. It would be bad enough to have to share the memory of eating the cremated meats humans were fond of—the very stink of them was enough to turn your stomach—but cooked plants . . . The telepath fumbled something out of a wrist-pouch and carefully parted the fur on one side of his neck before pressing it to the skin. There was a hiss, and he sank against the wall with a sigh of relief. His eyes slitted and he leaned chin on knees with a high-pitched irregular purr, the tip of his tongue showing pink past his whiskers.

Chuut-Riit wrinkled his nose and dismissed false compassion. How could you sympathize with something that was voluntary slave to a drug? And to an extract of sthondat blood at that.

"Yes, Chuut-Riit," Ktriir-Supervisor-of-Animals said. "Telepath's reading agrees with what the trained monkeys determined with their truth drugs." Chuut-Riit reminded himself that the drugs actually merely suppressed inhibition. "The attempt was a last-minute afterthought to the main attack of the monkey ship. Some gravitic device was used to decelerate a pod with these two; they came down in a remote area, using the disturbances of the attack as cover, and reached the city on foot. Their aim was to trigger the self-destruct mechanisms on your estate, but they were unable to do so."

Chuut-Riit brooded, looking past the kzin liaison officer to the human behind him. "You are not the human in charge of the Munchen police," he said.

"No, Chuut-Riit," the human said. It was a female. A flabby one, the sort that would squish unpleasantly when your fangs ripped open the body cavity, and somehow the holo gave the impression of an unpleasant odor. "I am Chief Assistant Axelrod-Bauergartner at your service, dominant one," she continued, giving the title in a reasonably good approximation of the Hero's Tongue. A little insolent? Perhaps—but also commendable, and the deferential posture was faultless. "Chief Montferrat-Palme delegated this summary of the investigation, feeling that it was not important enough to warrant his personal attention."

"*Chrrrriii,*" Chuut-Riit said, scratching one cheek against a piece of driftwood in a stand on his desk. This Montferrat-creature did not consider an attack on the governor's private control system important? That monkey was developing a distorted sense of its priorities. The human in the screen had blanched slightly at the kzin equivalent of an irritated scowl; he let his lips lower back over the fangs and continued:

"Show me the subjects." Axelrod-Bauergartner stepped aside, to show two humans clamped in adjustable plastic brackets amid a forest of equipment. These were two fine specimens, tall and lean in the manner of the space-bred subspecies. Both were unconscious, but seeming intact enough apart from the usual superficial cuts, abrasions, and bruises. "What is their condition?"

"No irreparable physical or mental harm, Chuut-Riit," Axelrod-Bauergartner said, bowing. "What are your orders as to their disposal?"

"Rrrrr," Chuut-Riit mused, shifting to rub the underside of his jaw on the wood. The last public hunt had been yesterday, the one to which he had taken his sons. "How soon can they be in a condition to run amusingly?" he said.

"Half a week, Chuut-Riit. We have been cautious."

"Prepare them." His sons? No, best not to be too indulgent. There was a badsmelling lot of administrative work to be attended to; he would be chained to his desk for a goodly while anyway. Let the little devils attend to their studies, and he would visit them again when this had been disposed of. Besides, while free there had been a certain attraction in the prospect of dealing with this pair personally; as captives they were just two more specimens of monkey-meat—beneath his dignity. "Get a good batch together, and have them all ready for the Public Preserve at the end of the week. Dismissed."

"Was that Suuomalisen I saw coming out of here?" Montferrat said.

"Unless you know another fat, sweaty toad in a linen suit looking like he'd just swallowed the juiciest fly on the planet." Yarthkin grinned like a shark as he settled behind his desk and pushed a pile of data chips and hardcopy to one side. "Sit yourself down, Claude, and have a drink. If it isn't too early."

"15:00 too early? That's in bad taste, even for you." But the hand that reached for the Maivin shook slightly, and there were wrinkles in the tunic. "But why was he so happy?"

"I just sold him Harold's Terran Bar," Yarthkin said calmly. Light-headed he laughed, a boy's laugh. "Prosit!" he toasted, and tossed back his own drink.

"*What!*" That was enough to bring him bolt-upright. "Why—what—You've been turning that swine down for thirty years!"

"Swine, Claude? What's so especially swinish about him?" Yarthkin leaned forward, resting his chin on paired thumbs. "Or have you forgotten exactly who's to be monkeymeat day after tomorrow?"

The reaction was more than Yarthkin had expected. A jerk, as if high-voltage current surged through the other man's body. A dry retching sound. Then, incredibly, the aquiline *Herrenmann* mask crumpled, slumping and wrinkling like a balloon from which the air has been withdrawn . . . and he was crying, head slumping down into his hands. Yarthkin swallowed and looked away; Claude was a collabo and a sellout, an extortionist without shame . . . but nobody should see another man this naked. It was obscene.

"Pull yourself together, Claude; I've known you were a bastard for forty years, but I thought you were a man, at least."

"So did I," gasped Montferrat. "I even have the medals to prove it. I fought well in the war."

"I know."

"So, when, when, when they let us out of the detention camp, I really thought I could help. I really did." He laughed. "Life had to go on, criminals had to be caught, we were beaten and resistance just made it harder on everyone. I'd been a good policeman. I still could be."

He drank, choked, drank. "The graft, everyone had to. They wouldn't let you get past foot-patrol if you weren't on the pad, too; you had to be in it with them. If I didn't get promotion how could I accomplish anything? I told myself that, but every year a little more of me was gone. And now, now Ingrid's back and I can see myself in her eyes, and I know what I am—no better than that animal Axelrod-Bauergartner. She's gloating, she has me on this and I couldn't, couldn't *do* it. I told her to take care of it all, and went, and I've been drunk most of the time since, and she'll have my head and I deserve it, why try and stop her it—"

Yarthkin leaned forward and slapped the policeman alongside the head with his open palm, a gunshot crack in the narrow confines of the office. Montferrat's mood switched with mercurial swiftness, and he snarled with a mindless sound as he reached for his sidearm. But alcohol is a depressant, and his hand had barely touched the butt before the other man's stunner was pointed between his eyes.

"Neyn, neyn, naughty," Yarthkin said cheerfully. "Hell of a headache, Claude. Now, I won't say you don't deserve it, but sacrificing your own liver and lights isn't going to do Ingrid any good." He kept the weapon unwavering until Montferrat had won back a measure of self-command, then laid it down on the desk and offered a cigarette.

"My apologies," Montferrat said, wiping off his face with a silk handkerchief. "I do despise self-pity." The shredded cloak of his ironic detachment settled about him.

Yarthkin nodded. "That's better, sweetheart. I'm selling the club because I need ready capital, for relocation and grubstaking my people, the ones who don't want to come with me."

"Go with you? Where? And what does this have to do with Ingrid?"

Yarthkin grinned again, tapped ash off the end of his cigarette. Exhilaration filled him, and something that had been missing for far too long. *What?* he thought. *Not youth . . . yes, that's it. Purpose.*

"It isn't every man who's given a chance to do it over right," he said. "That, friend Claude, is what I'm going to do. We're going to bust Ingrid out of that Preserve. Have a shot at it, at least." He held up a hand. "Don't fuck with me, Claude; I know as well as you that the system there is managed through Munchen Police H.Q. One badly mangled corpse substituted for another, what ratcat's to know? It's been done before."

"Odd you should think of that," Montferrat said, shaking his head dully. "For the past several days I have been regretting that I always kept out of the set-up side of the Hunts. Couldn't . . . I have to watch them, anyway, too often."

Odd how men cling to despair, once they've hit bottom, Yarthkin thought. *As if hope were too much effort. Is that what surrender is, then, just giving in to exhaustion of the soul?*

Aloud: "Computer, access file *Till Eulenspiegel.*"

The surface of his desk flashed transparent and lit with a series of coded text-columns. Montferrat came erect with a shaken oath.

"How . . . if you had that, all these years, why haven't you used it?"

"Claude, the great drawback of blackmail is that it gives the victim the best possible incentive to find a permanent way of shutting you up. Risky, especially when dealing with the police. As to the how, you're not under the impression that you get the best people in the police, are you?" A squint, and the gravelly voice went soft. "Don't think I wouldn't use it, sweetheart, if you didn't cooperate, and there's *more* than enough here to put you in the edible-delicacy category. Think of it as God's way of giving you an incentive to get back on the straight and narrow."

"I tell you, Axelrod-Bauergartner has the command codes for the Preserve! I can override, but it would be flagged. Immediately."

"Computer, display file *Niebelungen AA37Bi22*. Damned lack of imagination, that code . . . There it is, Claude. Everything you always wanted to know about your most ambitious subordinate but were afraid to ask, including her private bypass programs." Another flick of ash. "Finagle, Claude, you can probably make all this look like her fault, even if the ratcats smell the proverbial rodent."

Montferrat smoothed down his uniform tunic, and it was as if the gesture slicked transparent armor across his skin once more. "You appear to have me by the short and sensitives, *kamerat*," he said lightly. "Not entirely to my dismay. The plan is, then, that Ingrid and her gallant Sol-Belter are whisked away from under the noses of the kzin, while you go to ground?"

Yarthkin laughed, a shocking sound. "Appearances to the contrary, Claude old son, you were always the romantic of us two. The one for the noble gesture. Nothing of the sort: Ingrid and I are going to the Swarm."

"And the man, Jonah?"

"Fuck him. Let the ratcats have him. His job was done the minute they failed to dig the real story out of him."

Montferrat managed a laugh. "This is quite a reversal of roles, Hari . . . but this, this final twist, it makes it seem possible, somehow." He extended a hand. "Seeing as you have the gun to my head, why not? Working together again, eh?"

"All right, listen up," the guard said.

Jonah shook his head, shook out the last of the fog. Ingrid sat beside him on the plain slatted wood of the bench, in this incongruous pen . . . change-rooms for a country club, once. Now a set of run-down stone buildings in the midst of shaggy overgrown wilderness; the side open to the remnants of lawn and terrace was covered with a shockfield. He looked around; there were around two dozen humans with them, all clad alike in grey prison trousers and shirts. All quiet. The shockrods of the guards had enforced that. Some weeping, a few catatonic, and there was an unpleasant fecal smell.

"You get an hour's start," the guard said, in a voice of bored routine. "And you'd better run, believe me."

"Up yours!" somebody shouted, and laughed when the guard raised her rod. "What you going to do, ratcat lover, condemn me to death?"

The guard shrugged. "You ever seen a house cat playing with a mumbly?" she jeered. "The ratcats like a good chase. Disappoint them and they'll bat you around like a toy." She stepped back, and the door opened. "Hell, keep ahead of them for two days and maybe they'll let you go." A burly man rose and charged, bounced back as she took another step through the door.

Laughter, through the transparent surface. "Have fun, porkchops. I'll watch you die. Five minutes to shield-down."

"You all right?" Jonah asked. Neither of them had been much damaged physically by the interrogation; it had been done in a police headquarters, where the most modern methods were available, not crude field-expedients. And the psychists' shields had worked perfectly; the great weakness of telepathic interrogation is that it can only detect what the subject believes to be true. It had been debatable whether the blocks and artificial memories would hold . . . Kzin telepaths hated staying in a human's mind more than they had to, and the drug-addiction that helped to develop their talents did little for motivation or intelligence.

"Fine," Ingrid said, raising her head from her knees. "Just thinking how pretty it is out there." Tears starred her lashes, but her voice was steady.

Startled, he looked again through the near-invisible shimmer of the shockfield. The long green-gold grass was rippling under a late-afternoon sun, starred with flowers like living jewel-flecks. A line of flamingos skimmed by, down to the little pond at the base of the hill. Beyond was forest, flowering dogwood in a fountain of white against the flickering-shiny olive drab of native kampfwald trees. The shockfield let air through, carrying scents of leafmold, green, purity.

"You're right," he said. They clasped hands, embraced, stepped back and saluted each other formally. "It's been . . . good knowing you, Lieutenant Ingrid."

"Likewise, Captain Jonah." A gamin smile. "Finagle's arse, we're not dead yet, are we?"

"Huh. huh-huh." Lights spun before Jonah's eyes, wrenching his stomach with more nausea. Gummy saliva blocked his mouth as he tumbled over the lip of the gully, crashing through brush that ripped and tore with living fingers of thorn and bramble. Tumble, roll, down through the brush-covered sixty-degree slope, out into the patch of gravel and sparse spaghetti-like grass analog at the bottom. To lie and rest, Murphy, to rest . . .

Memories were returning. Evidently his subconscious believed there wouldn't be another interrogation. Believed they were dead already. *My fingernail. I have to escape. And that's a laugh. But I have to try. . . .*

He turned the final roll into a flip and came erect, facing in the direction of his flight; force the diaphragm to breathe, stomach out to suck air into the bottom of the lungs. His chest felt tight and hot, as if the air pumping through it was nothing, vacuum, inert gas. Will kept him steady, blinked his eyes into focus. He was in a patch of bright sunlight, the forest above a deep green-gold shade that flickered; the soil under his feet was damp, impossibly cool on his skin. The wind was blowing toward him, which meant that the kzin would be following ground-scent rather than what floated on the breeze. A kzin nose was not as sensitive as a hound's, but several thousand times more acute than a human's.

And I must stink to high heaven, he thought. Even then he could smell himself; he hawked and spat, taking a firmer grip on his improvised weapon. That was a length of branch and a rock half the size of his head, dangling from the end by thin strong vines. Thank Murphy that Wunderland flora ran to creepers. . . .

"One," he muttered to himself. "There ain't no justice, I know, but please, just *one*." His breathing was slowing, and he became conscious of thirst, then the gnawing emptiness under his ribs. The sun was high overhead; nearly a day already? How many of the others were still alive?

A flicker of movement at the lip of the ravine, ten meters above him and twenty away. Jonah swung the stone-age morningstar around his head and roared, and the kzin halted his headlong four-footed rush. Rose like an unfolding wall of brown-red, dappled in the light at the edge of the tall trees, slashed across with the white of teeth. Great round eyes, and he could imagine the pupils going pinpoint; the kzin homeworld was not only colder than Wunderland, it was dimmer. Batwing ears unfolding, straining for sound; their hearing was keen enough to pick a human heartbeat out of the background noise. This was a young male, he would be hot, hot for the kill and salt blood to quench his thirst and let him rest . . .

"Come on, you *kshat*, you sthondat-eater," Jonah yelled in the snarling tones of the Hero's Tongue. "Come and get your name, kinless offspring of cowards, come and eat turnips out of my shit, grassgrazer! *Ch'rowl* you!"

The kzin screamed, a raw wailing shriek that echoed down the ravine; screamed again and leaped in an impossible soaring curve that took it halfway down the steep slope.

"*Now, Ingrid. Now!*" Jonah shouted, and ran forward.

The woman rose from the last, thicker scrub at the edge of the slope, where water nourished taller bushes. Rose just as the second bounding leap passed its arc, the kzin spread-eagled against the sky, taloned hands outstretched to grasp and tear. The three-meter pole rose with her, butt against the earth, sharpened tip reaching for the alien's belly. The two met, and the wet ripping sound was audible even over the berserk siren shriek of the young kzin's pain.

It toppled forward and sideways, thrashing and ululating with the long pole transfixing it. He forced rubbery leg muscles into a final sprint, a leap and scream of his own. Then he was there, in among the clinging brush and it was there, too, convulsing. He darted in, swung, and the rock smashed into a hand that was lashing for his throat; the kzin wailed again, put its free hand to the spear, *pulled* while it kept him at bay with lunging snaps. Ingrid was on the other side with a second spear, jabbing; he danced in, heedless of the fangs, and swung two-handed. The rock landed at the juncture of thick neck and sloping shoulder, and something snapped. The shock of it ran back up his arms.

The pair moved in, stabbing, smashing, block and wiggle and jump and strike, and the broken alien crawled toward them with inhuman vitality, growling and whimpering and moving even with the dull-pink bulge of intestine showing where it had ripped the jagged wood out of its flesh. Fur, flesh, scraps of leaf, dust scattering about . . . Until at last too many bones were broken and too much of the bright-red blood spilled, and it lay twitching. The humans lay just out of reach, sobbing back their breaths; Jonah could hear the kzin's cries over the thunder in his ears, hear them turn to high-pitched words in the Hero's Tongue:

"It hurts . . ." The Sol-Belter rolled to his knees. His shadow fell across the battered, swollen eyes of his enemy. "It hurts . . . mother, you've come back, mother—" The shattered paw-hands made kneading motions, like a nursing kitten. "Help me, take away the noise in my head, mother . . ." Presently it died.

"That's one for a pall-bearer." The end of his finger throbbed. "Goddamn it, I can't escape!" he shouted at it.

Ingrid tried to rise, fell back with a faint cry.

Jonah bent over, hands moving on the ruffled tatters that streaked down one thigh. "How bad . . ." he pushed back the ruined cloth. Blood was runneling down the slim length of the woman's leg, not pumping but in a steady flow. "Damn, tanj, tanj, tanj!" He ripped at his shirt for a pressure-bandage, tied it on with the thin vines scattered everywhere about. "Here, here's your spear, lean on it, come *on*." He darted back to the body; there was a knife at its belt, a long heavy-bladed *wtsai*. Jonah ripped it free, looped the belt over one shoulder like a baldric.

"Let's move," he said, staggering slightly. She leaned on the spear hard enough to drive the blunt end inches deep into the sandy gravel, and shook her head.

"No, I'd slow you down. You're the one that has to get away." His finger throbbed anew to remind him. *And she's Hari's girl, not mine. But—* Another memory returned, and he laughed.

"Something's funny?"

"Yeah, maybe it is! Maybe—hell, I bet it worked!"

"What worked?"

"Tell you on the way."

"No, you won't, I'm not coming with you. Now get going!"

"Murphy bugger that with a diode, Lieutenant. Get moving, that's an *order*."

She put an arm around his shoulder and they hobbled down the shifting footing of the ravine's bed. There was a crooked smile on her face as she spoke.

"Well, it's not as if we had anywhere to go, is it?"

The kzin governor of Wunderland paced tiredly toward the gate of his childrens' quarters, grooming absently. The hunt had gone well, the intruder-humans were undoubtedly beginning a short passage through some lucky Hero's digestive system, and it was time to relax.

Perhaps I should have stayed to track them myself, he mused as he passed the last guard station with an absent-minded wave. *No, why bother. That prey is already caught, this was simply a re-enactment.*

Chuut-Riit felt the repaired doors swing shut before him and glanced around in puzzlement, the silence penetrating through post-Hunt sluggishness. The courtyard was deserted, and it had been nearly seven days since his last visit; far too soon for another assassination attempt, but the older children should have been boiling out to greet him, questions and frolicking . . . He turned and keyed the terminal in the stone beside the door.

Nothing. The kzin blinked in puzzlement. *Odd. There has been no record of any malfunction.* In instinctive reflex he lowered himself to all fours and sniffed; the usual sand-rock-metal scents, multiple young-kzin smells. Something underneath that, and he licked his nose to moisten it and drew in a long breath with his mouth half open.

He started back, arching his spine and bristling with a growling hiss, tail rigid. *Dead meat and blood.* Whirling, he slapped for the exterior communicator. "Guard-Captain, respond. *Guard-Captain, respond immediately*."

Nothing. He bent, tensed, leaped for the summit of the wall. A crackling discharge met him, a blue corona around the sharp twisted iron of the battlement's top that sent pain searing through the palms of his outstretched hands. The wards were set on maximum force, and he fell to the ground cradling his burned palms. Rage bit through him, stronger than pain or thought; someone had menaced his children, his future, the blood of the Riit. His snarl was soundless as he dashed on all fours across the open space of the courtyard and into the entrance of the warren.

It was dark, the glowpanels out and the ventilators silent; for the first time it even smelled like a castle on homeworld, purely of old stone, iron, and blood. Fresh blood on something near the entrance. He bent, the huge round circles of his eyes going black as the pupils expanded. A sword, a four-foot *kreera* with a double saw edge. The real article, heavy wave-forged steel, from the sealed training cabinets which should only have opened to his own touch. Ignoring the pain as burned tissue cracked and oozed fluids, he reached for the long hide-wound bone grip of the weapon. The edges of the blade glimmered with dark wet, set with a matt of orange-red hairs.

His arm bent, feeling the weight of the metal as he dropped into the crook-kneed defensive stance, with the lead ball of the pommel held level with his eyes. The corridor twisted off before him, the faint light of occasional skylights picking out the edges of granite blocks and the black iron doors with their central locks cast in the shape of beast-masked ancestral warriors. Chuut-Riit's ears cocked forward and his mouth opened, dropping the lower jaw toward the chest: maximum flow over the nasal passages to catch scent, and fangs ready to tear at anything that got past the weapon in his hands. He edged down the corridor one swift careful step at a time, heading for the central tower where he could do *something*, even if it was only lighting a signal fire.

Insane, he thought with a corner of his mind that watched his slinking progress through the dark halls. It *was* insane, like something from the ancient songs of homeworld. Like the *Siege of Zeeroau*, the Heroic Band manning the ramparts against the prophet, dwindling one by one from wounds and weariness and the hunger-frenzy that sent them down into the catacombs to hunt and then the dreadful feasting.

Chuut-Riit turned a corner and wheeled, blade up to meet a possible attack from the dropstand over the corner. Nothing—but the whirl-and-cut brought him flush against the opposite wall, and he padded on. Noise and smell; a thin mewling, and an overpowering stink of kzinmeat. A door, and the first body before it. There was little of the soft tissue left, but the face was intact. One of his older sons, the teeth frozen in an eternal snarl; blood was splashed about,

far more than one body could account for. Walls,
floor, ceiling; guts and splatters that dripped down in
slow congealing trails toward the floor. A *chugra*
spear lay broken by the wall, alongside a battered
metal shield; the sound had been coming from behind the door the corpse guarded, but now he could
hear nothing.

No, wait. His ears folded out to their maximum.
Breathing. A multiple rapid panting. He tried the
door; it was unlocked, but something had it jammed
closed.

A mewl sounded as he leaned his weight against it
and the iron creaked. "Open!" he snarled. "Open at
once."

More mewls, and a metallic tapping. The panel
lurched inward, and he stooped to fill the doorway.

The infants, he thought. A heap in the far corner
of the room. Squirming spotted fur and huge terrified eyes peering back at him; the younger ones, the
kits just recently taken from their mothers. At the
sight of him they set up the thin *eeeuw-eeeuw-eeeuw*
that was the kzin child's cry of distress.

"Daddy!" one of them said. "We're so hungry,
Daddy. We're so frightened. He said we should stay
in here and not open the door and not cry but there
were awful noises and it's been so long and we're
hungry, Daddy, Daddy—"

Chuut-Riit uttered a grating sound deep in his
chest and looked down; his son's *wtsai* had been
wedged to hold the door from the inside, the kits
must have done it at his instruction, while he waited
outside to face the hunters. Hunger-frenzy eroded
what little patience an adolescent kzin possessed, as
well as intellect; they would not spend long hammer-

ing at a closed door, not with fresh meat to hand, and the smell of blood in their nostrils.

"Silence," he said, and they shrank back into a heap. Chuut-Riit forced gentleness into his voice. "Something very bad has happened," he said. "Your brother was right, you must stay here and make no noise. Soon I . . . soon I or another adult will come and feed you. Do you understand?" Uncertain nods. "Put the knife back in the door when I go out. Then *wait*. Understand?"

He swung the door shut and looked down into his son's face while the kits hammered the knifeblade under it from the inside.

"You did not die in vain, my brave one," he whispered, very low, settling into a crouch with the sword ready. "Kdari-Riit," he added, giving his dead son a full Name. *Now I must wait.* Wait to be sure none of the gone-mad ones had heard him, then do his best. There would be an alert, eventually. The infants did not have the hormone-driven manic energy of adolescents. They would survive.

"Zroght-Guard-Captain," the human said. "Oh, thank God!"

The head of the viceregal household troopers rose blinking from his sleeping-box, scratching vigorously behind one ear. "Yes, Henrietta?" he said.

"It's Chuut-Riit," she said. "Zroght-Guard-Captain, it wasn't him who refused to answer, I *knew* it and now we've found tampering, the technicians say they missed something the first time, we *still* can't get through to him in the children's quarters. *And the records say the armory's open and they haven't been fed for a week!*"

The guard-captain wasted no time in speech with the sobbing human; it would take enough time to physically breech the defenses of the children's quarters.

"*Hrrnnngg-ha*," Chuut-Riit gasped, panting with lolling tongue. The corner of the exercise room had given him a little protection, the desks and machinery a little more. Now a dozen lanky bodies interlaced through the equipment about his feet, and the survivors had drawn back to the other end of the room. There was little sentience left in the eyes that peered at him out of the starved faces, not enough to use missile-weapons. Dim sunlight glinted on their teeth and the red gape of their mouths, on bellies fallen in below barrel-hoop ribs.

That last rush almost had me, he thought. An odd detachment had settled over him; with a sad pride he noticed the coordination of their movements even now, spreading out in a semi-circle to bar the way to the doors. He was bleeding from a dozen superficial cuts, and the long sword felt like a bar of neutronium in his hands. The blade shone liquid-wet along its whole length now, and the hilt was slimy in his numb grip, slick with blood and the lymph from his burnt hands; he twisted it in a whistling circle that flung droplets as far as the closing pack. Chuut-Riit threw back his head and shrieked, an eerie keening sound that filled the vaulted chamber. They checked for a moment, shrinking back. If he could keep them . . .

Movement at his feet, from the pile of bodies. Cold in his side, so cold, looking down at the hilt of the *wstai* driven up into the lung, the overwhelming

salt taste of his own blood. The one they called
Spotty crawled free of the piled bodies, broken-
backed but evading his weakened slash.

"Kill him," the adolescent panted. "Kill the be-
trayer, *kill him*."

The waiting children shrieked and leapt.

"He must have made his stand here," Zroght-Guard-
Captain said, looking around the nursery. The floor
was a tumbled chaos of toys, wooden weapons, printout books; the walls still danced their holo gavotte of
kits leaping amid grass and butterflies. There was
very little of the kzin governor of the Alpha Centauri
system left; a few of the major bones, and the skull,
scattered among smaller fragments from his sons, the
ones wounded in the fighting and unable to defend
themselves from their ravenous brothers. The room
stank of blood and old meat.

"Zroght-Guard-Captain!" one of the troopers said.
They all tensed, fully-armed as they were. Most of
the young ones were still at large, equipped from the
practice rooms, and they seemed ghostly clever.

"A message, Zroght-Guard-Captain." The warrior
held up a pad of paper. The words were in a rusty
brownish liquid, evidently written with a claw. Chuut-
Riit's claw; that was his sigil at the bottom. The
captain flipped up the visor of his helmet and read:

Forgive them

Zroght chirred. There might be time for that, after
the succession struggle ended.

"Gottdamn, they're out of range of the last pickup,"
Montferrat said.

Yarthkin grunted, careful to stay behind the po-

liceman. The transfer booth was an old one, left here
when this was a country club. It stood in a secluded
cleft below the rocky hill. Deactivated, supposedly
permanently, it appeared on no kzin records. His
hand felt tight and clammy on the handle of the
stunner, and every rustle and creak in the wilderness
about them was a lurking kzin. *Teufel, I could use a
smoke*, he thought. Insane, of course, with ratcat
noses coursing through the woods.

"Are they alive?" he asked tightly.

"The tracers are still active, but with this little
interfacer I can't—*Ingrid!*"

He made a half-step forward. A pair of scarecrow
figures stumbled past the entrance to the cleft, halted
with a swaying motion that spoke of despair born of
utter exhaustion. The man was scratched and blood-
ied; Yarthkin's eyes widened at the scraps of dried
fur and blood and matter clinging to the rude weapon
in his hand. Both of them were spattered with similar reminders, rank with the smell of it and the
sweat that glistened in tracks through the dirt on
their faces. More yet on the sharpened pole that
Ingrid leaned on as a crutch, and fresh blood on the
bandage at her thigh.

Jonah was straightening. "You here to help the
pussies beat the bushes?" he panted. Ingrid looked
up, blinked crusted eyes, moved closer to her companion. Yarthkin halted speechless, shook his head.

"Actually, this is a mission of mercy," Montferrat
began in his cool tone. Then words ripped out of
him: "Gottdamn, there are two kzin coming up, I'm
getting their tracers." Fingers played over his interfacer.
"They're stopping about a kilometer back—"

"Where we left the body of the one we killed,"

Jonah said. His eyes met Hari Yarthkin's levelly; the Wunderlander felt something lurch at the pit of his stomach at the dawning wonder in Ingrid's.

"Yah, mission of mercy, time to get on with it," he said, stepping forward and planting the projector cone of his stunner firmly in Montferrat's back. "Here." He reached, took the policeman's stunner from his belt and tossed it to Jonah. "And here." An envelop from inside his own neatly tailored hunting-jacket. He handed it to Jonah. "False identity, guaranteed good one. I couldn't get but one exit permit, but maybe you can manage that somehow. You'll have to get cosmetic work done to match, but there's everything you need in the room at the other end of the booth here. Money, clothes, contacts."

"Booth?" Jonah said.

"Yeah. Let's get going. You get the exit permit."

"Hari—" Montferrat began, and subsided at a sharp jab.

"You said it, sweetheart," Yarthkin replied. His tone was light, but his eyes were on the woman.

"I won't leave you here," she began.

Yarthkin laughed. "I didn't intend for you to, but it looks like you'll have to. Now get moving, sweetheart."

"You don't understand," Ingrid said. "Jonah's the one who has to get away. Not me. I don't matter, but he does. Give him the permit."

"The Boy Scout? Not on your life—"

"You can give it to me. No, don't move, any of you." The voice came from the transfer booth behind them. A woman's voice, sneering but triumphant.

"Efficient as usual," Montferrat said, with a tired

slump of the shoulders. "Allow me to introduce my ambitious chief assistant."

"Indeed, dear Chief," Axelrod-Bauergartner said as she strolled around to where everyone was visible. The chunky weapon in her arms was no stunner, it was a strakkaker, capable of spraying them all with hypervelocity glass needles with a single movement of her finger. "Drop it, commoner," she continued in a flat voice. "Thanks for disarming the Chief."

Yarthkin's stunner fell to the ground. "Did you really think, Chief, that I wasn't going to check what commands went out under my codes? I look at the events record five times a day when things are normal. Nice sweet setup, puts all the blame on me . . . except that when I show the kzin your bodies, I'll be the new commissioner."

The tableau held for a moment, until Montferrat coughed. "I don't suppose my clandestine fund account?" He moved with exaggerated care as he produced a screenpad and light-stylus.

Axelrod-Bauergartner laughed again. "Sure, we can make a deal. Write out the number, by all means," she taunted. "Porkchops don't need *ngggg*."

The stylus yawped sharply once. The woman in police uniform fell, with a boneless finality that kept her finger from closing on the trigger of the weapon until her weight landed on it. A boulder twenty meters away suddenly shed its covering of vegetation and turned sandblast-smooth; there was a click and hiss as the strakkaker's magazine ran empty.

Yarthkin coughed, struggled not to gasp. Montferrat stooped, retrieved his stunner, walked across to toe the limp body. "I *knew* this would come in useful," he said, tapping the captured light-pencil against the knuckles of one hand. His eyes rose to meet Yarthkin's, and he smoothed back his mustaches. "What a pity that Axelrod-Bauergartner was secretly feral, found here interfering with the Hunt, a proscribed weapon in her hands . . . isn't it?" His gaze shifted to Ingrid and Jonah. "Well, what are you waiting for?"

The woman halted for an instant by Yarthkin. "Hari—" she began. He laid a finger across her lips.

"G'wan, kid," he said, with a wry twist of the lips. "You've got a life waiting."

"Wait a minute," she said, slapping the hand aside. *"Murphy's* Balls, *Hari!* I thought you'd grown up; not enough, evidently. Make all the sacrificial gestures you want, but don't make them for *me*." A gaunt smile. "And don't flatter yourself, either."

She turned to Jonah, snapped a salute. "It's been . . . interesting, Captain. But this is my home . . . and if you don't remember now why you have to get back to the UN, you will."

"Data link—"

She laughed. "It would take hours to squirt all that up to *Catskinner* and you know it. Get moving, Captain. I'll be all right. Now go."

He started to protest and his finger throbbed unbearably. All right, but I'll wait as long as I can."

"You'll do nothing of the sort."

He hesitated for a second more, then walked to the transfer booth. Ingrid turned to face the two men. "You males *do* grow up more slowly than we," she said with a dancing smile in her eyes. "But given enough time . . . There are some decisions that should have been made fifty years ago. Not many get another chance. Where are we going?"

Montferrat and Yarthkin glanced at each other,

back at the woman with an identical look of helpless bewilderment that did not prevent the policeman from keying the booth.

"All three of us have a *lot* of catching up to do," she said, and disappeared.

"Well." Montferrat said dazedly. "Well." A shake of his head. "You next."

"Where did you send her?"

Montferrat grinned slightly. "You'll just have to trust me to send you there, too, won't you?"

"Claude—"

"You've been there. My family's old lodge. I've kept it hidden from—from everyone." He laughed slightly. "You've already had a head start with her. A few more days won't matter. But when I get there, I'll expect equal time. Now get moving, I have to set the stage."

"Better come now."

"No. First I see that the Sol-Belter gets offworld. Then I fix it so we can follow. Both will take time."

"Can you bring that off, Claude?"

"Yes." He straightened, and the look of the true *Herrenmann* was unmistakable. "It's good to be alive again."

S.M. STIRLING
and
THE DOMINATION OF THE DRAKA

In 1782 the Loyalists fled the American Revolution to settle in a new land: South Africa, Drake's Land. They found a new home, and built a new nation: The Domination of the Draka, an empire of cruelty and beauty, a warrior people, possessed by a wolfish will to power. This is alternate history at its best.

"A tour de force." .
—David Drake

"It's an exciting, evocative, thought-provoking—but of course horrifying—read."
—Poul Anderson

MARCHING THROUGH GEORGIA
Six generations of his family had made war for the Domination of the Draka. Eric von Shrakenberg wanted to make peace—but to succeed he would have to be a better killer than any of them.

UNDER THE YOKE
In *Marching Through Georgia* we saw the Draka's "good" side, as they fought and beat that more obvious horror, the Nazis. Now, with a conquered Europe supine beneath them, we see them as they truly are; for conquest is only the *beginning* of their plans . . . All races are created equal—as slaves of the Draka.

THE STONE DOGS
The cold war between the Alliance of North America and the Domination is heating up. The Alliance, using its superiority in computer technologies, is preparing a master stroke of electronic warfare. But the Draka, supreme in the ruthless manipulation of life's genetic code, have a secret weapon of their own. . . .

"This is a potent, unflinching look at a might-have-been world whose evil both contrasts with and reflects that in our own."   —*Publishers Weekly*

"Detailed, fast-moving military science fiction . . ."
                            —Roland Green, *Chicago Sun-Times*

"*Marching Through Georgia* is more than a thrilling war story, more than an entertaining alternate history. . . . I shall anxiously await a sequel."
                            —Fred Lerner, *VOYA*

"The glimpses of a society at once fascinating and repelling are unforgettable, and the people who make up the society are real, disturbing, and very much alive. Canadian author Stirling has done a marvelous job with *Marching Through Georgia*."
    —Marlene Satter, *The News* of Salem, Arkansas

"Stirling is rapidly emerging as a writer to watch."
                            —Don D'Ammassa, *SF Chronicle*

_____

And don't miss:
The Forge: The General, Book I
by David Drake & S.M. Stirling 72037-6 * $4.95
_____
Go Tell the Spartans, A Novel of Falkenberg's Legion,
by Jerry Pournelle & S.M. Stirling 72061-9 * $4.95

_____

Marching Through Georgia 65407-1 * $4.95 _____
Under the Yoke 69843-5 * $4.95 _____
The Stone Dogs 72009-0 * $4.50 _____

Available at your local bookstore. Or you can order any or all of these books with this order form. Just mark your choices above and send a check or money order for the combined cover price/s to: Baen Books, Dept. BA, P.O. Box 1403, Riverdale, NY 10471.

Name: _____
Address: _____

_____